A Tale of Two Jaguars

By

Robert G. Ewing

ISBN: 9798989840007

Published by Robert G. Ewing

Cover design by Mayuko Ewing

Dedication

The author thanks the members of the Tuesday Afternoon Writing Group, especially group leader Virginia Salazar, for many hours of proof-reading and editing.

The book is dedicated to the author's muse, Joan, who, long ago said, "We should try to write a novel." This one's for you, Red.

Chapter 1

Kitty signaled with a downward gesture of a red-tipped fingernail that she'd like a little more coffee. Meg, the waitress on duty at Toasties that morning approached with the pot of decaf and inquired:

"What's on your schedule today, Kitty?"

"Well, Malcolm and I are heading down to San Luis Obispo before noon" Kitty replied, as she took a final bite of her Belgian waffle.

"Malcolm?" Meg asked with a puzzled look. "I didn't know you had a new man in your life."

"No, Malcolm is what I named the Jaguar," Kitty explained with a smile. "It's named for Malcolm Sayer who designed her. He designed a lot of Jaguars before he died back in the '90s. I've had to learn a lot about Jaguars since I took on this missing person case."

She didn't mention that she loved that car more than anything she had ever owned or any man she ever knew. "The only thing I don't like about the old cat is she can't get XM satellite radio, which would really be a blessing on a long, boring trip."

"So, why are you going to San Luis," Meg asked.

"Oh, I'm stopping there first to visit a prisoner who is a Wiccan. He's got colon cancer really bad, and he wants my guidance as a Wiccan priestess about the afterlife."

"You mean you can visit a prisoner like, let's say, a Catholic priest could?"

"Yes" Kitty said. "There was a lawsuit back around 2013 brought by two women inmates over at Chowchilla. They were Wiccans and they wanted the state to hire a 'witch' as a regular chaplain. They got turned down at the state court in Fresno, so they appealed to the Federal court. They said there were no Jewish or Muslim women

1

in that prison, but the state was paying for a rabbi and an imam."

"So, they won?"

"Not really. The 9th circuit court, the Federal court up in San Francisco, ruled that there could be unpaid volunteers who were Wicca if the inmates were sincere in their belief, but they would not be paid by the state, so the case drags on."

"But the prison lets you visit with this inmate?" Meg asked.

"Sure, but I have to go through all the hoops that any visitor to a prison does, which took a while, in my case because of my felony conviction all those years ago."

"So, who is this guy?"

"Oh, Felix was Jake's First Sergeant when they were both in 'Nam and Laos. Jake found legal work with movie and TV producers, and Felix became a hired killer, what they call a 'hit man'."

"So that's it? You're going to San Luis and then you'll be back?"

"No", Kitty replied, "I'm going to be gone most of the week. My clients, the Shepherd family, want to give me some more clues as to where they think Maximillian, their missing brother, may be. And then I'm meeting with a guy named Goldfarb. He's an independent film producer of some obscure bits of work who thinks that witches might be big at the box office. I met him once when I worked for Jake O'Malley."

"So, what would you be, the starring witch?"

"No, he thinks that when Sundance has this show called 'A Discovery of Witches' which is filmed in England, and 'Sabrina the Teenage Witch' is coming back on TV, that there may be a call for a revival of something like 'Bewitched' which was big on TV in

2

the 1960s. So, he might hire me as a consultant, so that he doesn't insult the Wiccan community too much, if you get the idea."

"So, when are you leaving," Meg asked as Kitty fished in her purse for the cash to pay her bill.

"Oh, the post office counter should be open now. I've got to get some stamps to mail some letters to my wicked witch friends in England. Then I've got to put some expensive fuel in Malcolm and get my bag packed. I'll be on my way about ten after this fog lifts. I hope to see you Friday for my lunch."

"Oh, one last question before you leave. Where do you carry your broom in that Jaguar?"

"Very funny, Meg. Watch it lady or I'll put a spell on your fry cook that will make him a health hazard."

"Okay, sorry about the wisecrack. Have a good trip and be safe in that overpowered antique of yours."

"Oh, I'll be fine," Kitty, said as she reached the door. "I've got to be back by Friday 'cause I have a date with Clairol. Can't let those gray hairs get the upper hand as long as I've got 'Loving Care'. So, I should see you about lunch time."

"Loving Care," said Meg. "I thought that red was natural."

"Oh, it is, but at my age it needs a little help. See 'ya later," Kitty said as she exited onto Lighthouse and crossed Congress to the Post Office.

Chapter 2

As Kitty entered the post office, she first went to check her mailbox. She sometimes wondered about the wisdom of spending the money to have a mailbox, but always came back to the convenience of not having to worry about mail deliveries during her absence when traveling. She also liked the idea of being able to give potential clients her business card with the address:

K.T. D'Literie
Research and Enquiries
P.O. Box 513
Pacific Grove, CA 93950

She particularly liked the fact that her box had the two numbers "sacred" to her Wiccan faith. There were five basic elements of her faith, and the lunar calendar had 13 months, while 13 was the number symbolizing change and good luck to a Wiccan. She also liked the "enquiries" touch; it sounded a little like Sherlock Holmes.

Having emptied the box, she headed for the counter where she was greeted by the clerk on duty, Josephine Nguyen. "Good morning, Ms. D'Literie. How may I help you?"

"Good morning, Josephine, and I must say I'm impressed by your pronunciation of my unusual French name. I don't get that often around here."

"Oh, you know, we almost all learned French in school in Vietnam and picked up a little English when you Americans showed up," replied Josephine.

"Well," said Kitty, "I had a card in my mailbox that indicated that there was a package for me too large to fit in."

"I'll be back in a couple of minutes" Josephine said, and disappeared into the back rooms of the building.

Kitty hoped that the package contained some of the course catalogs that she had requested from Californian State University Monterey Bay (CSUMB), U.C. Santa Cruz and San Jose State College. It had been just over thirty years since she had been in a college classroom, but if she could get a master's degree that hopefully would lead to a full-time job in a library. All she could get now was part-time work in library technical services, and that was based on her library duties in prison.

"Here you are, Kitty," Josephine announced as she handed over the package. "Feels like it might be a book."

"Well, judging by the return address it's the catalog I requested from CSUMB. This will help me decide my next move," Kitty replied.

"Now, what else can I get you," asked Josephine.

"I need a roll of the first class 'forever 'stamps and a sheet of ten of the international 'forevers'. And I notice that the price has gone up on all of them again."

"Yes," Josephine replied, "the internationals went up a lot, from $1.00 to $1.15, and the first-class domestic stamps are now 55 cents. So that will be $55 plus $11.50 for a total of $66.50. Now, which design do you want on the internationals, the green succulent or the red poinsettia?"

"Oh, I'll take the poinsettia, but I sure liked the old ones with the globe design and the $1 price a lot better."

"Okay, put your card in the reader and I'll print your receipt," said Josephine.

"Thanks, Josie." said Kitty as she picked up her purchases and mail. "Now I've got to get home and pack and be on the road by noon. I'll see you next week and maybe you'll have another package for me."

She was out the door and over to the Jaguar in twenty steps, and it was a short drive down Lighthouse to her condo. She looked at the old Jeep parked at the curb and thought, "Someday I've got to part with Eugene. It's looking less likely I'll ever use him again to explore the backcountry here or down south. It's just that the old beast reminds me of Jake and the times we went into the wilds looking for a film location. That's gone now, unless this guy Goldfarb has something in the great outdoors for his movie project. Oh, well, maybe that will be revealed before this week is out. Now, I've got to get packed, check with Mrs. Sanchez on pet-sitting the cat and fuel up Malcolm."

A quick call to Mrs. Sánchez, who agreed to check in on Pyewacket twice each day to ensure that she was fed and her litter box emptied. Then Kitty turned to packing. This took a bit of time since she could only fit one suitcase into Malcolm, and she had three different "audiences" to deal with in the four days ahead.

First came the visit with Felix in the prison at San Luis. The rules prohibited certain colors being worn by visitors, even volunteer clergy. Orange was banned, but she never wore anything in her entire life in that color except during her days in the prison in Chino.

The state of California also said, "No blue denim," so the Ralph Lauren jeans she loved so well would be OK for the drive down the coast, but not at the prison. Also out were dark green pants, or a tan blouse or jacket; too similar to the guards' uniforms. No underwire bra lest it set off the metal detector. She would wear her silver Wicca pendant with the pentagram and crescent moon design, but they would make her take that off upon entry. She wondered about that last rule; would a Catholic priest or other Christian clergy have to remove a cross hung 'round his or her neck?

So, she decided upon her very conservative grey and black-flecked wool jacket over a plain white blouse, with the black pants and the black flats over the black knee-highs. "I'll look more like a Quaker than a witch, except for the pendant," she mused to the cat. "Oh, well, whatever it takes to get in and see old Felix, maybe for the last time before he goes to Summerland. I'll do the healing spell with him, but I think all he really wants is to hold a woman's hand for one last time."

Then it would be down to Burbank to meet with Goldfarb. "Pye," she said to the observant Siamese feline, "I'll go with the bright yellow jacket for that meeting and the black pants again, and the pendant. If he wants a witch advisor for his movie, I'll give him one, but it won't be some old crone. I'll be sure to put on the Revlon lipstick, the one labeled, 'Wine with everything.' You can't get much redder than that!"

"Now the last stop on Thursday will be with the Shepherds. I think the dark blue jacket and pants over the white turtle neck and minimum jewelry. I think that the string of pearls and the soft silver rose lipstick will create a nice businesslike look. Nothing flashy, just a mature woman who looks like she knows how to find people."

With the suitcase packed and her cosmetics in the small flowery tote along with her phone charger and tiny alarm clock she was off to the Shell station and her trip to southern California.

Chapter 3

Kitty's first stop was the Shell station at the corner of Lighthouse and Park Street. She needed to be sure that the Jaguar had enough fuel because there were few places along Highway 1 to refuel, except the Chevron station in Big Sur.

As she pumped the high octane, over-priced fuel into Malcolm, she thought to herself about how much she disliked doing this. "Why can't California be like Oregon, where it's illegal to pump gas into your own car? Oh sure, it's just a way to create jobs for teenagers and school dropouts, but the fuel there is less expensive than in California. No one complains about the extra help, especially women motorists and the elderly."

Refueling done and her credit card and receipt in her purse, Kitty drove down Lighthouse to Forest, hung a right and took the Jaguar down a gear for the climb up to the intersection with Highway 68. As she passed city hall and the police station she thought about trying to befriend some of the officers on the local police force. They could be of help in her search by telling her if the person she was looking for was in a prison somewhere.

As she passed the north end of the Presidio of Monterey, she thought about the stories that Jake used to tell her about his time there, learning the Vietnamese and Hmong languages. Now, 5% of all Hmong speakers in the world live in California, mostly in farming communities. It was at the Presidio that Lieutenant Jacob O'Malley had met Sergeant Felix Morris, the man whom Kitty was going to see in the prison at San Luis.

Highway 68, labeled the Holman Highway after a family prominent in the Pacific Grove business community, swept down through twists and turns that let Kitty enjoy the nimble handling of the old Jaguar. As she caught the green light at the entrance to the Community

Hospital, she thanked her lucky stars that she had never had to test the skills of their trauma team. Once past the Pebble Beach tollgate for the 17 Mile Drive, it was a sweeping right turn into the traffic on Highway 1, also known as the Cabrillo Highway. Once past the light at Carmel Valley Road, she wouldn't see a traffic light for 95 miles until she neared Hearst Castle.

Now it was time to give Malcolm a chance to show what he could do as he headed south into the Big Sur. Radio and cell phone service was pretty spotty along this segment of the California coast thanks to the Santa Lucia mountains between the coast and the Salinas Valley. Kitty didn't mind. Silence, except for the Jaguar's muffled roar, was conducive to thinking back over time. The first time she had ever seen this section of the road was the summer of 1978. Her mother and father were going to Monterey, and Kitty, their only child, was with them. The road seemed scary. A ten-year-old girl doesn't care much about scenery. Sadly, it was the last trip they ever took together.

Her mother became a widow in 1978. Her father died on a business trip from Sacramento to San Diego. The plane crashed. No one survived.

Between her father's insurance and a settlement by the airline she and her mother were able to continue living in their Silver Lake home. Her mother sold the family business within a year. Her mother never recovered emotionally from the loss of her spouse. She began to neglect her health and died when Kitty, then 20, was in her junior year at UCLA.

Kitty passed through Big Sur about 11 a.m. and her goal was to reach the hamlet of Lucia and the little convenience store there. The family that controlled the property, five generations and 100 years after they had created Lucia on a cliff above the ocean, owned a small hotel and an over-priced restaurant. Their convenience store, and stretching her legs for a few minutes, was all that Kitty needed. A bag of chips, a can of Sprite and the view to the south was perfect for her. The sun was shining, the beaches below were uncrowded, and the traffic had been light. Sightseeing tourists tended to get out of her way when the Jaguar appeared in their rear-view mirror, and she was not reluctant to flash her headlights at anyone who seemed oblivious to a fast-moving car overtaking them.

Her quick snack over, Kitty was back on her way south. Thirty miles more, and in a half hour she would be in San Simeon. She thought about a stop at Piedras Blancas to take a look at the huge herd of elephant seals. The seals had decided, a few years earlier, to make this part of the coast their personal playground. Sometimes you could not find a parking place, because the tourists had also discovered Piedras Blancas.

It was fun to watch the big, fat seals in action. The huge older males, fighting each other for the female of their dreams, was especially funny to Kitty.

At the traffic light at San Simeon, Kitty looked for the parking lot for the Hearst Castle. She had done the tour there a few times. She liked to see what was new at the gift shop. As a major source of revenue for the state park, you could find a good menu at the restaurant, and the best public restrooms on the entire central coast.

Kitty had lost contact with an old gal who had been a tour guide at the castle for many years. Bev had been a friend of Kitty's mom, had been trained as a nutritionist and worked for Weight Watchers. She had decided to say goodbye to Los Angeles and its crowds and move to Cambria, just south of San Simeon. At first, she volunteered at the castle, then took the job as a tour guide. Recently, she had moved to Florida to be near family members and Kitty lost track of her. She had welcomed Kitty into her home on several occasions after

Kitty had been released from prison. Bev believed that "second chances" were important and were best given by older and wiser friends.

Kitty liked Cambria, and her next stop would be at the Fireside Inn at Moonstone Beach. With about 20 motels in town, why pick that one? First, unlike some of its competitors, it didn't require that you stay for a minimum of two nights, and it gave her access to the beach for a good after-dinner walk. Second, the motel was small, so she could park Malcolm right in front of her room, just for safekeeping. Also, the Moonstone Bar and Grill was only a short walk away.

She spent some time after dinner walking and thinking about her meeting the next morning with Felix. He was another of those post-Vietnam war "wrecks" you might encounter in any homeless encampment. The difference was that when Felix left the army in 1978, he didn't have a lot of skills that might have been useful in civilian life. What he did have was a great deal of skill in killing people. Jake, who had been Felix's commander, was able to find work in Hollywood advising on war-related movies. Felix found that there were people in Hollywood who would pay handsomely to have someone else die in an alley in what appeared to be a nasty robbery attempt. Jake had found that he could make a living helping movie and TV producers and directors, finding a location for a scene in a western movie that required a desert or a mountain setting.

Felix found good places in the Mojave Desert where a carefully selected spot could be prepared as an unmarked burial spot. Two different callings, one respectable and well paid, the other… well, respect is lovely, but cash is always appreciated.

The trouble with that life choice is that when your employer comes under suspicion for the disappearance of an industry rival, he or she might just swing the fickle finger of fate in your direction. That is exactly what his "employer" did to Felix.

When Kitty met with Felix the next morning, she would remind him of two tenets of Wiccan philosophy. The first, which she had taught him, says, "And it harm none, do as ye will." Felix had clearly broken that rule, as not only were individuals killed but also harm was done to their dependents, friends, loved ones and maybe business associates. The other tenet that seemed applicable to Felix said, "Whatever you do comes back to you three times." Do something good for someone and you will be rewarded three times over. Do harm and you can expect three times the misery you caused to others to befall you. Felix had been apprehended because a "client," wanted to make a deal with a prosecutor for a lighter sentence. He was convicted and sentenced to life in prison without the possibility of parole. Now he was in pain due to an illness which could have been treated earlier if he had been in a more respectable line of work.

Kitty was not going there to judge. She too, had done wrong. She used knowledge gained while taking classes in interior design to meet a class requirement, as well as information she gained while working for a catering firm. She knew where and when to enhance her modest income by stealing valuable jewelry from the homes of people who had allowed her class to look around the interior of their Bel Aire or Beverly Hills home, or who had employed a caterer for a big party which required wait staff.

Luck, and maybe brains, as much as fate played a role in her eventual apprehension and conviction. Some of the thefts were blamed on a "bling ring" of young people with whom she had no ties. They were engaged in the same type of crime at about the same time.

She was only charged with one of her crimes, due to a lack of evidence which she had managed to conceal.

12

She had been wise enough to say she would plead guilty to the one charge and save the county of Los Angeles the expense of a trial if she got a favorable deal.

Since her crime was non-violent and only property was involved, the prosecution was willing. The police could label another case closed and turn their efforts to other crimes. Today in California she would probably have been given an even lighter sentence and earlier release due to the pressure to reduce prison overcrowding throughout the state.

Kitty prepared herself for bed with the knowledge that there was little she could do for Felix tomorrow morning. She felt an obligation, not only to an old friend of a friend, but also to another human being. He had made bad choices and, unlike her, would never have the chance to go back and get a "do-over." She also saw it as an application of that tenant of her faith; "And it harm none, do as ye will." What she would and could do might make a dying man's final days a tiny bit better, and harm no one.

Chapter 4

Kitty was up early on Saturday morning. The hours for visiting an inmate at the prison began at 7:30 a.m. and she wanted to be on her way again before noon. She had her letter from the Department of Corrections approving her visit. Felix had listed her as "clergy" under the "extended family, mentoring" category of visitors. Getting the approval from the Department of Corrections (DOC) took longer than expected due to her felony conviction almost thirty years before.

She dressed as she had planned before leaving Pacific Grove, very conservatively. No clothes in orange, blue, green or tan. It was going to be a sunny day, but her sunglasses would have to be left in the car along with a change of clothes in case something about her appearance upset the guards. She had nothing on with metal buttons or wires, so she should be OK when scanned by the metal detector. Now it was time to head down Highway 1 to the prison.

There was already a line of cars coming up Highway 1 toward the prison parking area, so Kitty decided to park outside and walk to the gate. With the top up on the Jaguar, the alarms set and everything locked, it was time to face the prison bureaucracy.

She knew what to expect from her own days in Chino. The guard, clad in the tan shirt and green pants of his uniform asked, "Who are you visiting, Ma'am?"

"Inmate Felix Morris, hospital wing, east facility," Kitty replied.

"ID and DOC approval documents please."

She extracted her driver license and the DOC paperwork from her purse, a quick examination and comparison with the list of approved visitors and it was time for the metal scanning. As expected, she had to shed her Wiccan pendant and turn over her purse to be returned when she departed. Once past the metal detector she was on her way to the east facility.

The east facility held inmates with medical conditions and those regarded as minimum risk for escape or violence. A guard conducted her to a large room with chairs and tables, much like any large dining area.

"The inmate will be brought down shortly," the guard informed her.

"When my visit is over, I'll need to talk with Warden Gastelo about funeral arrangements," Kitty responded.

"OK, ma'am, talk to me again before you leave and we'll see if she can see you today, or maybe you'll have to come back tomorrow."

"Thanks, I'll look for you later," Kitty responded.

The room gradually filled with other visitors. Kitty realized that she was about the only middle-aged white woman in the room. There were individuals like her, but also women accompanied by children. She knew that the corrections people felt that the presence of the family members lead to a better level of rehabilitation, and also reduced the level of recidivism among parolees.

Her wait was only about fifteen minutes. She hadn't seen Felix in many years, so the sight of this dried-up, feeble old man in a wheelchair was a bit of a surprise. Felix had been a "lean, mean fighting machine" when Jake had first introduced him to her. Now he was just an old man with the angel of death almost visibly riding on his shoulder. He sure wasn't going to live up to one of his Vietnam War era sayings: "Live fast, die young, have a good-looking corpse."

"Hey, Felix, long time no see," Kitty exclaimed.

"Hey Red, I'm glad you could make it. Where did you have to come from?"

"Just up the coast at Pacific Grove. I'm only a short drive from the Monterey Presidio," Kitty responded.

"The Presidio. That seems like a hundred years ago. Can you still see the harbor from there, or did it all get built up?'

"No, you can still see the harbor and Fisherman's Wharf from there. There are a couple of big new hotels near the old customs house, but the view from the Presidio is still like it was in 1961 when you were there."

"Yeah, over fifty years ago. I understand that Fort Ord is gone now?" Felix asked.

"Oh, yeah, they closed it about ten years ago. It took almost that long to clean up all the unexploded mortar rounds and grenades, but now parts of it are a university. A big area on the east side is now a National Monument. People can go hiking on trails or take bike rides. They do make a big thing about staying on the trails, because there might still be some things that could go "bang" lying about in the brush. There's even a housing tract, with nice homes, over near Reservation Road" Kitty explained.

"So, you live in Pacific Grove. Is it still the quiet town it was back in the '60s?" Felix asked.

"Oh sure, it's really quiet, except on a couple of weekends. There's always a big crowd when the Pebble Beach golf tourney is going on in February. It really gets crowded during Car Week."

"What's Car Week?" Felix asked.

"Actually, it's about ten days right around the middle of August. Back in the '70s an enthusiast with money started having races out at Laguna Seca. You might recall the track that was built there on Fort Ord land around 1957. He started having races for old sports cars at the same time as the big car show over at Pebble Beach. The whole thing just grew into ten or twelve days of shows, auctions and races. Thousands of people with big bucks to spend show up. That really has an effect on

16

Pacific Grove," Kitty explained. "But enough about that, let's talk about you."

"Well, what you see is what the mortician is going to get, and soon," said Felix. "The cancer is stage four, it's terminal, and so my '20 to life' is going to be the death of me. I don't have any family, at least none that I know of. I want you to take care of all the details about my funeral and so on."

Kitty responded, "I've already started looking into funeral arrangements. I remember that Jake had it all planned out and paid for before he took his own life. So, I see three options for you. One, I looked at burial at a national cemetery like Riverside, where Jake is. There's still room there, so I checked with the VA, and they would take care of the paperwork. Then I ran into a problem."

"Well," Felix said, "it is the VA, so problems have to be expected. So, what is it?"

"I thought that Riverside was the solution until someone at the VA told me about Title 38, United States Code, section 2411. It reads that no one can be buried in a National Cemetery if they have been found to have committed a capital crime. That is what the section says. So, I could try to slip it past the VA, but when they see that your body will be coming from a state prison, they'll shoot the plan down," Kitty concluded.

"Great! God only knows how many Viet Cong I killed in 'Nam, but I off some screen writer's agent and I'm not allowed to be buried with other 'Nam vets. Probably the law was written by some Congressman who protested the war in 'Nam and burned his draft card," Felix mumbled in pain.

"OK," Kitty interjected, "but there are other options. One involves money, but I'll help as much as I can. You could be cremated and have your ashes scattered at sea, or you tell me a place and I'll do the scattering. Then there is one that would meet the Wiccan standard."

"What do you mean," Felix asked.

"The standard I'm talking about is that whatever you do comes back to you three times. You did wrong, so you got sent to prison, have cancer, and will be denied a veteran's burial. That's three things. The other option is to donate your body to a medical school. That is a good deed, so three good things happen. One, it doesn't cost you or me anything. Two, you will help train doctors who could save lives. And three, there will be people who will live because of the doctors who learned from your death. Heck, your skeleton might even end up on display in a medical school classroom."

"Are you sure that anyone would take this body of mine?" Felix asked.

"Yes, I am. I know because I've asked people who have had similar situations, and both UCLA and USC medical schools will take your body. I'm pretty sure that UC Berkeley would do the same, and I can ask people at Stanford next week about their policy," Kitty responded. "But you will have to make out a will soon. Make it clear that you want me to be in charge of the details about your body. If you tell me what you want, I'll talk to Warden Gastelo before I leave today."

"OK, you've got me sold on the body donation to a medical school idea if it can be done. I can get help with making a will right here, but right now I'm feeling really bad, so I'm going to cut this visit short. How about you put a witch's curse or blessing on me before you leave, you red-haired pagan."

"All right," Kitty said, "put your left hand right over wherever it hurts the most. Now I'm going to hold your right hand and put my right hand on your forehead. Close your eyes while I whisper the words of the healing ceremony. This is like the ceremony the Japanese Shinto

18

religion follows. They call it 'Reiki', and it is known to lower your blood pressure and reduce pain. Just think about where your spirit will go when this life ends. We Wiccans call it Summerland. It's like the heaven of the Jews, Christians and Muslims, but in our religion there's no gate keeper like Saint Peter judging you."

"Thanks, Kitty," Felix said. "Where do you go from here?"

"Before I leave, I want a few words with the warden or her staff about your care. Then I'm off to Burbank to meet with a guy who thinks he'll create a TV series featuring a witch. After that I meet with a family who wants me to find a missing relative so they can close up the will of a parent and get on with their life. Write to my mailbox in Pacific Grove; here's my card. And don't forget to make a will so I can take care of your funeral. I'll probably see you again before you make that trip to Summerland."

"So long, Red. Be safe," Felix said as he wheeled his chair away.

Kitty caught the eye of the guard and reminded him of her wish to see the warden about Felix's funeral arrangements. She was escorted to the administrative offices where she met one of the few female wardens of a men's prison in the United States.

"Ms. D'Literie, a pleasure to meet you. I understand you are 'mentoring' one of our inmates, Felix Morris. How may we help you?" the warden asked.

"I'm basically looking after the disposal of his body. I think he is going to make a will asking that his body go to a medical school. My job will be to find a school that will accept his remains, perhaps USC, UCLA or Stanford. Am I correct that getting his body transported is not a problem?" Kitty asked.

"No, it's pretty routine with the aged 'lifers' here. We have a funeral home here in San Luis Obispo which will pick up the body and make the arrangements to get it delivered to whichever school you choose. Are there any special religious needs involved?" the warden asked.

"No, we Wiccans don't go in for ceremonies like Catholic Masses or memorial services, especially when the deceased has outlived or lost all contact with family. I'll work with the VA to see if there are any legal complications, but Federal law prohibits him being interred in a National Cemetery. If he changes his mind and wants to be cremated the process could be pretty cut and dried. I'll leave you my card, but I'll be in L.A. County for the balance of the week, so it might be hard to get in touch with me," Kitty concluded.

"Well, have a safe trip, and we'll keep you informed of Mr. Morris' condition. Goodbye."

Kitty made her way back to the prison gates, collected her belongings, went through a final search to be sure she was carrying nothing out, and headed for the Jaguar. She had to stop next to Malcolm for a minute to compose herself. The time with Felix was all pretty businesslike, but the subject of death did not make her feel lighthearted. She knew she would think about death as she drove south.

She turned off the alarms, put the top down, placed her unused spare clothes in the "boot" as the English called it, and fired up Malcolm for the trip to "beautiful downtown Burbank." She wanted to get there before Autobooks closed.

Chapter 5

Kitty had the Jaguar headed south on Highway 101 in a few minutes and began to wonder why she had felt so light-headed after she left the prison. Was it just seeing Jake's old sergeant in such sad shape? Suddenly it dawned on her: low blood sugar.

"Damn, heck and H-E-Double LL" she thought. "I forgot to eat breakfast!" In an hour she could get off Highway 101 and go to Solvang and Mortenson's Bakery. A good Danish pastry in a town built by Danes with a cup of coffee and she would be set for the journey to Burbank.

Timing was important now. She had to reach the Autobooks store in Burbank before the shop closed at six p.m. It wouldn't be open again until Tuesday, and she had a commitment at the easternmost corner of L.A. County then. While she enjoyed her late-morning breakfast she calculated her next move. Logic told her that the right move was to get back on 101 and head south. She was only 150 miles from Burbank, about two hours of driving time. "No," she thought, "that section through the Valley, on a Saturday afternoon? I'd better add another hour. That gets me there about three p.m."

Then romantic nostalgia kicked in. "What if," she thought, "I went to Santa Ynez and took Highway 154 over San Marcos Pass. I haven't been that way since Jake scouted the old stagecoach route for one of Huell Howser's videos about California."

The road over San Marcos Pass wouldn't be as fast as the coastal route that most travelers would take, but Kitty and Malcolm weren't most travelers. It would be a good workout for Malcolm, and if the bicyclists weren't too numerous it would be fun. She could even check to see if the old Cold Spring Tavern was still there. It was the place back in the 19th century where the stagecoach stopped to change horses and give passengers a break. It was the only place she had ever heard of that served, when available, venison, kangaroo and bear steaks. Yes, time to take "the road less traveled" as the poet, Robert Frost, once put it.

A quick stop on the way out of Solvang to give Malcolm more fuel and she was on her way again. As she had hoped, the biking crowd was more interested in going over to Los Olivos for wine tasting than climbing up the pass. She was in Santa Barbara in an hour, and now it was only a two-hour drive to Burbank.

As she had feared, the section of Highway 101 that ran from Topanga Canyon Blvd. in Woodland Hills to the junction with the 405 was a nightmare in the early afternoon. She did not enjoy the "dance step" of accelerator, brake, and clutch repeated every ten feet. She endured it and survived, making the transition to Highway 134 that took her to the Hollywood Way off-ramp. Up Hollywood Way toward the Warner Brothers lot, and when she spotted Porto's Bakery on the corner of Magnolia, she knew she was on time to visit Autobooks.

The shop, which is small but truly unique, was actually named Autobooks-Aerobooks. It had been founded around 1950 by an old racer named Harry Morrow. Harry was a greater supporter of racing, competing in tiny race cars called Formula III. Harry died in 1980 and the new owners moved the shop down Magnolia to be next door to the Porto's Bakery. It was in that shop that Kitty had first come into contact with Autobooks.

Kitty parked Malcolm on the side street next to the shop. She greeted an employee as she entered, saying "Wow, this is different from my first visit back in 1997. I was looking for the shop down by the bakery. By the way, I'm Katherine D'Literie, and I guess that you're the owner."

22

"Well," the young woman responded, "I'm Kate Bryne, and I'm managing the store while the owners are at a book sellers conference. When they bought the store in 2007, they could afford the rent near Porto's. Like everything else in California property, the rent just went up and up. Then the old original shop, where we are now, became available in 2010 so they jumped on the chance to move the business back to where it began."

"It's not as roomy as the one down the street," Kitty responded, "but I like what has been done with it. I remember going to the other location and the guy who helped me was very nice to a woman who didn't know much about old cars."

"Well, if it was the late 1990's it might have been Doug, one of the owners then. What were you looking for at that time?"

"Oh, my employer at that time, Jake O'Malley, was consulting on a police procedural TV show at the time. The plot was about crooks stealing classic or vintage cars and shipping them to collectors in Asia or South America. The writers knew nothing about those cars and wanted to read up on the subject. I waltzed in and bought some books and magazines for the writers to get familiar with the subject in a hurry. I guess some of it rubbed off and I got interested myself," Kitty explained.

"Okay, what brought you here today, besides that lovely E-type Jaguar you parked out there?"

"Well, among other projects I'm meeting on Tuesday with a client who wants a family member located. I've got to gather a lot more information about the missing person, but I know that he is obsessed with collecting, buying and selling vintage sports cars, especially a particular Jaguar. I want to learn more about the market in general, and where would be the best place to encounter someone who is in the market for such cars.

"You mention a Jaguar. You'll see that we have an entire shelf of books that cover the entire range of cars from that manufacturer. Is there one that your subject is especially interested in?" Kate asked.

"What I know so far is that the man I'm to look for became very interested as a boy in the C-type Jaguar, which I understand is really very rare."

Kate directed Kitty's attention to a segment of the Jaguar book display. "We have a couple of books on that model of Jaguar. If you want an introduction, I'd suggest 'Jaguar C-type & D-type' by Brooklands Books. It includes reproductions of articles written about the cars from 1951 to 1960. That will give you some talking points if you're dealing with real enthusiasts."

"Okay," Kitty replied, "do you have anything about the value of one of these cars today?"

"To be very frank and honest, if your man is looking for one of them to buy then he better have bags of money. I've never seen one. There were only about 50 of them ever built, and the last one sold in England about 30 years ago for 200,000 pounds. If your man is serious, he's looking for, pardon the cliché, the Holy Grail," Kate said.

"So, who might know where these rare creatures are," Kitty asked.

"I'd try two sources," Kate replied. "Go online and look for the Society of Automotive Historians. They used to have a chapter here in Southern California, but the chapter just died off. They are an international group with lots of members in the British Isles. Someone in the organization should be able to help you. Also, look online for British car clubs. They may only recruit MG owners, for example, but they probably know of a club for Jaguar owners that you could talk to."

"Well, thanks, Kate. You've given me some clues. I'm going to the Petersen Museum tomorrow. I hope one of the docents there can be of some help."

"There is a museum in San Diego that has a large data base to help automotive writers. You might also try looking for the Millen Museum in Oxnard, up the coast. The owner is crazy about French cars, but he might give you some clues," Kate suggested.

"I also plan to spend some time during 'car week' this summer," Kitty added. "What with all the auctions and shows I just might get a few more leads as to where the C-types are hiding now."

"Well, I do wish you luck. It won't be easy to find a missing man who is looking for a very rare car. And before you leave, can I sell you a couple of other publications? Classic and Sportscar is full of ads for rare cars and dealers in the United Kingdom. The recent issue of Classic Jaguar has more of the same but is focused more on selling or restoring that make of British cars."

"Okay, I'll take them and thank you again. It's been a long day getting here from San Luis Obispo, and I'm starved. I'm off for a late lunch at Porto's, and then I have to find my hotel on Glenoaks. I'm sure I'll be back this way again this year, and I appreciate all the guidance."

"Hey, you're welcome," Kate replied, "and you have my best wishes on your quest."

Kitty put her purchases in the Jaguar and headed down Magnolia for Hollywood Way. After a nice lunch she looked forward to a room with a comfortable bed and taking a relaxing shower. She was planning on dinner at the Coral Café on Burbank Blvd. and then trying to set up a meeting with Mel Goldfarb. She wondered what the would-be TV mogul would have to offer the witch of Pacific Grove.

Chapter 6

After a light lunch at Porto's, Kitty checked into her room at the Hampton Inn. She wanted nothing so much at that moment as the chance to shed the prison-approved outfit she had worn all day. She loved bright colors, but that didn't sit too well with the Department of Corrections.

Now, after a relaxing shower and a change into her favorite jeans and a loose blouse, she decided to give Mel Goldfarb a call. As expected, all she got was his voice mail and so she left a message.

"Mr. Goldfarb, this is Katherine D'Literie. I'm in Burbank and I'd like to get together to hear your movie ideas. I'm going to get dinner at the 'Coral Café' on Burbank Blvd. If you can, join me around seven; or we can try their brunch tomorrow morning." She gave him her cell phone number and the number of the front desk and ended the call.

As she lay back on the bed, letting the fatigue of the drive from San Luis ease away, she thought about how strange it was, all these years later, to be back in "movie land." Her mind wandered back to the years when she first met Jake O'Malley and this adventure had begun.

It was a wintery night in Palm Desert, December 1996. The air was clear and dry but bone-chilling cold if you were outdoors. She was working as the hostess at the 'Casuela's Café' on Palm Canyon Drive when a man she immediately assigned to the "retired military" category entered and asked for a table for one. She also made note of the gold ring on the fourth finger of his left hand.

She made her judgments based on a couple of features. First, the haircut: nobody, except an ex-Army man, or a retired Marine, would wear his hair cut that short. Secondly, he walked with a slight limp, indicative of some long-ago injury. She had some bad memories of military men, active or retired, that were a hangover from her two-year marriage that ended in divorce.

"This way sir," she said, and she directed the man to a table near the bar. "Jose will be your waiter, and he'll be with you in a moment. May I get you something to drink while you wait?"

"Yes, if the bartender has Jameson, I'll have a shot, neat," he replied.

"Well," she thought, "an Irishman of some sort, but that's a California accent if I ever heard one."

"I'll be right back with your drink, sir," she replied and set off to see what Johnny could do about that very specific request.

The restaurant wasn't very busy that cold December evening. She took some time to go from table to table as the owner-manager often did to see if the customers were happy. She noted that her new customer had settled on the enchilada dinner with a margarita replacing the Irish whiskey and she inquired, "Everything to your satisfaction sir?"

"Yes, young lady, it's all good. I've not been in here for a few years and decided to give it another try. You know, after you've lived somewhere for thirty years you just sort of take places like this for granted. They're just there, like the stop sign at the end of your block and you, well, you sort of overlook them."

"Well, I'm glad you decided to give Casuela's a try again. Hope we'll see you in here in the future. Now I'd better get back to the front counter. Nice talking to you," Kitty responded.

And so, a routine began. The customer would appear about eight on a Thursday evening, order a shot of Irish whiskey, have a dinner with a margarita and leave about ten p.m. Then one Thursday night he didn't appear. A month went by, and Kitty thought that they had lost a valued, regular customer. And then he reappeared.

"Good evening, sir. Your regular table?" Kitty greeted him.

As she got him seated, she commented, "I thought we had lost you as a customer. It's good to see you back."

"Oh, you hadn't lost me. I just started a new line of work, and it took me south of the border," he replied.

"Sounds interesting. Maybe when things are lighter here, you know, less busy, you can tell me about it. That is, if it's not too top secret," she responded.

"No, I'd enjoy telling you about it. And maybe you could tell me a little about yourself, if that's not too much to ask," he replied.

And so it was that Kitty learned that the mysterious customer was named Jake O'Malley. He had been scouting locations in the Sonoran Desert for a western movie that Sony was planning to film later in the spring.

She also learned that she was correct about her initial impressions. Jake was a retired Army officer who got into the movie business through a "side door." He had worked as a consultant on several movies that had a military or Vietnam War theme.

"Does your wife worry when you are gone for a month south of the border?" Kitty asked.

"My wife doesn't mind," Jake replied with a sigh. "She died back in '95. She had ALS, and dying was a slow, agonizing process," he concluded with a pained look.

"Oh, dear God, I'm so sorry. I shouldn't have asked," Kitty said, a tear appearing in each eye as she put her hand to her mouth.

"It's okay," Jake responded. "That's one reason you see me here so often. I never could cook worth a damn, so I decided why bother to learn at my age. So, I eat out almost every night. And it's not just her cooking I miss, or her company. She helped me a lot in my work when she wasn't taking care of our three kids."

"Do you still have kids at home?" Kitty asked.

"Oh no, they are all pretty much out on their own. The oldest boy is 26 and works in investment banking up in the Bay area. His brother is 24, and after law school he plans to join the Army and work in Judge Advocate General. We'll see how that works out in a year or so. And my daughter is in her junior year at CSULA. Plans to go into teaching elementary school. I only worry about who she may be dating and what that might lead to. And what about you? I don't see any rings on that left hand."

"I'm divorced," Kitty replied. "Have been since the spring of '96. You've probably heard that saying 'When I'm not near the one I love, I love the one I'm near.' That's what happened to me. PFC McEwan became CPL McEwan and was transferred to Fort Carson in Colorado. The terms of my parole at the time were that I couldn't leave the state. So, I stayed in Seaside, kept working at Tarpy's.' Alex fell in love with a girl who worked at the PX at Fort Carson. So, we divorced, and I moved down here. My parole officer got me this job, and I better get back to it. I hope to talk to you some more later."

Kitty was closing up and ready to go home at ten p.m. when the cook closed the kitchen. Jake had left moments before. When she tried to start her aged but trusty Honda Civic nothing happened. A dead battery in the dead of night.

Then Jake appeared and said, "Let me call a tow truck and have the car hauled to the dealer in Cathedral City. And do you need a ride home?"

"Well, I do, but home's a long way from here. I live in Desert Hot Springs where all the other low-income folks and retirees can afford to live."

"Good grief, that's miles from here. Why didn't you rent in Indio?" Jake inquired.

"Because when I say low income, I mean LOW INCOME, and Desert Hot Springs is what I can afford," she retorted.

"I understand," Jake replied. "We'll follow the tow truck to the dealer, and you can leave a note on the windshield. Tell them to replace the battery and check out the charging system. I'll get you home and you can get a cab to the dealership tomorrow. Is all that okay with you?"

"Thank you. I really appreciate your kindness. This is quite a car you've got here."

"Oh, The Jaguar?" Jake exclaimed. "I got it shortly after Jane died. I guess buying it was some sort of self-indulgence to offset the grief, and I'd wanted one for a few years. It's almost 30 years old, but it was always well maintained."

With the Honda on the hook of the tow truck, the trip to Desert Hot Springs began. Jake asked the question Kitty knew would come up, as it almost always did.

"So, you were on parole. Whatever for? You don't seem like the criminal type," Jake inquired.

"I got a three-to-five-year sentence for one count of theft and one of burglary," Kitty responded. "I got paroled just a little short of the three years. That was way back in 1992. Then I moved to Monterey County, at my parole officer's direction to be away from the temptations of Beverly Hills, and I got married."

"So, this was all after you went to school? I assumed from your speech patterns that you went beyond high school."

"Yes, you're looking at a UCLA graduate. B.A. in American Literature and Culture, class of 1988."

"So, did you do any post-grad study while you were locked up? I've heard some inmates take extension classes."

"No," she replied, "but they put me to work in the prison library because of my degree. I learned some skills there. It was good to do some research into the laws, in case I ever need to argue about a traffic ticket."

"Well, here we are at the Hot Springs area," he said. "Point me to where you live, and I'll wait in the car until I see that you're inside and have a light on. I'd like to talk to you some more about your research skills. I just might be able to give you more than just a ride home. Now, goodnight, and be safe."

At that point her reverie was interrupted by the ring tone on her phone.

"Hello, this is Katherine D'Literie."

"Hi. This is Mel Goldfarb. I'm glad you called. I can't join you this evening, but brunch tomorrow is something I can do. What time are you talking about?"

"How about 10:30, Mr. Goldfarb. I want to go to the Petersen Museum in the afternoon, so that would be my best time frame."

"I'll see you at the 'Coral' at 10:30. But how will I recognize you? It's been a long time since you worked with O'Malley"

"That's easy," she replied. "Just look for the tall redhead in the bright yellow jacket. Thanks for returning my call. I'll see you tomorrow."

"I look forward to meeting you, and have a good night," Goldfarb said as he ended the call.

"Okay," Kitty thought, "that's all set. Now it's time to see what the cooks at the 'Coral' can do for me." She grabbed her purse, phone and keys and set off to see if the valets had taken care of Malcolm properly.

Chapter 7

It was Sunday morning, and Kitty liked to sleep in on such a day. She sometimes thought about people she knew and their Christian faith. To her, Sunday was a day when, if the planets aligned correctly, she might enjoy good fortune, as in "make some money." That however required that she burn a yellow candle, which for a Wiccan traveling far away from home can be a problem. You don't exactly call down to room service and ask for, "a pot of decaf, two croissants with jam, and if you have one, a yellow candle."

Fortunately, her beliefs taught her that gold was a metal associated with Sunday, so her gold chain around her neck would be part of the ritual. And in Wicca one increases the power of the ritual by a chant or a dance while singing and clapping her hands. So, what could she sing while she took her shower that might deal with wealth or fortune?

The first tune that came to her mind was "Diamonds Are a Girl's Best Friend," as sung in a movie by Marilyn Monroe and Jane Russell. Well, it was diamonds and gold that got her three years in prison, and she couldn't recall all of the words. Then the song made famous by Doris Day came to mind. Even Kitty could sing "Que sera, sera, whatever will be will be" in the shower, then dress for brunch at the Coral Café and whatever would be would be.

At 10:20 a.m., Kitty was seated at a table at the Coral, positioned so she could keep an eye on the door. As planned before she left Pacific Grove she was wearing her bright yellow jacket and black pants. The suitcase wrinkles from the trip to Burbank had been nicely pressed out, and her white blouse looked as it had on the day she bought it at the Carmel Plaza. And the red lipstick, she hoped, made her look somewhat younger than she felt. Fifty-one years old, and here she was hoping to make an impression on a would-be movie magnate. "This must be him," she thought as a short, balding man of indeterminate middle age approached her table.

"Ms. D'Literie? I'm Mel Goldfarb. Hope I haven't kept you waiting," he said, as she rose to offer her hand.

"Glad to meet you, Mr. Goldfarb. Mind if I call you Mel? And most people just call me Kitty, because my initials are K.T."

"Okay, Kitty it is. How was your trip down from Monterey?"

"Oh, it was a mixed bag. Yesterday morning I spent time with a dying inmate at the so-called Men's Colony in San Luis Obispo. Yesterday afternoon I was over at Autobooks on Magnolia doing a little research, and last night I was here at the Coral for dinner."

"Wow, that's quite a day. I take it you didn't fly in to our Bob Hope airport," he asked.

"No, I seldom fly. I'm not wild about TSA at the airport. It's crowded and uncomfortable on the plane and I'd end up renting a car anyway. I like driving my old Jaguar when I can."

"Ah, that old E-Type I saw outside might be yours. Anyway, shall we order something and then talk a little business?"

Kitty got the waiter's attention, and they placed their orders. She wasted no time getting to the reason she was here, asking "Mel, what do you think I can do for you in this movie project you mentioned?"

"Okay, here's what I have in mind. Witches, vampires, and demons, all that sort of thing seems to have some sort of attraction for a young demographic today. Probably just a fad, but if I can cash in on it, why not?"

"Do you have any writers lined up?" Kitty asked.

"I do, but their experience is mostly with what I would call the 'action hero' genre. They see everything through the view of comic books, which seems to be big these days."

"And are you looking to do a single feature-length movie, or a TV series with weekly episodes?" she asked.

"Oh, definitely the latter. With all the cable channels and streaming options looking for content, that's the way to go," he replied.

"And what about finances," she asked. "The startup costs must be huge."

"That I've got a handle on," he replied. "Again, people see opportunity in these many outlets all competing for an audience share. They view it as an investment."

"And you, what have you done in the industry? I don't recall your name on many credits," she asked.

"Well, you probably won't like to hear this, but do the names Vivid or Miracle mean anything, as in 'If it's a good picture it's a Miracle'?"

"Okay, I think those two production companies were solely related to what is euphemistically called 'adult entertainment,' or what the rest of us would call 'porn.' Am I correct?" Kitty asked with a trace of a scowl on her face.

"You've got it on the first take," Mel replied. "But I'm out of that now and looking to make some money in a more, shall we say, respectable part of the industry."

"Well, that's good to know, but I'm not sure I want my name tied up with someone who is trying to become respectable. Which leads me to a question you'll find curious and maybe insulting. Are you on parole by any chance?"

"Why on earth would you ask a question like that?" Mel asked. "No, I'm not on any parole or any type of probation."

"I asked," Kitty responded, "in your own interest. Anyone on parole who talks to me runs the risk of being rearrested and sent back to prison. Parolees are not allowed to be in the company of a convicted felon in California, which sadly is what I am."

"Good grief, what did you do to get convicted, and when was this?"

"Many years ago, back in the 1980s. Let's just say that I watched too many episodes of the Pink Panther movies and the LAPD version of Inspector Clouseau finally caught up with me," Kitty explained. "But enough about crime and punishment. What kind of movie or TV series are you planning? What's the basic plot idea?"

"Well, and I'm serious about this, I think that we could do a sequel to the movie Witch Hunt, from back in 1994. If you don't recall it, the plot was that a private investigator, played by Dennis Hopper, got himself hired to catch a husband who was cheating on his wife. His investigation gets him involved with a local politician who is sure that a coven of witches is messing up everything in Los Angeles and he must stop them. I think a series of maybe twenty episodes could be worked around this private investigator getting drawn into a public investigation about this crazy politician's idea."

"Okay," Kitty responded. "I'll let you know up front here and now that I'm what's called in Wicca a solitary. I don't belong to a coven and never have. I've got nothing against them, but I never liked what colleges call 'Greek society,' that is sororities and fraternities, so I do my thing on my own."

"So, if we had a single witch encountering our private eye you could give advice?" Mel asked.

"Sure, but don't expect me to share with your writers how to cast spells or anything like that I'll tell you that there are many diverse covens, and they often pledge to secrecy. They are as numerous and divided as the denominations of Christianity," Kitty explained.

"So how did you get into witchcraft?" Mel asked.

"I first met some Wicca in prison, back in the early 1990s. My family was Catholic, but I began to drift away after my mother died when I was just starting college. I had read about the Salem witch trials and got curious, so I read more while in prison. Then I found that you could actually take classes online, if you could pay. I gradually learned enough, at about $50 per month, to be certified as a Wicca priestess."

"So, you can actually be considered a form of clergy? Isn't this whole thing some sort of New Age cult movement?" Mel asked somewhat skeptically.

"Come on, Mel. You went through bar mitzvah, right? I don't know where she crops up in your version of the Old Testament, but in the King James Version of the Christian Bible they mention the Witch of Endor. King Saul tried to wipe out all witches, but he ended up consulting 'a woman that hath a familiar spirit' at Endor. Endor exists. It's a little town near Mount Tabor. Saul consulted with her because he thought the Philistines would wipe him out. She had a vision, probably ESP, and she said she could connect him with the prophet Samuel. So, we who believe are not some new phenomena. We go way back!"

"Okay, my apologies. I see if I'm going to go down this path with a story involving a witch, I'm really going to need a consultant. I also noted from your questions a little while ago that you seem to have a grasp of the movie industry. How did that happen?"

"Back in 1997 I was working at a restaurant, and I met a man named Jake O'Malley. He was a Vietnam vet who had been widowed a couple of years before. He did some consulting for producers on scripts tied to Vietnam, and later other war movies. Then he got into location scouting for both movies and TV shows. He found out I was educated, had some research skills which his wife used to do for him, so he hired me. He had a pretty big home in Palm Desert, met a lot of entertainment industry folks and my job went from researcher to, I guess you might call it, major domo. You know, the 'Gal Friday' that keeps things organized around the home and the business. I became his companion if he went to a social event or some awards show in the Hollywood area. I just absorbed a lot of knowledge without any formal training."

"Well, I think we could work something out between us to our mutual advantage," Mel stated. "How long are you going to be around the L.A. area?"

"I'm going by the Petersen Museum over on Wilshire after I leave here. I've got to meet with the curator or a docent about the research I need for my new client. Tonight, I'm going to dine at Taix on Sunset; got to maintain connections to my French roots. Tomorrow I've got to make contact with the Veterans Administration and the UCLA medical school for my friend in San Luis. And Tuesday I meet with the new client who wants me to try to find a long-lost relative. Then, I'll be happy to head for home in Pacific Grove," Kitty concluded.

"Wow, you really have a lot of irons in the fire, as the saying goes. So, give me your card, and here's mine. It's probably easier to contact me online than on the phone. Let's stay in touch, and I'll keep you informed about where the 'private eye' story line is going."

"I will, Mel. I'm glad we've met and maybe something creative will come of this. I'll stay in touch," Kitty concluded.

She picked up the tab, waved the waiter over with her credit card and within a few minutes she and Malcolm were headed over the Cahuenga Pass on her way to the Petersen Museum.

Chapter 8

Once past Cahuenga Pass, Kitty looked for the off-ramp for Highland Avenue. Traffic was light for an early Sunday afternoon in Hollywood. As she passed the intersection of Highland and Sunset Boulevard she noted that Hollywood High School hadn't changed much over the ten years since she left Southern California for the calm of Pacific Grove. She made a right turn onto Sunset and drove west toward Fairfax Avenue.

Fairfax was a street she remembered from childhood. Before he died her father took her to see what he called "the original Farmers Market." He wanted her to see and sample some of the products of farms and food vendors. He seemed to have a special affection for the corned beef sandwiches of one market stall called Magee's Kitchen, and the baked goods of a place called Dupar's. He would buy her a sandwich that was far too big for a ten-year-old girl, and then a pastry from Dupar's she could have for breakfast the next day. Then, while they ate their sandwiches, he would tell her about coming to baseball games at a stadium long gone, and how he never did like the Dodgers coming to Los Angeles. Now, like the Hollywood baseball team he loved, he was gone, suddenly and violently in that plane crash. Her mother seldom went near the Farmers Market as she wanted to be sure that the settlement money from her husband's death would last as long as possible. Now she too was a fading memory.

Kitty only had a short distance further on Fairfax to the intersection with Wilshire Boulevard. That section of the street was called, for reasons she never understood, the "Miracle Mile." She often wondered if the "miracle" was that traffic ever moved on Wilshire. On the southeast corner of the intersection, she reached her destination, the Petersen Museum.

She remembered the museum from a time she attended a social gathering held there sometime around 2003 or 2004. Jake often took her along to these "soirees," as he called them, as his companion. He always introduced her to the Hollywood crowd in attendance as his research assistant. He also referred to her, if in conversation with someone from the military or with a military background, as his "S-2." That is an Army term for the intelligence officer of a unit.

Jake had realized long ago that a woman could pick up on points of conversation and so-called "body language," those subtle gestures and mannerisms that a man might never even notice. Then add the fact that a woman, in conversation with another woman, might find things revealed that might be of value when assessing whether the woman's male companion was trustworthy and reliable. In the often less than straightforward world of Hollywood such clues could be of value when deciding one's level of involvement with some proposed project under consideration.

Many men scorn and often scoff at the concept of "feminine intuition." Jake was not one of these men. He knew that many species rely on instinct to let them know when situations were different or even dangerous. He felt that women were more instinctive than men in many ways, and that this was often labeled intuition. He also felt that this intuition was another source of potentially useful "intelligence," so he encouraged Kitty to "listen to her instincts."

Kitty also knew that many women to whom she was introduced probably had an instinctive reaction to her job title. She sensed that some of them probably reacted with the unspoken thought "Research assistant my foot! She's his mistress, has been for years." Kitty didn't let the unspoken reaction just roll off her back. If anyone

39

inquired about what she was researching, she would tell them about her other duties.

Jake often was gone from home for a week or two looking at potential locations for an upcoming "shoot." Once he was gone for an entire month to Thailand. He had quickly figured out that Kitty could fill that major domo role that she had mentioned to Mel Goldfarb. Twice each month Anna and Alejandra came to clean the entire house. Once each week Lorenzo and Roberto came to edge, mow, trim and rake. Once each week Sally came to do the laundry, make the beds and wash windows. Every day, Rufus and Winston, the two Welsh Corgi dogs, had to be fed and taken for a walk, and on occasion taken to the veterinarian. Of course, the four cars had to be maintained and used to keep them functioning properly, and from time to time there arose a need for a plumber or painter. If Jake were hosting a dinner gathering of some sort, Kitty would hire one of two professional chefs that she knew to do the meal preparation as neither she nor Jake had any interest in cooking. Jake knew he needed someone to supervise all of this, plus ensure that the bills got paid and a budget maintained. So, the research assistant pretty quickly became the major domo. No matter what the skeptics and the busybodies might fantasize, there was no sexual activity in the relationship.

Kitty sometimes had wondered what she would have done in those years in the late 1990's when Jake took her into his life as a researcher. What if he had made any romantic overtures? She was in her early thirties then, so it wasn't improbable. Jake was in his mid-to-late sixties and widowed. Would she have consented? She didn't know, but she could understand that other women might be skeptical. All she knew was that such a proposition never came up. Jake never made a "pass" at her, and always kept the relationship a professional one during their ten years together. What about her feelings; did she love him? All she could say was that she cried her heart out on that November afternoon in 2006 when he took his life on Mount San Jacinto.

Now here she was on a Sunday afternoon in the spring, back in the Petersen Museum. She could recall when it was the Orbach's Department Store, one of many stores that had lost the struggle against the Goliath of the East Coast, Macys. The Petersen family, whose wealth came from publishing Hot Rod and other motor magazines, bought the building out of the bankruptcy process and converted it at great expense into an automotive museum. The evening that she and Jake had attended the soiree the occasion was two-fold. First, the entire underground level of the museum was remodeled and was to be renamed "The Vault." This would be where cars could be stored by the dozens and only viewed by groups of "important people" at designated times. The second reason for that gathering was to announce that added to that collection in "The Vault" would be the extremely rare Jaguar XK-SS owned by the late movie star, Steve McQueen, who had died far too early in life in 1980.

It was to talk to Chris, the docent in charge of "the Vault" that had brought Kitty to the Petersen this time. She also wanted to see what the $90 million spent in 2015 by the Petersen estate on new renovations had done to the place. After parking the Jaguar in the attached three-story parking structure and paying her admission she explained to the docent near the entrance her interest in talking with Chris. Before she knew it she was on the elevator and whisked down to the Vault where Chris awaited her.

"Hello, Chris. I'm Kitty D'Literie. We've met once before at the grand opening of this display."

41

"Welcome to the Petersen, Kitty. I understand you want some information on rare Jaguars."

"That's correct. On Tuesday I'm meeting with a family that is trying to settle an estate and to do so they hope I can locate a long-lost heir. The only major clue I have at this point is that he is wild about Jaguar competition cars, particularly the XK120C and the XK-SS, which is even more rare. What I want is a contact name, someone who can tell me where these rare cars can be found. If I can start there maybe I can pick up the trail of the missing heir."

"Well, Kitty," Chris replied, "I can say that your best bet is to contact the Society of Automotive Historians. The SAH has hundreds of members, each of whom has a special interest. They can direct you to those members who have a serious interest in Jaguars. Their email address is simple: www.autohistory.org. I also know that in Canada there is a college professor who knows a lot about Jaguars and other historians. So those would be the best places to start."

"What are the chances that any Jaguar C-types or an example of an XK-SS will come up for sale at an auction," Kitty asked.

"I'd say about zero. And if your missing man isn't careful, he might be looking at a very carefully crafted replica. Two firms in the U.K. are turning out some really authentic looking replicas, which to the real hard-core collectors are like art forgeries. No, getting your hands on one of the original fifty XK120C models would be like the plot of the McQueen movie, The Thomas Crown Affair. To get one he'll have to steal one."

"Well, thanks Chris. I'm going to go back upstairs and look at some of the public displays before I go on my way. And I hope I'm not going to get myself into a missing manhunt that becomes a search for a thief. Do you ever get any attempts at theft here?"

"The only theft attempts," Chris replied, "are on the first floor where the bookstore and the items of clothing, like T- shirts, are on sale. I'm sure though that some visitors fantasize about stealing a Corvette or rare Porsche, but none have tried to my knowledge."

Kitty took a quick tour of the museum and stopped for a bite at the snack bar on the first floor. Then it was time to reclaim Malcolm and take a little side trip on her way to the Echo Park area and the Taix restaurant.

Kitty found herself in a nostalgic mood. She hadn't been anywhere near the home she left so long ago to attend UCLA. Her knowledge of Los Angeles told her that to reach the house on London Street in the Silverlake areas she could go east on Wilshire to Vermont Avenue or, she thought, go back up Fairfax to Beverly Boulevard and go east on Beverly. "Yes," she decided, "that's the better way. There'll be less traffic than on Wilshire."

So, she made her way to Beverly Boulevard, made the right turn and headed east. She made her way east on Beverly until just past Vermont, and soon enough she was on London Street. Once there she wished she hadn't come that way. As someone once wrote "You can't go home again." The house, built, she was once told, by her grandfather, was now an ugly dump occupied by people who didn't look too friendly or neighborly. "Forget it. It's part of the past, not my future," she thought.

With a little more time to kill before dinner she decided to visit the old French Quarter. She had noted that parts of Los Angeles now had what looked like designated ethnic neighborhoods. She knew that the area of Fairfax south of Wilshire was always a Jewish neighborhood. Now she saw signs telling her that she was passing Koreatown, and part of Sunset Boulevard east of the Hollywood Freeway was labeled Thai Town, and near Western Avenue was Little Armenia. If she had stayed on Beverly, she would have entered Filipino

43

Town. Where she headed now had been for a long time labeled Chinatown.

In 1860 it was the French Quarter, with a hospital. The French Benevolent Society had a prepaid health plan. You could be covered by the plan for $1 per month, and your "co-pay" was 50 cents for each visit to the doctor. The Society bought the four lots next to the doctor's house and built the French Hospital. To make sure that everyone knew whom they were, the Society commissioned a bronze statue of Joan of Arc to be placed on the lawn in front of the hospital.

Kitty wanted to see if Joan of Arc still stood on guard before the old building. She did. Kitty headed the Jaguar back to Sunset. Time to go to Taix and get some French onion soup and a Basque dinner.

Chapter 9

Kitty didn't have as much trouble finding a parking place near Taix as she had expected. "Good," she thought, "the Dodgers aren't playing at home so I may be in luck getting seated."

As she surveyed the menu, she took note of the items she really wanted. The French onion soup was $8.50, a small salad was going to cost her $5.00 and the salmon filet in champagne sauce was going to be $25.95, and she was sure it would all be good. "Wait," she thought, "this is Sunday. I wonder if they still offer the Sunday Supper Special?"

The waiter assured her that the "Special" was still available. "And what does that include this Sunday?" she asked.

"We start with a green pea soup, your choice of any salad, and the chef's choice of the entrée tonight is the French style chicken pot pie. For dessert you have your choice of different flavors of sherbet, and the price is $25."

"I'll take the Special, with a small green salad, and add a glass of Pinot Grigio," Kitty said. She began to think about what this trip to southern California was costing her, and so far, it had all been outgo with no income. As she waited for her soup, she began to think about the dollars she wasn't making on this venture so far.

"Once I get back to Burbank and the Hampton Inn, I'm going to call the Biltmore and get a room there for Monday and Tuesday nights," she thought. "Yes, it'll be more expensive, but I can contact the Veterans Administration and the UCLA Medical School and go there if it's necessary at this point. Then I'll call the International Jewelry Center and see if Avedis is still there. If he is, I can just walk over there from the

Biltmore; it's just across Pershing Square from the hotel. I've got to start watching the 'bottom line' a little bit more than I have."

As she enjoyed her dinner, she also enjoyed looking around the room at the other diners, mostly couples, from the elderly husband and wife to the young couple who probably were on a "get acquainted" date arranged on the internet. She thought about the way Jake and she had met back there in Palm Desert years ago when a restaurant was her employer. If she hadn't been working there, she probably would never have met him.

She would never have been his employee and wouldn't be driving the Jaguar she first saw on that night when he came to her rescue and gave her a ride home. Jake had continued the pattern of Thursday night at Casuela's with an enchilada dinner and a margarita. He had always made certain to be around as she ended her workday and chatted with her about her education. He seemed to be most interested in what she wanted to do in the future.

About three months after they first met, he asked if he could meet her before her work began on the following Monday. "Sure," she said, "that's easy, because like most restaurants we're closed on Monday. Where do you want to meet?"

"How about we meet around noon at the California Pizza Kitchen on Palm Canyon Drive? I've got an offer I want to present to you."

"Okay," she responded, never bothering to ask where this might be leading. It didn't worry her as she thought, "Whatever it is, he's either after my body or my brain, and I'd probably be glad to offer him either one if the idea he presents sounds good."

In a way it was both that he wanted, but not in the way she had anticipated. After they got a pizza and some

46

beer, she opened the conversation with, "Well, Jake, so what is the offer?"

"It's pretty simple." He responded. "I need to employ a person who has some background in, shall we say, looking things up. Let's call it research. One who can look things up online, in a library, or a hall of records. Someone who can go out and ask questions while I'm away looking for a place for a director to stage a movie gunfight. A person with a good education, some skill with words, who has an open and friendly personality. Someone, I think, like you."

"Well," Kitty responded, "that all sounds pretty promising, and frankly, rather flattering. Now, if I can be blunt about it, what's in it for me?"

"That's what I like, straight to the point," Jake said. "What I propose, to start, is that you would be a full-time salaried employee, starting at a flat sum of $750 per week, which I'm *not* defining as eight hours a day, five days per week. Bear in mind I'm not talking about punching a time clock. Some days may be just free time, while others may be long, boring, and eye-straining. And, if you don't mind, I have another 'perk' which you can accept or reject."

"Well," she responded, "the wages sound good, especially since as the hostess at Casuela's I only get a small percentage of the tips the waiters receive, plus the hourly minimum wage $5.15. You're offering to triple my weekly income. So, what's the 'perk' you brought up?"

"Well, it would require moving on your part. When my late wife got ill with ALS, I knew that we would soon need round-the–clock nursing help. I had our garage modified, adding a small apartment where a nurse could stay when my wife was asleep. It's not much bigger than a hotel room and it's just sitting there empty. It's yours to use if you want the job, free of all charges

47

except that you pay for the phone and the Internet connection."

"So, I'd be living on your property rent free? That would be one helluva 'perk.' What would your kids say about the arrangement?"

"I don't think there would be any negative reactions. They know I need help with research and fact-finding, often involving finding locations for filming and learning just who owns a piece of property. Also, what do they want for the use of the location. Then there are local governments to deal with and their rules and regulations for having filming within their territory. It's amazing how many trucks, all of them taking up large parking spaces, that it takes to shoot just a few feet of film. These are some of the things my wife did when she was alive and well. As for the kids, they still have rooms should they wish to visit or even move back home, heaven forbid."

"Give me until Thursday evening to think about it, and if I have any more questions, I'll bring them up then," Kitty said. "I do have one more question at this point. What will the neighbors think, and what do you think their reaction will be, seeing a strange woman on your property?"

"I don't worry much about the neighbors. It's not like we live within a few feet of each other. This is, regardless of the size of the house, the desert. Everyone may know who's who but, unless there is some big disturbance, nobody really gives two hoots about the neighbors. They know who I am and about my sometimes-lengthy absences, but they just go about their lives and leave others alone."

"All right. As I said, I'll see you on Thursday and give you my decision, or ask any other questions," Kitty concluded. And with that their first business meeting came to an end.

Kitty knew that the offer was too good to turn down, but she thought, "What's the harm in a little bit of the 'hard to get' approach." She did think of one concern, which indicated that she was more aware about personal finances than the usual thirty-year-old woman. She brought that issue up during their Thursday evening talk.

"Jake, I'm really interested in your offer, but I have two questions. First, will I be an employee, or what they call an independent contractor? I'm still young, but I won't always be. I think of things like Social Security and who is paying into it."

"Kitty, you'll be an employee of Old Warrior Trust, a limited liability corporation, which owns the real estate and the vehicles stored there. Income taxes and Social Security come out of your pay just like at the restaurant. The corporation also offers a medical plan through Kaiser Permanente, in case that was the next question you were going to ask."

"Wow," Kitty exclaimed, "you really have this thing organized. I like that, so I'm going to say yes to your offer, and tomorrow I'm going to give Casuela's my two-week notice." So, on that evening in the fall of 1997, K.T. D'Literie became a full-time employee of the Old Warrior Trust. Within a month she had moved out of her tiny apartment in Desert Hot Springs and into the small apartment attached to the four-car garage in Palm Desert.

As Kitty finished her orange sherbet dessert, she realized that it was time to stop traveling down "memory lane" and get organized for what she needed to do on Monday and Tuesday. She took out her little notebook that she always carried in her purse and noted, in no particular order, the things she needed to do the next day. She wrote: Contact VA and UCLA, call Avedis Sarkisian at the Jewelry center, get directions to the Shepherd

49

house in La Habra Heights and contact Janet Nguyen in Westminster.

"There," she thought, "that ought to keep me busy tomorrow. Then I'll check out of the Hampton Inn, and if Avedis is available I'll go see him before I go to the Biltmore. If he can do for me now what he did for me before, my 'cash flow' situation should improve."

She called over the waiter and settled her bill, adding a nice tip, got Malcolm fired up and was on her way back to Burbank. If all went well in the coming week, she'd have a new assignment and be "home and dry" as the English say, once again in Pacific Grove.

Chapter 10

It was Monday morning, and Kitty had already begun her plan for the day. She had called the Biltmore and reserved a room for two nights. Now, once she was sure she could get a real person on the phone, she would start dealing with the agenda she had set for herself last night before she left Taix.

She had added one more item to the list. She would call Mel Goldfarb and let him know that she would send him an e-mail in a week and give him the names of some local Wiccans. She wasn't sure about all the work that being a "consulting witch" might entail. "Consulting Witch," she thought, "sounds very professional. Didn't Sherlock Holmes call himself a 'consulting detective'? Maybe I'll add that to the description on my business cards."

While she waited for business offices to open for phone calls, she treated herself to the free breakfast at the Hampton Inn and packed for departure. No need to look too business-like today, so the comfortable jeans and a blouse would do.

At nine A.M. she called the Veterans Administration in Westwood. She briefly explained to the benefits officer what the situation was with Felix in prison and death imminent. Since he desired to have his body donated to a medical school, would the VA help with any related expenses?

The answer was bureaucratically straightforward. Since the veteran was dying in a non-VA facility, and would not be buried in San Luis Obispo County, the VA would pay up to $300 for expenses related to disposition of the remains. Felix's executor, which would be Kitty, would have to pay the bills and submit the death certificate and receipts to the VA and then wait for the VA to settle the claim.

The UCLA Medical School was next on her "to call" list. Their answer was simple. They would accept a body that did not die of a communicable disease, was intact, the cancer hadn't metastasized to other areas of the body and the body was within 75 miles of the school. If the body was more than 75 miles away, then the executor had to come up with the extra cost of transportation.

The USC Keck Medical School had almost the same response, adding that there were three forms to be completed before the person's death, including a vital statistics form. The statistics form was intended to determine if the deceased was in a category that the school was looking for to aid in their research into diseases of the elderly. USC also had the 75-mile radius rule. This meant that there would be out-of-pocket costs to her as the executor.

"This is getting a little bit complicated," Kitty thought. She would have to get a more detailed estimate on the cost of transportation versus the cost of the cremation option. It looked like she would be back at San Luis before Felix died.

Her fourth call was to the International Jewelry Center on Hill Street. When the switchboard answered her, she asked to be connected to Avedis Sarkisian. A familiar voice came on at the third ring. "This is Mr. Sarkisian. How may I help you?"

"Avedis, this is Kitty D'Literie. Remember me? It's been a long while since we did any business."

"Kitty, where on earth are you? It's been years since you and I last did some business," came his response.

"I'm in L.A. for a brief while," she responded. "I wonder if I can stop by your office later this week. Also, do you still have that connection in Mexicali?"

"I do, kiddo, so I guess this will be another sales opportunity?" he asked.

"Yes, and it should be the last one. I have to contact my associate in Orange County, but I'd like to drop by sometime around noon on Wednesday and give you the package, if that's okay with you."

"That'll be fine," Avedis said. "Give me a call when you are ready to meet, and I'll join you for lunch. Where are you staying?"

"I'm going to be at the Biltmore this evening so maybe lunch there would be good," she said.

"That sounds good, Kitty. I'll look forward to your call."

Avedis Sarkisian was, if you haven't guessed, of Armenian heritage. His family history played a part in how Kitty dealt with her, shall we say, ill-gotten goods. His family had been forced to flee from the terror of the Ottoman Empire during the genocide of World War I. They, like Jews who were smart enough to flee Germany after Hitler came to power in 1932, converted everything they could sell into diamonds and precious stones. Diamonds and gems can be easily concealed when crossing international borders, and are a much more universal currency than gold. The Sarkisians fled south into Persia, today's Iran.

They prospered in business there, and when many years later the Muslim fundamentalists overthrew the Shah the next generation of Sarkisians were unwelcome as Christians. Again, property was sold; the proceeds were converted to "rocks" and the family fled, first to Egypt and then to the United States. Some of the family bought farmland in the Imperial Valley near El Centro. Avedis found a slot in the Jewelry Exchange and later at his new location in the International Jewelry Center.

Avedis had never asked Kitty, when she first approached him in 1998, where her small hoard of "stones" came from. He probably surmised that they weren't an inheritance, but that was not his business. His business was to buy and sell diamonds, gemstones and precious metals to buyers around the world. He knew that most of the gold, for example, would be going to India where that metal was valued greatly as jewelry for weddings and anniversaries. He knew that the diamonds would very possibly be going to Venezuela. High-ranking government officials and military officers there were acquiring "stones" in preparation for flight when the corrupt government was overthrown.

His assignment would be to go to a dealer in Mexicali who had contacts in Mexico City who, in turn, would make the "cargo" available to dealers in South America. He also knew that gems were easier to move across the border going south than the stolen cars that came across the same border. It had been this way for Jews fleeing Germany and Armenian Christians fleeing the Turks.

Kitty's next call was to Janet Nguyen. Janet and Kitty met years before when they were students at UCLA. Janet's family had fled South Vietnam before the fall of Saigon in 1975. Her father had acquired a small complex of workshops on Hoover Street in Westminster, and many small Asian-owned businesses operated out of these shops.

Janet was the one person she called when she was arrested in 1989. She came to the West L.A. police Station on Butler Avenue, just a block south of Santa Monica Boulevard. Kitty's instructions were simple and direct. "Janet, I've been arrested and I'm going to be gone for a while, probably a couple of years. Here are my car keys and the key to my apartment. I want you to retrieve my car; you know it, the little Honda 600, before it is towed. It's on the 300 block of Bel Air Road.

"I want you to ask your dad if it can be stored in one of his shops. Don't worry about maintenance, just get it parked and leave it be until I get out. Then get my clothes out of the apartment and tell the landlady to cooperate with the police when they show up to search it, which they will do."

"What did you do, for heaven's sake, to get yourself arrested," Janet asked.

"What I did was not realize that a so-called 'baby camera' could be operating when no one was home and could be linked directly to the LAPD. I was arrested before I got to my car with the gold jewelry."

"Don't you want me to call a lawyer," Janet asked.

"I'm not going to waste time and money on a defense. I'll take a plea of guilty and ask for a minimum sentence. With no criminal record I should be out before too long. I'll stay in touch with you as much as they'll let me. But just get my car out of that neighborhood and stashed away. Can you do this for me?"

"Are you sure you don't want me to sell the car," Janet asked. "And where should I put your clothes and stuff?"

"Above all," Kitty replied, "do not sell that car. It's more valuable to me than it looks, and I can't tell you why. Just stash it somewhere safe and keep the keys. If the DMV comes looking for fees let me know and I'll sign the 'non-operative' paperwork."

"Okay," Janet said, "I'll get a taxi ride up to Beverly Glen and find the car, and then go by your apartment on Normandie. Do you owe any rent? What do I do with any clothes that I can't stash in the car?"

"No," Kitty said, "the landlord has my rent and cleaning deposit all paid up. Just give any excess clothes, shoes, and so on to Goodwill. Now, get on your way because I see they want to send me to central jail for booking. Thanks, and I'll stay in touch somehow."

Now here she was, almost thirty years later, readying herself to call Janet. Janet got her degree and became interested in politics in the Vietnamese community in

Orange County. She hitched her career to a young Vietnamese man who ran for a number of offices. First, he was on the school board in Costa Mesa, then on the city council. Now he was a member of the California State Assembly.

Janet kept the Assemblyman's office in the district running and serving the local citizens, and had stayed in touch with Kitty over the years. Kitty had reclaimed the little Honda 600 in 1992 and retrieved a small metal box that had been concealed under the back seat of the tiny car. The car was put back on the road and sold to a local college boy. Kitty entrusted the metal box to Janet while retaining the key. Only once before, around 1998, had Kitty asked Janet to bring the box to her. It was after that meeting that Kitty had business to conduct with Avedis Sarkisian.

Her call to Janet was short as she was ready to check out of the Hampton Inn and drive into downtown L.A. When Janet answered the phone at the office Kitty said "Janet, it's Kitty. I'll be in La Habra Heights tomorrow. Can I meet you at your father's grave tomorrow afternoon around three?"

"I can meet you there Kitty," Janet responded. "Do you want me to bring the 'treasure chest' as before?"

"Yes, and this should be the last time. I'll not burden you with that problem any further. It's been long enough and it's time to bring an end to the arrangement. I'd like to make a donation to the candidate's campaign fund. So, are we all set for Tuesday at three?"

"I'll see you then, Kitty," Janet said. "Drive safe on those twisty roads in the Heights."

"One more call," Kitty thought, "and I'm out of Burbank and on my way to L.A." The remaining call was to Napoleon Shepherd in La Habra Heights. Someone employed by the family answered, and Mr. Shepherd came on the line.

"Hello, Mr. Shepherd. This is Ms. D'Literie. I'm in Burbank and on my way into L.A. I wondered if we could meet tomorrow before noon?"

"That would be a good time," Shepherd replied. "Why not make it ten in the morning?"

"That would be very good, Mr. Shepherd, as I have another appointment in mid-afternoon in Westminster. What I need is directions to your home in La Habra Heights."

"Take the 60 freeway from East L.A. to exit 16. That's Hacienda Boulevard and you can take that south into La Habra Heights. At the traffic light at West Road go right for about a mile or so and look for Cloister Drive. Make a left there and we are at the very end. Depending on the traffic you might get here in an hour. Did you get all those directions?"

"I've got them, Mr. Shepherd, and I look forward to meeting with you tomorrow morning," Kitty replied. "Goodbye until then."

With the phone calls done it was time for Kitty to check out of the Hampton Inn and head for downtown Los Angeles. She intended to see three things that were new since she had left southern California in 2008. First, the Disney Concert Hall on Grand Avenue, and nearby the new Broad Art Museum. She also knew that the new Catholic Cathedral was worth a visit. Then she could check into the Biltmore and rest up for the long day she would have tomorrow. She wanted to prepare a list of questions to pose to the Shepherds, and then on Wednesday she could have lunch with Avedis and start heading home for Pacific Grove on Thursday. It would be good to get back to her normal dull life in the library for a while.

Chapter 11

By four in the afternoon Kitty was more than ready to check into the Biltmore, get to her room, and take off her shoes. Touring the concert hall, the art museum and the cathedral was a bit more walking than she had anticipated. It was well worth the effort, but now she needed a bit of rest before dinner.

Checking in at the Biltmore brought back a flood of memories. Changes in recent years under new owners had reduced the number of guest rooms by half, but some things would never change. Now with the status of "historic" bestowed on the old building things would stay as they were for years.

What she was especially glad to see was the long galleria, over 300 feet long, paneled in gleaming wood and adorned with a mural ceiling. An Italian artist who had also done work at the White House and the Vatican had painted the murals in the late 1920's. She entered the lobby off Grand Avenue, and the sight of the galleria and the walk down it to the elevators took her back to the summer of 1987.

She was dating a young man who had just graduated from UCLA. They had been to a show at a nearby theater. Her date, no, let's call him her lover, Mark, took her hand and guided her down the galleria to the Gallery Bar. He had arranged for a table for two and a late-night supper. When they were done, he led her across to the elevators and up to his room on the fourth floor. She knew what was about to take place and she thought, "Well, it will certainly be more comfortable than our previous encounters in the back seat of his Chevy, plus a lot safer than that dusty pullout off Mulholland Drive."

So, she and Mark made love, they got room service for breakfast, and he drove her back to her apartment in Westwood. She knew it was goodbye, probably forever, as he kissed her and said he had to pack and be on his way. Law school at Columbia University awaited. She knew she might never see him again, and she was right. She was his "summer love," and by her next summer she was beginning her short criminal career. Oh, there had been a few letters, but she knew that his law school course work and internship would occupy his time and mind. She remembered it all as she rolled her suitcase down the galleria and onto the elevator.

For dinner Kitty felt like taking a short walk down Grand Avenue to the Water Grill. She had been there several years before with Jake and recalled that they always had good seafood. She had become quite the seafood enthusiast since moving to Pacific Grove but this night she knew was going to be a bit different. She also remembered that she was supposed to be paying attention to her budget.

Kitty had never developed a love for oysters, but the Water Grill menu listed 16 different types of oysters, half from the Atlantic, and the other half Pacific. "Okay," she thought, "I'm skipping down the menu to other appetizers." She ordered a jumbo blue crab cake to start, ignoring the grilled wild Spanish octopus. "I've met some Spanish octopus," she thought, "but it walked on two legs and smelled too much like garlic." She ordered the tomato salad with avocado, and went for the Ecuadorian swordfish with an olive and anchovy tapenade. A glass of Riesling from Alsace to wash it down, and if her waistline permitted an iced cherry sundae for dessert. She thought, "As the Brits say, 'in for a penny, in for a pound' or 'you only live once' and this will be my big night out so to hell with the budget. I hope the Shepherd family isn't a bunch of tightwads. We'll start to find out tomorrow." And at $105 plus the tip the budget truly had "gone to hell."

She spent time in her room jotting down questions she would need to ask the Shepherds about their missing relative, Maximillian. "Who," she wondered, "names their sons for French emperors and an Austrian who got executed for trying to take over Mexico? A family named Shepherd sounds about as Anglo-Saxon as you can get."

A light breakfast in the Biltmore Rendezvous Court and Kitty was ready to get on the road by nine in the morning. Once she got free of the downtown gridlock, she found the trip eastward to La Habra Heights easier than expected. All the traffic congestion was going westward into the city center. Malcolm, her Jaguar, seemed to like the climb up Hacienda Boulevard, and he certainly got a workout on West Road. Just as ten o'clock came up on her watch she finished the trip to the house on Cloister Drive.

It was, as she had anticipated, a large house with a view south into Orange County. She guessed that after dark you could probably see the lights of Disneyland from up here.

A man who appeared to be about 65 years of age greeted her at the door. He extended a hand and said "Ms. D'Literie, I'm Napoleon Shepherd. Won't you come in?"

"I'm glad to meet you sir," Kitty said. "The trip went as quickly as you said it would, and the traffic was light."

"I'm glad to hear that," Shepherd said, as he led her to a comfortable living room with that great view to the south. "I'd like to introduce my sister, Josephine, and my younger brother, Augustus."

"I'm glad to meet you all," Kitty said, while in her mind she thought, "They must all be named for imperial family members. How bizarre!"

"Let's get right to the point of your visit," Napoleon said. "We want you, if possible, to locate our brother

Maximillian. We have neither heard nor seen him in about ten years. Our mother, who was widowed for several years, died 13 months ago and we would like to settle her estate. I'm the executor, as the oldest child, and the property is to be sold and the proceeds to be divided evenly between her surviving children. We can't do that until we know if Max is alive or not."

"Well, I'd love to give the search a try, but I'm going to need more information. I'd start with the vital statistics: date and place of birth to begin, and Social Security number if available. Any recent photo of Max would also be a great help to me."

"I can give you all of that before you leave. What else would help?" Napoleon asked.

"Well, did he ever marry, or father any children?"

"That we don't know," Josephine interjected. "When we last saw him he was single, but he had been dating someone he met in college. If it went beyond that we don't know."

"Okay, college. Where, when, degree earned?" Kitty asked. "He may be in their alumni records, a member of a fraternity, or asked for a transcript to be sent."

"Pomona College, a B.A. degree in Literature or English, about 30 years ago," Augustus replied. "He did work doing freelance writing for various publications like the New Yorker. He is probably doing that for some publication if he is still alive."

"Next," Kitty asked, "where are some places that you know he has lived, either in California or other states? Did he ever live overseas?"

"Well," Napoleon replied, "he particularly liked the San Francisco Bay area. That's where he was born, and we lived in Berkeley until he was about 12, then we moved here.

"After college we only saw him for holiday gatherings, like Easter or Christmas, and then he'd be gone. I do know he lived in and worked in Ireland for some time. They give a nice tax break to income earned by writing. Part of their national heritage, I guess."

"Next area," Kitty asked, "Did he have any special hobbies or avocations. You mentioned classic sports cars in your letter to me. How did that start?"

"Yes, he liked old sports cars from the 1950's, especially if they were English. He would be very interested in that Jaguar you drove up in," Napoleon said.

"And how did that interest get started?" Kitty asked.

"Our Dad used to take us to races when we were little. I think he was a frustrated Walter Mitty. You know, the kind of man who dreams of exciting deeds but who lives a life of quiet but lucrative drudgery. Max saw some interesting cars and dreamed of owning some. I'm pretty sure he has bought and sold some exotic cars."

"You said in your letter that there was one he seemed, when last you saw him, to be obsessed with. I think you said it was a Jaguar."

"Yes, Dad talked a lot, when we were kids living in the Bay area, about a race that was actually held in Golden Gate Park in the City around 1950 or 1951. The winning car was a Jaguar, something they called a C-Type, and the guy who drove it was a young dilettante named Masten Gregory. In his dreams I think Dad wished he could have been Gregory, and that dream seems to have transferred to Max."

"If Max had acquired a car like that it would be registered and heavily insured," Kitty said. "My contacts in the auto history area and the collector car insurance business may be able to help if that is the case. I have another area you might be able to help me with. Did Max have any health concerns that might require the care of a specialist, such as a heart condition?"

"Well, if he did, he never let on," Napoleon said, "but given that we haven't seen him nor heard a word from him in ten years, who knows? I can see that he might have developed a condition in his late 50s, but we don't know. I can give you the name of our family doctor whom he might have consulted."

"One more thing," Kitty said. "May I have the name of any family lawyers whom he might have contacted? It may be that he knows of his mother's death and wants to know if he is in the will."

"That I can give you before you leave. Are there any other bits of information about his life that you'd like to dig into?" Napoleon queried.

"Oh yes. Did he have any religious preferences? Contact with a church might give us a clue," Kitty responded.

"Ah, he did often express an interest in Buddhism. For all we know he gave up the pursuit of wealth and exotic cars and went into a monastery," Napoleon said with a chuckle.

"Well, I can think of places where that could happen. I have one last question for now if it's not too impolite. How did your parents, especially your father, earn a living? It must have been a good income to afford this lovely home."

"One word," Napoleon said. "Oil. Dad met Mom in Saudi Arabia where he worked for Aramco, and she was training nurses in one of the kingdoms hospitals. Coming here was part of their long-range plan. You see, these hills are part of a chain that runs from down there in the south," as he pointed toward Orange County, "that runs up to Los Angeles. The chain is broken in segments by rivers; the Santa Ana, San Gabriel, Los Angeles. There is a fault that follows and probably created the line of hills. Wherever there is a fault you might find oil. That's how it was in Montebello in the early 20th century, and the Whittier hills a bit later. Dad looked for and found some

63

oil and even today we earn a little from a few of those east L.A. County wells."

"That's very interesting," Kitty said, "my geology lesson for the day. There is one item of business we need to deal with before I leave. That would be my fee. As this search is not my only responsibility, I plan to spend no more than 20 hours per week doing research and making enquiries. My fee will be $15 per hour plus expenses. I'll submit all receipts for expenses at the end of each month, along with the hours worked on the search. Is that agreeable to you?"

"It sounds reasonable to me," Napoleon said, looking at his siblings for their reactions. "I say we give it a year, and if you find nothing, we will take legal action to declare Max dead, or whatever our lawyers advise. Then the estate can be divided. What kind of expenses do you think you'll encounter?"

"Well, there will be a lot of phone calls, many long distance, even to the British Isles. I think I may hire a college student to look at property records, death indexes for each state, and motor vehicle records, that sort of thing."

"I'll document it all and keep good records of all expenditures. Just bear in mind that finding someone who doesn't want to be found is very difficult without police power, such as search warrants. It may get a bit sketchy if any hacking of computers is involved," Kitty concluded.

"Okay, we have a deal," Napoleon concluded. "I expect weekly e-mails letting me know your progress. I do wish you the best of luck in your research."

"Now I must be on my way," Kitty said, "because I am meeting an associate in Westminster in a couple of hours. One final question: where can I get lunch near Whittier?"

"Just get back on West Road and go to your left. That will drop you off at the Boulevard and there are several restaurants in the Whittwood Mall, which will be directly in front of you at the traffic light. If you go east on Whittier Boulevard to Beach Boulevard, also called Highway 39, you can go south on Beach directly to Westminster."

"Thank you all," Kitty said. "I'll report anything I find within a month's time. Goodbye, and enjoy the rest of your day."

Chapter 12

As Kitty drove the Jaguar off Cloister Drive and onto West Road she couldn't help thinking, "Now I have a very challenging task ahead. Max Shepherd is going to be hard to find in a year unless I can pick up his trail through the auto-collecting world. One thing that his family couldn't give me was his credit card numbers. If I had that, I could trace where he stayed, ate, bought things. Oh well, I'll get some help when I'm back in Pacific Grove."

The twists and turns of West Road were a fun drive in the Jaguar. She loved the growl of the motor as the exhaust notes echoed off the pavement. She was at the intersection with Whittier Boulevard in minutes. Entering the sprawling parking lot of the mall she noted that there was a Red Robin restaurant. "Just the thing," she thought. "A hamburger, some fries and a coke. What a contrast with the dinner I had last night at the Water Grill."

The contrast turned out to be more than just the choice of food. Red Robin is popular with young adults and groups of teenagers, so the music was loud and whatever was currently popular. The basic problem was the design of the building. Whether deliberate or just a design flaw, the room served as a giant echo chamber. Not just for the music, but the clatter of plates, glasses, utensils, and conversations reverberated off the walls and ceiling and were thus amplified. Kitty was glad for the chance to get some lunch, but as she left and looked across the parking lot she thought, "Next time it's Panera Bread for lunch." Then it was back into the car and down Whittier Boulevard into Orange County.

As she drove through La Habra, Kitty thought to herself, "I wonder why the movie studios don't seem to do much filming in this part of the county?" She could not recall a single instance when Jake had asked her to research a site in the area. Maybe it was the local cities deciding that filming would be a burden or an annoyance for their citizens. Or it could have been just the force of habit, where a director would decide, "Chatsworth is more familiar than Fullerton, so let's use Chatsworth for that scene."

Beach Boulevard came up pretty quickly and Kitty turned south into the heart of the county. La Habra gave way to Buena Park and soon she was motoring past Knott's Berry Farm. Now an amusement park that competed with Disneyland, in the past Knott's had been a very legitimate farm, producing various fruits which Mrs. Knott had turned into jam and a commercial success. Meanwhile, Mr. Knott was sponsoring the very anti-Communist John Birch Society. "Maybe," she thought, "that's why the studios avoid the 'O.C.'. We're not in 'liberal land' anymore, Malcolm."

She continued south on Beach Boulevard through Anaheim, but nowhere near Disneyland, then into Stanton and Garden Grove. All these names applied to cities, using that term very loosely, which were probably fields of string beans and pumpkins in 1945. Long before she was born people, like Eli Broad whose museum she had just visited, saw flat land that could easily be turned into one housing tract after another. As she crossed Westminster Boulevard, she knew that her goal was near.

The Westminster Memorial Park Cemetery occupied the entire block of land between Beach Boulevard and Hoover Street north of Bolsa Avenue. The cemetery and its history go back a long time. Kitty knew that somewhere in the older part of the property, near the north end of the cemetery, were the graves of 20 men who had fought on opposing sides in the American Civil War.

Kitty was headed for the southeast corner of the cemetery to an area that had been unused before 1975. Now it was the burial site of many Vietnamese who had fled to the United States when Saigon fell to the North Vietnamese Communist regime. It was there that Kitty was to meet Janet. She waited at the base of the flagpole where the flag of South Vietnam was raised every day.

Janet was very punctual and appeared right at three in the afternoon. They strolled over to the Nguyen burial plot, and then took a seat on the steps of the pagoda that was a feature of the cemetery. Janet asked "Kitty, this is it for this little metal box? You're all done with that part of your life?"

"Yeah, I'll take it to my contact tomorrow, and he'll begin to work to make the contents into… probably pesos and then dollars."

"Would it be okay for me to see what's in there," Janet asked. "Almost thirty years I've been protecting the contents in one way or another, and I've never seen what's in there."

"Sure," Kitty said. "At this time of day on a weekday we're not likely to see anyone else. That's one reason I like to meet here. Besides that, your dad is here now, and without his help in storing the little Honda I might not have this box."

Without further comment Kitty produced the key and opened the metal box, which was lined with some sort of red felt. Inside lay six emeralds of various sizes, a quartet of small rubies that had once adorned a ring, and a number of blue opals mounted in a bracelet.

"The emeralds and the rubies look like they were once part of a piece of Jewelry," Janet said. "How did they end up loose like this?"

"You're right. I removed them from their settings. Easier to store a loose collection than a bulky necklace.

68

The rubies were in a ring that I actually inherited," Kitty said.

"What about the opals. Why are they still in their mounting?" Janet asked.

"One thing I learned in my jewelry class, and yes, I did take a class to learn the basics, is that opals are very heat sensitive and require special care. I was afraid I'd damage them. Probably never should have taken them in the first place."

"So, why on earth did you steal these things then?" Janet asked. "Look at all the difficulty you created for yourself. I never thought you were stupid, but I've always been puzzled by your choices."

"Okay, I'll tell you," Kitty answered. "When I graduated, I found that there wasn't much call for students of American Literature and Culture. Sure, I could have gone into teaching after another year of classes, but I never liked the idea of teaching in the first place. Also, I'd been in the homes of those rich folks in Bel Air and Brentwood. I'd seen what these women wore, and I was envious. That's a sin right there in your Catholic religion."

"Yes, it is a sin, and in your case, it seems to have led to theft. How did you think you'd get away with this behavior, these actions?"

"Well," Kitty responded, "I never went into a house that was occupied at the time. People can be so dumb at times. For example, have a catered bon voyage party and then be gone for weeks. The red-haired girl who was a waitress comes back the following night when she knows no one will be at home. Surprise! Your emerald necklace is gone."

"Yeah, but you got caught, so who's the dumb bunny? Would you try it nowadays?"

"Good grief, no," Kitty answered. "In the 1980's even the rich people very seldom had the security that a middle-class family can get now. People now have complex alarm systems, cameras monitoring both inside and outside, security companies that respond to alarms, and they live in gated communities. I was also lucky, in a way that the LAPD figured some of the burglaries were done by a gang or a ring of thieves. They caught me leaving with some gold jewelry and they figured the other burglaries were the work of the gang. I never dissuaded them of their errors. They had caught a thief, the loot was recovered, the prosecutor could take a win and the insurance company was happy with no payout for a loss."

"So, you went to prison and now there are things which you cannot do, correct?"

"Yes, I lost the right to vote until my parole was over. I can't possess a gun, can't travel outside the United States, and I can't be a licensed private investigator or lawyer."

"So, you are permanently damaged in terms of your life?" Janet asked.

"Well," Kitty replied, "I have hope if I can find a competent lawyer. There is now a way to get a felony reduced to a misdemeanor or even wiped off your record. It has to do with what lawyers call a wobbler. I could have been charged with either a misdemeanor or a felony. That's what would happen today. Under Penal Code 17(b) I might get the conviction reduced to a misdemeanor. Other sections of the Penal Code can be used to 'expunge' my conviction since I've been a 'good girl' for years."

"So, you have hope. Aren't you endangering that hope by even possessing these gems?" Janet asked.

"No, that's why I've waited so long. The statute of limitations on my original crimes has expired. The statute of limitations on theft is four years in California. I

70

can't be accused of grand theft based on my having the contents of this metal box."

"Well, I'm glad there is some hope for you, Kitty," Janet said. "I wish you well on your new endeavor, and I hope we'll stay in touch."

"No worries there, Janet. You're my oldest and most trusted friend, and we'll always be connected. As I said over the phone, I want to make a contribution to your employer's campaign for re-election. How do I make out the check?"

"Make it out to 'The Committee to Re-elect John Tran', and I thank you for helping us this way."

"Okay, here's my check for $250, and I'm going to hit the road back to L.A. At this hour it'll probably take me until after six p.m., but it's got to be done."

With a quick embrace the two women went their separate ways. Kitty debated the best way to get to downtown Los Angeles at that time of day, and decided, as she put it, "There is no 'good way'. I'm close to the 405 freeway, but it's under construction for widening. The I-5 is good until you reach L.A. County. I think I'll just go back up Beach Boulevard to La Habra and look for a Mexican restaurant for dinner. After 7:30 I'll bet traffic into downtown will be lighter."

Thus, it was that she found herself at El Cholo on Whittier Boulevard in La Habra. After all those years at Casuela's in Palm Desert one thing Kitty knew was what a good Mexican restaurant was like. This place, she decided, was one of the good ones.

Chapter 13

Kitty enjoyed her dinner at El Cholo. Since she had arrived at five p.m., she could take a seat anywhere she wanted and watch the elderly couples arrive. She liked to contrast this place with the two Mexican restaurants that were most familiar to her.

Like Casuela's in Palm Desert, El Cholo was roomy but was better lighted, and like Casuela's it didn't get a lot of customers before 6:30 or 7:00 p.m. on a weekday evening. She remembered how Jake would always show up on a Thursday and stick around until closing to chat with her. Those evenings had resulted in a major change in her life, and they were a pleasant memory of over 20 years ago.

For contrast, she thought about the other Mexican restaurant that had become a part of her life. Peppers, on Forest Drive, just a few doors off Lighthouse Avenue in Pacific Grove, could not have been more different. With the possible exception of a cold mid-week night in December, when no one except the most dedicated Mexican food lover would be in the place, Peppers was always crowded. It was small, basically a couple of storefronts joined together. One did not get to linger very long because the line of people waiting for your seat would be out the front door and down the sidewalk.

Kitty settled in to enjoy her chips and salsa, followed by what she often called "Jake's entrée," two enchiladas with beans and rice. When asked if she wanted another margarita she thought, "Why not. One for Jake's memory, and one for the road." Then she settled back to enjoy her drink and watch the after-work crowd arrive. Some had probably driven all the way from work in Los Angeles, and others from the opposite direction at Irvine. La Habra was where you came to recuperate and get yourself ready for tomorrow's "rat race."

With her conversation with Janet still fresh in her mind and the memory of Jake's job offer from almost 20 years ago having been brought back by her choice of restaurants, she began to think about that job offer. She had finished her parole in 1997, but the stigma of "felon" still was stuck to her name. The fact that she was the hostess at Casuela's, and before that at Tarpy's, and not a waitress was because her parole officer who got her the jobs had made it clear that she was not to handle money. He felt that she might be tempted to shortchange either the customer or the employer, so let's not give her a chance to be tempted.

So why did Jake take that chance on her? Why give her a very good salary, a place to live and within a short time a lot of responsibility in running his business? She would never know now; Jake had been dead for over ten years. Was it the allure of the UCLA degree, a common denominator for both of them? Or was it that memory he had from his undergraduate days?

She remembered that once, before he made her the job offer of a lifetime, that he asked her during one of their chats at Casuela's, "Did your mother also go to UCLA?"

"No," she had replied, "I think she may have taken some classes at a junior college, but she was working for a buyer at a major department store when she met my father. Why do you ask?"

"Oh, just a passing thought. When I was at UCLA in the 1950's I was in a couple of French classes with a girl who looked a lot like you."

"Well, did you ever date her?" Kitty asked.

"No, I discovered that she was already dating a classmate of mine in Army ROTC, and it didn't seem too gentlemanly to get involved," Jake replied.

"So, what was it about me that reminded you of her?"

"Oh, some physical characteristics. Like you, she was tall and had red hair, and also her personality. Like you, she was very much at ease having a conversation with people. So, I just thought I'd ask."

Whatever his reasons, Jake had done what many employers would have balked at, hiring someone with a felony conviction on their record. For that reason, Kitty would never forget what she owed the late Jake O'Malley.

By 7 p.m. El Cholo was filling up, so Kitty calculated that "if they're all home now the roads will be less crowded." So, after a quick "pit stop" and settling her dinner bill Kitty went out to the parking lot and fired up her sleeping Jaguar. "Time to hit the road, Malcolm. Get me and my treasure chest back to the Biltmore," Kitty said.

The following morning Kitty had breakfast again at the Rendezvous Court, and then she got packed up to leave. She made arrangements to have a table for lunch at the Gallery Bar with Avedis Sarkisian, and to check out leaving her luggage with the concierge. She calculated that if she got on the road by 1:30 p.m. she could be home in Pacific Grove by nine that night. It would be good to sleep in her own bed once again. The first thing to do after breakfast was to call Avedis and finalize the arrangements.

As usual, Avedis answered his phone on the second ring. Kitty said, "Good morning, Avedis. It's Kitty and I'm ready to make that delivery. How do you want to make the exchange? We could do it here at lunch, or I could come over to your office now."

"If you don't mind," he replied, "could you come over to my office, and we can put your property in my safe?"

"Sounds good," Kitty replied. "I'll walk over and make the delivery. Do I need any special arrangements to access your floor?"

"No, just be prepared to show your identification and expect to be treated just like you were going past TSA at the airport. They'll check your purse and make sure that you're not armed. Then take the elevator up to my floor. My office is down the corridor to your right. The number is 310."

"Okay, I'll be over about 11. If you're free, we can have lunch here at the Gallery Bar."

"Good. I'll see you around 11, and I'd love to do a quick lunch with you. See you later," Avedis concluded.

Kitty had grabbed a copy of the L.A. Times to read before she set off for the Jewelry Center, so she spent some time catching up on the "show biz" columns in the Calendar section. She took note of who was "shooting," and where the crews would be in the Business section. Yes, she was long gone from the business of Hollywood but "old habits die hard."

She also remembered that she was going to call Mel Goldfarb, so she dug his number out of her purse and placed the call. As expected, she was sent straight to voice mail, so she left a short message.

"Mel, it's Kitty. Before I leave L.A. I want to let you know there are three Wiccans locally who might want to consult with you. I'll send you their names by email tomorrow when I'm back in Pacific Grove. Take care of yourself and stay well."

With that bit of business out of the way it was time to hike across Pershing Square to the International Jewelry Center on Hill Street. The process of getting into the building was just as Avedis had described. It all made sense. Robberies of jewelry stores were certainly not unheard of, and to rob a wholesaler or designer of jewelry would be a major criminal coup. The armed guards, both uniformed and plain clothes, were polite but very much in control. Kitty even had to produce the key and open the small metal box that had played a big part in her life up to the present.

Once in Avedis' office she felt she could relax. She had known him since about 1999 or 2000. She had learned of his existence at one of those gatherings of Hollywood "types" when she had commented on one woman's lovely and unique jewelry. When told, "It was custom made for me," she promptly asked "By whom? How do I meet this craftsman?"

On her first trip to the office of Avedis Sarkisian she had offered the diamonds she had "mined" from pieces of jewelry she had "acquired." When asked. "Where is the setting you removed these from?" she responded, "Have you ever been to the pier in Santa Monica? Perhaps someday a guy fishing from that pier, or a scuba diver will find something in the water there." Avedis had never pressed her for any details. The less he knew of the provenance of these "girls' best friends," the more comfortable he would feel.

She made herself comfortable across from Avedis at his desk and opened the little metal box. He examined the emeralds first and asked, "Do you have any ballpark figures on the value of these?"

"Well," Kitty replied, "I know that emeralds, like other gemstones, are not valued like diamonds. And I would guess that the fact that they have been cut might affect the price, but dollar value? I have no clue."

"Okay," Avedis said, "Here's a short lesson. The first area you judge is color. That's the highest priority. You want an emerald to be so dark that you can't see through it. That's 60% of the value, and these stones are very good."

"What are the other factors?" Kitty asked.

"The next one is clarity, that is that there are no interior blemishes. These passed that test easily. Then we look at cut. These would get an A grade; they are so well done. Then, there is carat; how much does it weigh."

He put the largest stone on a small scale and remarked, "One carat in 1/5 of a gram. This one is right on 3.4 carats, so I'd guess it will go for about $1500."

"Is there anything else to look at?" Kitty asked.

"Well, if this were an uncut stone, we'd look at the country of origin. Some places mine better quality stone, Afghanistan in particular. But that is irrelevant here. Now there are five smaller emeralds here. I assume they all are similar, so I'll estimate, and that's all it is now, that all six would bring about $6,000."

"Good. Now what about the opals?" Kitty asked.

"Are you sure you want them dismounted? I can do it, but if they are leaving the country they might sell for more just as they are in this bracelet."

"I'll leave that to you," Kitty responded. "I think the bracelet is, let's say, 'clunky'. I would never wear something that big on my wrist, so I'll leave the call on that up to you."

"Either way," he said, "I'll guess that I can get you another $1,000 on the opals. I have a thought on the little rubies, so hear me out. Were they in a ring before this?"

"Yes, a ring I inherited from my mother. I never saw her wear it, so it must be something she inherited, maybe from my grandma. Does it make a difference?"

"It might," he replied. "They are so small that they would work better in the ring. Did you save the ring they were set in?"

"No, it had no sentimental value to me, and I knew nothing of the background, so I took the stones and dumped the ring. Bad move, I guess."

"Well, they still have value, so I'll see what I can get, but don't expect some big sum beyond what we get for the emeralds," Avedis concluded.

"Okay," Kitty said, "I leave it all in your hands, but I'm going to keep the little box if you don't mind. It will bring back memories each time I look at it."

"You know, I'm surprised," Avedis said. "Most people wouldn't walk around with a little metal box holding gems, and you don't even seem to be armed. Don't you have a gun to protect yourself?"

"Good grief, no," Kitty responded. "I'm not allowed to possess one, wouldn't know how to use one, and the only time I've ever handled one was when Jake asked me to bring him the .22 caliber pistol he kept in the house in Palm Desert."

Kitty added, "That's the gun he took with him on the aerial tram into the mountains to kill himself, so I don't like to be around them. They just give me bad memories."

"Do you have anything to protect yourself, moving and traveling around by yourself?" he asked.

"Oh, I'm very good with pepper spray," Kitty said, "and I take a self-defense class in Pacific Grove. I feel that the best defense is to just be aware of your surroundings, and always be looking for an exit. Oh, and don't be walking along talking or texting on your phone, oblivious to all around you."

"Well, I can see that you've given the issue some thought, which is good." Avedis said.

"How about we take a walk-through Pershing Square and get lunch at the Biltmore," Kitty said. "I've reserved a table in the Gallery Bar. After lunch I'll reclaim my bags, get the valet to bring me my car, and I'll be on my way back to Monterey Bay."

"I'm with you, young lady," Avedis said. "I'll just put these stones in my safe and we'll be off."

With that they left the Jewelry Center, and within the hour the tall redhead in the old blue Jaguar was on Highway 101 headed north.

Chapter 14

It took Kitty about eight hours to drive from Los Angeles to Pacific Grove. She would have been there sooner, but a stop for fuel at King City led to dinner at the small diner there.

Once in the house there was Pyewacket, her loveable cat, waiting to greet her and ask, "What's for dinner, sweetie?" "Just give me a few minutes, Pye," Kitty said, "and I'll get you some food. It doesn't look like you've missed too many meals while I've been gone. I do need to get my suitcases in and unpacked. I'll be doing laundry tomorrow."

Once things were unpacked Kitty got the cat some of her dry food and saw that Mrs. Sanchez had been doing her job. The litter box was clean, and the cat obviously had been eating well. Kitty knew that she would see Mrs. Sanchez the next day and settle her account. Then it was time for a warm shower, a fresh nightgown and a familiar bed.

Up at what she liked to call "the crack of dawn" on Thursday she got her laundry started and began sorting out the jackets and pairs of slacks that would need to go to the dry cleaners later in the day. She was about to start toasting an English muffin when there was a loud banging on her front door. "Can't be Mrs. Sanchez," she thought. "She'd use the key I gave her to get in."

She opened the door to find a policeman at the entryway, and a black and white patrol car pulled up right behind the Jaguar. She was never thrilled to see a policeman "up close and personal." Bad memories of a dark street in Bel Air and the feel of cold steel handcuffs on her wrists came back all too readily.

"Good morning, ma'am," the officer, whose nametag told her that he was officer Mulbrae, said, "Are you Ms. D'Literie?" he asked.

"Yes, I am," she responded. "Is there some problem?"

"Well, there is, and I hope we can resolve it without any difficulty," he replied. "Is that old Jeep parked on the street yours?"

"Yes, it is," she answered.

"Well, I was here on Tuesday, and a lady, who I think was called Sanchez, answered the door. She said you were out of town on business, and she gave me your name. That's why I'm here this morning."

"So, what is it that brought you here at mid-week?" Kitty asked. "I've been down in Los Angeles on business and Mrs. Sanchez came by daily to take care of my cat. I'm puzzled as to what I've done wrong to bring you here?"

"Okay," he replied. "The reason I came by in the first place is because that old Jeep is breaking a city ordinance. If a car is parked on a street without moving in Pacific Grove for over 72 hours it can be towed and impounded, and you have to pay a pretty good-sized fine to get it out of impound. That Jeep is breaking the law, so to speak."

"So, you came by earlier this week to do just that and found out I was out of town. So why didn't you have it towed then?"

"Well," he answered, "Ms. Sanchez told me you were gone, and that it had something to do with witchcraft, and that if I messed with that Jeep before you got back, you'd put a spell on me or maybe the entire city. So, I had to see just what I was dealing with. I don't want to be turned into a toad or something."

Kitty, laughing and smiling, said, "Mulbrae, why don't you come in while I try to finish preparing my breakfast, and I'll clue you in on the wonderful world of Wicca. After I finish dressing properly, I'll get the Jeep out of the street, assuming I can get it to start, and I'll be a good little old witch again."

"Okay," he said as he entered. "I could use a cup of coffee if it's no trouble. I want to enforce our codes, but not at the expense of someone who was out of town on business."

"Look," she said, as she poured two cups of coffee," I'm like the only Wicca, which is the correct word for witch, in P.G., maybe the whole of Monterey County. Mrs. Sanchez thinks I'm some sort of rarity, like a penguin who got out of the aquarium. When you knocked, I thought it was her coming to check up on my cat, as I hired her to do. I've been down to San Luis to see an old friend who's dying of cancer, and to make contact with some folks who think I can, maybe, find a family member who's been missing for a decade.

"I also saw some old friends in L.A. and Orange County. Only in San Luis did I try what you might call witchcraft. I tried to help ease the suffering of an old man who served with my former employer."

"What military branch did they serve in?" asked Mulbrae.

"Felix, he's the guy who's dying, and Jake, the guy I used to work for before he died, were both Special Forces in Laos and Vietnam. They met just a few miles away at the Army Language School at the Presidio. Incidentally, the Jeep and the Jaguar were both given to me in Jake's will. They both mean something special to me."

"Well, thanks for the coffee. I've got to get back on patrol. I'll tell the sergeant that you'll have the Jeep out of the street by noon, right?"

"Oh gosh, yes," Kitty replied. "I've got to take Malcolm to the shop at Mattson's, you know, the repair place up by Laurel. Then I'll walk back here, and Eugene can get me to the Cypress Cleaners and the Grove Market."

"Wait," he said. "Who are Malcolm and Eugene? I thought you lived here alone."

"Oh, sorry," she said. "Malcolm is what I call the Jaguar, and of course, aren't all Jeeps named Eugene?" She paused for a moment and said, "You're right, I live here alone, and there's no men in my life, more's the pity. I've been divorced since 1996, but that's another long-ago story, just like old Fort Ord."

"Well, I've really got to go now," he said, "but maybe I'll come back by some other time to make sure you're okay. You know, to protect and to serve, like the motto says."

"That would be most welcome, officer. I'd like to talk to you about my assignment to find a missing relative, and see if the police could aid in any way."

"Have a good day," he said as he walked toward the black and white police unit. "I'll be in touch, just to be sure you're safe."

"Goodbye, and be careful out there," she said as she closed the door.

"Well, Pye, what do you think of officer Mulbrae?" she asked the cat, who simply stretched, rolled on her side and went to sleep. "This might lead to something more interesting than recovering the books at the library."

Once properly dressed she moved the Jaguar out onto the street and put Eugene the Jeep in the driveway. Then she drove the Jaguar down Lighthouse to town, did the right turn onto Grand, and pulled into the crowded lot of Matteson Auto Repair. She asked Ernie, the mechanic on duty, if she could leave the car, even if it was overnight, to have all the fluids checked and the engine oil and filter changed. He assured her they would be done by five that afternoon. Then she began her two-mile walk back home.

Once there she called Mrs. Sanchez to let her know she was home, and to have her drop by about three in the afternoon. Then came the major trip of the day, to the Cypress Cleaners shop on Grand, then over to the Grove Market on Forest Avenue.

She wondered if there would ever come a time when she would have to use the old cliché about "the way to a man's heart is through his stomach?" She shuddered at the thought, reflecting on her limited culinary skills. Oh well, one conversation with a middle-aged cop about her parking routine doesn't need to lead to a dinner for two.

With the groceries loaded into Eugene, it was back home to meet Mrs. Sanchez and pay for the cat's care. Mrs. Sanchez was very prompt, and Kitty heard all about "the charming police officer that came to talk about towing your Jeep away."

"Yes, Mrs. Sanchez, officer Mulbrae was by this morning, and we got it all worked out. I really ought to get rid of one or maybe both of these old cars, but I hate to part with them."

"Well, dear," Mrs. Sanchez responded, "you probably should get yourself a nice little SUV. Maybe a three-year-old Hyundai or something like that."

"That would make sense," Kitty replied, "but where's the fun in that? I like being behind the wheel of that Jaguar, top down, wind messing up my hair. Oh rats, that reminds me I've got to get my hair trimmed and a decent shampoo. So, Mrs. S. what do I owe you?"

"Well, six days, at $20 per day. Let's make it $100 even and call it the friends and family discount."

"Okay, here's my check, and you have my thanks, I know I'll have to call upon you again. I foresee a future where I go four times a year to southern California. Of course, I may find the missing heir tomorrow, but while I believe in magic that would be too long a shot to have any chance. So, I thank you, Pye thanks you, and I also thank you for giving that policeman my name. Maybe something good will come of that before too long."

"I hope that something does happen for you. Remember, if all else fails, just try some of that Love Potion Number Nine." And with that the cat lady was gone.

Chapter 15

Saturday morning, Kitty usually liked to sleep late, but not today. For some reason she felt that she wanted to look a little bit better than usual, and she knew she needed an appointment with a hairdresser. Getting an appointment on a Saturday morning was probably a reflection of poor planning on her part. There were two salons she usually went to, but she would have to wait until nine a. m. for the first one to open.

Wave Length, on Lighthouse Avenue, would be open at nine, but it wasn't her favorite. On a Saturday, Wave Length would very possibly have every single beautician working on members of a bride's wedding party. That was their specialty. Some brides wanted every woman in their group of bridesmaids to not only dress the same, but also have the same hairstyle. Kitty thought this was "madness with a capital M." Some of the girls were even expected to have their hair dyed to match the bride's color.

The other choice she had, and the one she preferred, was Prim Hair, which was also located on Lighthouse. The shop didn't open until ten a.m. on Saturdays, and it closed at four p.m., so her "window of opportunity" would be smaller. Chrystal was the shop owner and head beautician and always had a full book of appointments. She didn't work alone, however, so just maybe one of the other stylists would have an opening. She decided she would wait until ten and take her chances.

She didn't wait until ten, but decided to dial the Prim number at 9:30, and she was right. Chrystal was there early to get things organized. Kitty asked about getting an appointment for a trim and shampoo and was told, "Honey, you've got to be kidding. I'm booked all day and most of next week, but you're in luck if you want to try someone else. I rented a chair to a gal who used to have her own shop near L.A. She doesn't have any local clients to speak of yet, so if you want to take a chance Karen can see you at, let's see, ten thirty this morning."

"Put me down for 10:30. After a week of driving an open car to L.A. and back I'm a mess and I need help. Maybe Karen and I can swap stories about SoCal," Kitty said with a sigh of relief. Now it was time to get dressed.

Whenever she got her thick, red hair cut Kitty always put on an old, somewhat worn, loose-fitting blouse and an old pair of jeans. She knew that no matter what care was taken she would end up with hair clippings down her back, a sensation she had disliked since she was a child. Get the haircut, then get in a little workout and finish the morning with a shower. Then she would have to get busy with the job of finding the elusive member of the Shepherd family.

She had decided to start a file on the case and label it "Pimpernel." She remembered reading, as a child, stories written early in the 20th century by an English baroness named Orczy about a fictional English noble whom everyone thought was either stupid or lazy. He was Sir Percy Blakeney, and he would rescue French aristocrats and get them to safety in the British Isles. He would always leave behind a small scarlet flower, a pimpernel.

Kitty's mother told her that her ancestors came to America in a way similar to that story, escaping the Reign of Terror and coming to America with the help of the man who would become President, Thomas Jefferson. Looking for the missing Shepherd heir made her think of the little couplet that her mom would recite:

"They seek him here, they seek him there,
Those Frenchies seek him everywhere.
Is he in heaven, or is he in hell,
That damned, elusive Pimpernel."

So far, the file was pretty thin. She was going to e-mail Napoleon Shepherd three bits of news. First, she had zero success getting any information from the family lawyer, Montagu Beaulieu, when she had asked if Max Shepherd had been in contact with the lawyer regarding his mother's estate.

Secondly, she had contacted the people at Hagerty Insurance, who insured both her Jaguar and her Jeep, with regard to the potential market value of the C-type Jaguar that Max seemed to be interested in acquiring. The result of that inquiry was that even the worst looking, least desirable Jaguar of that small group of fifty would be valued at $9,000,000 for insurance purposes. If the car looked to be of the best quality of preservation or restoration the value would rise to at least $17,000,000. Max would have to win the lottery to have a chance of buying one of those Jaguars.

Kitty also wanted the family to open an account with Ancestry.com and provide a sample of Napoleon's DNA. She would be researching to see if Max showed up on any of the death records of the fifty states, and if there were any unidentified male bodies in a morgue somewhere, then DNA matching with a brother could eliminate Max from the ranks of the dead. A long shot, but that's what this whole case could be in the end.

The final bit of information she would ask the Shepherd family to provide would be about the possibility of any past encounters with law enforcement. She was going to ask the local police to see if Max was serving time in a prison somewhere as "a guest of the state."

With that level of planning done it was time to head east on Lighthouse to the Prim Hair shop. She asked for Karen and was directed to a short woman who appeared to be about 30-something with short dyed-blond hair.

"Good morning, I'm Kitty D'Literie and I'm your 10:30 appointment."

"Hi, I'm Karen Lavine, and what can I do for you today?"

"Okay, I need my hair cut back, and I like it to come down no further than the nape of my neck," she said, gesturing to where she would like her hair to end as she got herself seated. "I'd like it thinned a bit overall if you can, and then I want a real nice shampoo when the trimming is all done."

"No problem. I can see the basic shape you've been keeping it and I'll get it just right. So let me get you covered up and we'll get on with it."

"So, Karen, I understand you're new to Pacific Grove and you had your own shop in the L.A. area. Where was it? I was just down there earlier this week."

"Well, I worked at shops in the southeast part of the county; Downey, Pico Rivera, and different shops in the Whittier area. Then I got a chance to rent a small shop of my own in Whittier. It had two chairs, so I was sometimes able to rent the second one out."

"So, what happened to bring you so far north," Kitty asked.

"Oh, there were a number of setbacks. The first was a break-in where a bunch of supplies and equipment were stolen. If you can't take care of your customers, even for a short while until you get re-supplied, they just drift off. That's especially true when there are lots of other shops they can go to, and there are in Whittier. There was even a 'beauty college' where a customer could get a cut and set very cheap if they were trying to save a few dollars."

"That can't have been all that happened to bring on such a big move," Kitty said.

"Yes," Karen replied, "there were worse things to come. My boyfriend and I got married and he went into 'I'm the boss' mode. I wasn't making much; the second chair rental idea seldom worked out, and then he insisted that we buy a house in Montrose. Do you know where that is?"

"It's somewhere around Glendale or Crescenta Valley if I remember right," Kitty responded. "That must have been a very long way from your shop."

"Exactly. The trip to work was killing me, and if I complained he'd just say 'Well, quit trying to run a business and stay home and take care of our needs.' That really meant 'take care of me like a wife is supposed to do.' I wasn't ready to give up the idea of having my own shop, so I divorced him and moved as far away as I could afford. I learned this shop had an open chair and I could start over in a whole new game."

The setting now changed to the sink for the shampoo. This was really an indulgence for Kitty, who always shampooed her own hair at home. The conversation also shifted to how Kitty came to be here in P.G.

"Were you always here in Pacific Grove," Karen asked.

"Oh, no," Kitty replied, "I came here in 2008 about two years after the death of the man I worked for over about seven or eight years. It took two years to get his estate settled and I took my share of the estate that he left me and moved here from the Palm Springs area."

"So why did you pick Pacific Grove out of all the places you could have gone?"

"Well," Kitty replied," I worked in the Monterey area for about three years, starting in 1992 or '93 when I got out of prison on parole. I was married to a G.I. at Fort Ord, but that ended in divorce after two years, so I went to the desert in '96. While working there I met the best man I never married. He gave me a big chance; good pay, lodging, and I learned a lot about how to run a business. His death left me with enough dough to move here, get settled, find a part-time job, and now I'm trying to get my own business started."

"Wait," Karen said, "did you say the words prison and parole in that sentence?"

"Yeah, you just cut the hair of a felon, and I must say, now that it's getting blow-dried, that it's a better cut than I ever got at the Chino Women's Prison."

"I know it's rude to ask, but since you brought it up, what did you do to get sent up? I'll tell you; I've never known someone who spent time in prison. Maybe overnight in jail for drunk driving on New Year's Eve, but that's minor league stuff."

"Well, I'll tell you more the next time I'm in here, but I've got to get back home and get a little workout in before I hit the shower. What do I owe you?"

"Let's make it $60, and I do hope to see you again in a couple of weeks. That hair of yours really is thick, and there's a lot of it even if you keep it pretty short. So, until next time, have a good week."

Kitty was out the door and into the Jaguar before noon. She decided to have a quick workout of sorts before she showered. A quick change of shoes and she was jogging down Lighthouse to Point Pinos, then north to Del Monte Boulevard and back to Lighthouse to complete a four-kilometer lap.

She arrived to find that now slightly familiar black and white patrol car parked near the condo. Yes, it was Officer Mulbrae at her front door. She said, "Officer, we have to stop meeting like this. People will talk."

"Sorry, Ms. D'Literie. I just stopped to see if you were okay, and I wondered why, since you have a garage, both cars are parked outdoors?"

"All right, detective," she said, observing him a bit flustered at the use of the title which didn't apply. "Step into my home and I'll show you, without a warrant, what lurks in my garage."

She opened the door from the small foyer to the garage and said, with a bit of a flourish, "Observe, officer, the deep dark secret of the middle-aged witch."

What officer Mulbrae saw was a complete but compact gym, down to a punching bag suspended from an overhead beam. There was a weight machine, a stationary bicycle and a treadmill.

"Wow," said Mulbrae, "I never took you for a fitness fanatic upon first contact. You must really be in pretty good shape."

"Not a fanatic, just a girl who feels she needs to be ready to maybe protect herself."

At that point Kitty launched a left jab, a right cross and a swift kick with her right foot into what would be the groin of her hapless punching bag if it had been a man.

"Now that you know why my garage holds no cars, let me tell you that I'm working on a solution before winter arrives. You may know Mrs. Murphy, the 83-year-old lady who lives next door. She can't drive, lost her license, poor old girl, and sold her car. I'm negotiating with her to rent her garage for my cars and pay her $100 a month. I think she'll agree if I mention that the police keep coming around because my cars are outside and in the street."

"No fair, dragging in a cop who's just trying to improve the safety of the neighborhood. That's not the only reason I dropped by. I have patrol duty tomorrow, but I have this evening free. I wondered, Ms. D'Literie, if you would join me this evening for dinner at The Fishwife over on Asilomar. I usually dine alone there on Saturday evening, so I know there's a small table reserved by the window."

"I'll be glad to join you, officer, on one condition. People call me Kitty, but what do I call you besides officer?"

"My given name is Angus, and how does 6:30 this evening sound?"

"I'm okay with that, but I want to give you a warning. I hope our going to dinner doesn't cause you any problems in the future. I don't know how your employer would feel about a sworn police officer dining with a felon."

"I'm okay with it, and I can see we might have more to talk about at dinner than your choice of drinks. I'll pick you up about 6:15?"

"I'll be ready," she said, giving the punching bag another swift kick and heading for the shower.

Chapter 16

While Kitty showered, she began to plan what she should do to prepare for the dinner date offered so suddenly. She was pleasantly surprised at the offer considering that Angus Mulbrae had only seen her up close on two occasions. On Friday morning she had hardly been a vision of loveliness wearing her nightgown and bathrobe. Just a short time ago she was wearing a loose and worn-out blouse, scruffy jeans and was all sweaty from her run after her haircut. What on earth must he have been thinking when he asked her to join him for dinner?

As she toweled herself off, she thought, "What am I going to wear this evening? All my best outfits are in the dry cleaners." She had answered that question with a snap decision before she showered. Shave her legs, or leave them alone for now? "Oh heck," she thought, "I'm just going to wear a pair of pants. If Angus expects a dress, he'll have to wait for something fancier than the Fishwife."

She looked at her meager "going out" wardrobe and decided two things. First, she had a clean white blouse, which she would wear with her green jacket. Her back-up pair of black slacks would be just fine, and her black flats would make a complete "date ensemble." Since she wouldn't be driving, she could use a small purse that she hadn't taken out of a dresser drawer since the days of those "soirees" that Jake would take her to in Hollywood. It was a suitably flashy little bag with a gold chain she could use if she wanted to hang it over her shoulder. She kept it together with a little token she had been given from Tiffany's in a pretty cloth bag in unmistakable Tiffany blue. Ten years, and she had never found a use for it since those days of "wine and poses," as she liked to call the Hollywood scene.

Her last thoughts on the subject of appearance came down to lipstick color. She decided to go with the Revlon color labeled "Soft Silver Rose." Not as bright a color as her favorite "Wine with Everything" red, but she felt that might make her look too brash.

All "tarted up," as Jake used to say about her when they were going out; she was prepared when her doorbell rang at 6:10 in the evening. Angus looked properly "Californian Casual" in a lightweight sport coat and grey slacks. "Good," she thought, "He wore a dress shirt but no tie. Much more relaxed, and less likely to feel uncomfortable."

"Hi there," she greeted him. "You look a good bit different out of uniform. I like the look."

"And you," he said, "Look a heck of a lot better than you did this afternoon. Not that you looked bad, just a lot more attractive. I must have made you feel ill at ease because of the way I showed up this afternoon. I just better shut up and get you into my car."

"No, you're right," she said. "I was not at my best either yesterday morning or this afternoon. I just needed some 'basic repairs' after a week on the road."

As she got into his car, a late model Ford Mustang, she commented, "I wondered what a policeman would drive in his off-duty hours. I'm glad to see that it's not a Crown Victoria or some other version of a patrol car."

"Yes," he said, "I bought this three years ago in L.A. just about the time I decided to take the job here."

The Fishwife was located where Asilomar Avenue ended at Sunset Drive. It was a small restaurant with a good selection of seafood and absolutely no parking, unless you got lucky and found a spot at the curb on Sunset. It was 6:30 on a late spring evening, and it was cold already, as they were only yards away from the Asilomar State Beach and adjacent conference grounds.

Kitty was glad to get inside and out of the cool evening air.

Drinks were ordered, Kitty, a mojito and Angus, a margarita, and the perusal of the menu was under way. Angus asked, very straight forward, "So what's this about you and the word felon? I'm just curious because you look more like a schoolteacher or a librarian."

"Oh great," she thought; "he thinks I look like a librarian. I should have gone with the bright red lipstick, a couple of ounces of Chanel #5, and the two-inch heels."

"Well," she said, "I believe I should be open about my legal status, especially when knowledge of it might be helpful to someone. Not mentioning it, only to be discovered later, might make someone think I was trying to put something over on them. I'm not ashamed of that condition; it's just a fact of my life. I intend to use the law to change my legal status, hopefully next year."

"I did a dumb thing," she continued, "right after I got out of college, got arrested, took a plea with prison time and spent almost three years locked up. I finished my parole, but the word 'felon' stays with you forever unless you can get it expunged. I plan to work on that for the next 12 months."

"I won't press you for any details now," he said, "and I do know that the label of felon can have really bad effects on life, careers, opportunities. So let me tell you a little about me."

"I'm all ears," she said. "I like the 'getting to know you' part of a relationship, although I probably shouldn't use that word yet."

The waiter, asking if they had any questions or could he take their order interrupted them. Kitty wanted a cup of clam chowder and the Salmon Lafayette for her entrée. Angus went with the garden salad and the Shrimp Veneto.

"Okay, over to you," Kitty said. "How'd you end up patrolling the crime-ridden streets of Pacific Grove?"

"When I graduated from high school in Ohio in 1984 at age 18, I had little or no interest in education. The Army was going into its all-volunteer mode after Vietnam, so I joined with the idea of getting a skill. I became an M.P., you know, Military Police, and I could have left after 20 years with a pension in 2004. The Army was basically pressuring experienced personnel to stay in, because we were in Afghanistan, and then Iraq. I reenlisted for another six years and got out in 2010. I decided to take some courses at a community college in criminal justice, and I did well. Hell, I knew more than most of the instructors. In 2012 I got into the L.A. County Sheriff's academy in Whittier, and when I graduated, I heard about the job here.

"It doesn't pay as well as the LAPD or the L.A. Sheriff, but if you stay with the sheriff, you spend your first year, or more, pulling duty in the jail. So, the job in Pacific Grove sounded very attractive."

"Please pardon my being nosy," Kitty said, "but I didn't hear the words 'wife' or 'marriage' anywhere in that story."

"I came very close a couple of times," he replied. "Once in Texas while at Fort Hood, and another while on duty in Germany. The Texan decided that the idea of moving somewhere every two years or so was not what she wanted. She wanted a stable home and a couple of kids, so we parted ways. The German gal? Well, she simply wasn't American, as best I can describe it. There is an American culture or civilization and not everybody is comfortable with it. So, I ended that relationship and took my next posting to Korea. And how about you, Miss No Rings on Left?"

"Married once, right across the bay at Fort Ord. I was on parole, my parole officer got me a job locally and I met Pfc. McEwan. Whirlwind romance, marriage in the chapel on base, and after a little over a year he got promoted to corporal and was assigned to Fort Collins in Colorado. A parolee can't leave the state, so I stayed here and kept my job. He met another gal, asked for and got a divorce. My P.O. got me a similar job down in Palm Desert and there I met Captain Jake O'Malley, USAR, Special forces in Vietnam and Laos. He was working as a consultant on war movies, and then as a location scout for westerns and some TV shows. He hired me and within a year or so I was pretty much running his business. He called me his 'major domo' and his researcher. It was one hell of an interesting life."

"So, what happened to bring you back to Monterey?"

"In 2006, when he was about 73, Jake decided, for reasons I don't know, to end his life. I know he never really got over the death of his wife and was in some degree of pain from old Vietnam era injuries. Maybe the VA doctors found something like an Agent Orange syndrome killing him. One fall day he just announced he was going to take a trip on the Palm Springs aerial tram before the ride closed for the winter. He asked me to bring him the .22 caliber pistol he kept around the house. He said it was 'just in case I meet a coyote.' He went up to Mount San Jacinto and killed himself. His body wasn't found for a couple of days."

"So, I cried my eyes out for a week, got the VA to help with the burial, and with the help of his three adult children I wrapped up his estate. He left me that Jeep and the Jaguar, and enough money from the sale of the property to a developer to relocate. I chose here, far from Palm Desert."

"Wow, that's quite a story, and all I've done is track down AWOL soldiers, arrest drunken, brawling G.I.'s and train to arrest drunken brawling civilians. So, what's this thing you thought I might help you with?"

"I'm trying," she said, "to find a member of a family in L.A. County who hasn't been seen by his siblings for ten years. He's entitled to one quarter of a pretty good-sized estate, but where is he? What I want to know first is if he is still alive, and I know how to research death records. Next, is he in prison? Can you, or any police force, look at databases and see if this person is incarcerated somewhere? He is also a nut about classic British sports cars, so I'm looking at that life interest to see if he has surfaced at any auctions or events like that. The family has said that they'll give the search one year, and then they'll go to court and try to have him declared dead."

"I get what you're looking for," Angus said, "and I or the computer guys at the station might be able to help you with the prison records search."

"That would be great," Kitty said, "but the last thing I want is you or any member of the P.G. police force to get in any trouble, especially with my criminal record."

"I've thought of a way to cover that," he replied. "I'll just let everyone on the force who asks know that you are my C.I."

"Your what?" she asked.

"My confidential informant. Most cops, even those who walk a beat or in a patrol car cultivate a relationship with someone, often an ex-con, who can give them information on crimes, either ones they are working on or things that might be coming up. You can be my C.I. on let's say property crimes and auto theft. Then no one will think it strange for us to have a meal together, like tonight."

"Oh boy, I could become a 'snitch' or 'rat' like the gals in the 'joint' would always express contempt for. Heck, it's all right with me. It might help in the future if a judge is deciding whether to expunge my record and lets me be a full citizen again. So, yes, I'll be your C.I.

Now, let's get us some tea or coffee and a couple of pieces of their key lime pie."

As he enjoyed his pie and coffee, Angus asked, "Where do you think this thing goes next?"

Lowering her cup of tea and her dessert fork, Kitty replied, "Well, do you mean 'next' in the short or the long term? In the short term, where this evening goes is you drive me back to my place, walk me to the door, I give you a hug and a kiss on the cheek, thank you for a nice evening and go inside."

"And is there a long-term scenario?" he asked.

"Yes, there is." she replied. "You give me a call next week, and here's my card with my number on it. You tell me when you're free and then we go to dinner where I choose. In this scenario the place I choose is Peppers, so I hope you like Mexican food. Then I make the reservation, I pick you up, I guess at the 'cop house,' as we ex-cons might call it, in my Jaguar and we go to dinner, my treat."

"And after dinner?" he asked.

"Well, that depends," she responded. "Maybe there'll be a movie we can agree on either here in PG or over at the multi-plex at the Del Monte center. If we end up over at Del Monte, then we could go to Cold Stone Creamery for some ice cream. Either way, we'll come up with something we both would like to do. While on the 'like to do' subject, how do you feel about ballroom dancing?"

"Good grief," he replied, "I've never done it, but I'm willing to take lessons. The Texan I mentioned earlier tried to get me to try that line-dancing that they do there and that did not interest me."

"Okay," she said, "that's a little bit, just off the top of my head, what I think the 'next' might be. I'm interested in getting to know you better, but you've got to understand that I've been on my lonesome for a good long time. I'm used to being on my own and in charge of my life. Also, I've got commitments I've made to people. I'm planning to start work on a master's degree, and there's a producer in North Hollywood who wants me to be the consulting witch on a movie. Oh, and I work 20 hours a week at the library. Like they say, I have many irons in the fire."

"All right, I'll leave it at that," he said. "I'm glad you want to see me again, and I get it that you want it to be an equal relationship. It won't hurt my ego, or my wallet either, if you want to pay for our next date. I do consider this a date, and I look forward to the next one, especially with such a good-looking woman."

With that, he settled their bill and they headed for the Mustang at the curb.

Chapter 17

Sunday morning, and it appeared to Kitty to be a fine spring morning. She had much to accomplish, the first thing being a good run out toward Pebble Beach. As she ran, she could think of the things that she should begin work on.

She would email Mel Goldfarb to inquire about the status of the movie project. She really didn't want to become deeply involved with the "consulting witch" idea, but neither did she wish to slam that door completely shut.

Her research into the market for C-type Jaguars had yielded four leads, all in the U.K. They all claimed that their replicas were of "impeccable build" or "superb condition" or "a mechanical masterpiece," not to mention "a racing legend you can enjoy every day." Prices on these replicas ran from just under $1,000,000 for the one with the nice touch of "factory blueprints included" to $350,000 for the three-year-old "masterpiece." In other words, hardly the $9,000,000 to $17,000,000 for one of the real original C-types. Would Max Shepherd settle for an obtainable copy if he could not buy or steal an original? She would contact each of these vendors in the hope that Max had been in touch with any of them.

She would also contact that college instructor in Ontario, Canada, who, she hoped, could put her in touch with a fellow auto historian who would know where the originals were. That could be a tricky business, because some private collectors might not want anyone to know what was in their collection. If one of the original 50 cars were located in the U.S.A., it would most likely be that owner whom Max would approach to ask about any potential for a sale in the near future.

She had located the web sites of the major auction houses where a car such as this would probably be consigned for sale. Topping the list would be Bonhams, with offices in both the U.K. and the U.S.A. Coys had an auction site in London, and Sotheby's held auctions all over the U.S.A., as well as most of Europe. They all welcomed interested buyers to register as bidders and to buy the catalog for any upcoming sale to learn what would be offered for sale. The question for her was would they tell her if Max Shepherd was a registrant? The odds seemed against her there, as the firm would want to preserve the privacy of the potential buyer.

She would need to employ, on a part-time basis, someone who might be able to pry such information out of other people's computers. That meant she would need to contact the job placement office at California State University Monterey Bay and the Monterey Peninsula College. She thought, "I'll wait until Monday morning to make any phone calls to either college."

Her run completed, she decided to put in a few minutes in her "garage gym." She only used the treadmill on those mornings when it was too cold, dark, foggy or rainy to be unsafe running on the poorly lighted streets of Pacific Grove. Today it would be fifteen minutes with the weights, concentrating on upper body strength, and an equal time on the stationary bike. Then it was time for a warm shower followed by breakfast and a morning with the Sunday edition of the Monterey Herald. It was going to be a very lazy day for Kitty once the newspaper had brought her up to date on the latest crime reports in Monterey County, plus all the national, state or local political news. She also enjoyed the huge real estate section of the Sunday paper, and thought about going to a couple of "open house" showings just for the fun of it.

She dropped the paper and spent several minutes thinking about her dinner with Angus Mulbrae. The next move was up to him. She did wonder how this relationship might develop. She felt it would be nice to be involved with someone, much as she had been with Jake. It was awkward, she had discovered, to be the lone unaccompanied female at some group function. There was, for example, an annual fund-raising gala held for the benefit of the library that she was involved in. That, however, was just part of her job at the library, so her attendance was required. She noticed that the vast majority of people attending such an event were couples, married or not. So, her social life was, and had been, virtually non-existent for several years.

Such, she figured, was the fate of the solitary Wicca. Others around her might have been at some church function this morning, but she had elected many years ago to follow a different path. She had considered joining a group that read and discussed books, but again most of the members were women. She guessed that what she really missed was any regular contact with the male of the species.

Then again, she valued the condition of being able to "paddle her own canoe" as an old saying went. No, she wasn't going to give up that autonomy, but if the opportunity arose, she wouldn't mind a man in her life. They could be useful if managed properly, and one might prove to be a better companion than her cat. She would have to give that situation more thought.

In the afternoon she called up Mary Brown, who was her boss at the library. She wanted her to know that she was back in town and would be at work tomorrow, but at a later time than usual. She explained that her first task would be to get back to the shop and retrieve the Jaguar. She could walk there as she had when she dropped the car off, but she decided that using the Monterey Salinas Transit bus, known locally as MST, would save her some time and energy. With the car back on the road she would get over to the library and put in her four hours of ensuring the physical health and well-being of part of the collection. When she had been there nine days earlier, she had been working with books in the mystery section of the collection.

As the day began to wind down, she finished off the most recent book by Michael Connelly. It was obvious that the days of the retired LAPD detective Harry Bosch were coming to an end. "How," she wondered, "will the author bring an end to his greatest character. Will he die in a shoot-out with some robber, or will he take his retirement pension and move to Nevada because taxes are low and his ex-wife lives there?" Then she remembered that Harry's ex-wife, a professional gambler, had died in a shoot-out in Hong Kong.

One of the best benefits of her job at the P.G. library was the ability to know when the latest novel, especially mystery stories, would be on the shelves and available for checkout. "Yes," she thought, "it's like insider trading on the stock market, but it hurts no one." So, as the day ended, Kitty prepared a low-cal TV dinner and settled down to watch 60 Minutes and Masterpiece Theater. Tomorrow she would be fully back into life in Pacific Grove.

Chapter 18

Monday, Tuesday, Wednesday. Another week in the life of Katherine Teresa D'Literie, library technical services. Oh, there were a few breaks in an otherwise dull-as-dishwater week. On Monday our heroine took the bus to Forest Avenue and went to Matteson's shop to retrieve Malcolm. Ernie, the mechanic, informed her that Malcolm would need some extensive work in the near future.

"Have you ever thought of selling the Jaguar?" he asked. "I mean, it's a collectible car now, still in pretty good condition and you could probably get somewhere between 80 and 100 grand for her."

"Ernie," she replied, "I may have to sell the old dear someday when I'm desperate for money, but not yet. That car is, well, it's sort of what I am. It's a part of my past, and it'll be a part of my future for a while longer. So, tell me what the old beast needs, and I'll bring it back later in the month when you have the parts in hand. Deal?"

With that business completed it was off to the library for her daily four hours of work. Before leaving the library at 2:30, she did some research on the computer to see what a 1966 Jaguar XKE might sell for. Ernie was right. She might be able to squeeze $80,000 out of the sale of old Malcolm, but what would she drive around in after he was gone?

She went further online to see what a new Jaguar convertible would cost her. $91,000 to $126,000 with a V6 motor and all-wheel drive, or $73,000 with a four-cylinder motor. "Good Lord," she thought, "Jake had paid $30,000 for a 30-year-old Malcolm back in 1996. I guess I'll just keep the old beast a while longer. I just love the looks I get when I drive it around town."

Tuesday, and another trip to retrieve her property, this time her clothes at the dry cleaner's. At the library the new book to be processed was the latest by author Rhys Bowen, with the title "The Tuscan Child." "Sounds like a departure from her usual English setting," Kitty said to Mary Brown. "I'll put myself on the waiting list and see what it's about in a couple of weeks."

She also got a positive response to an email she had sent to Napoleon Shepherd. She had asked for more information on Max's work history and education. She thought maybe something there would help her look for him with potential employers.

She now learned he had gone back to college as a graduate student when it appeared his journalistic career might end, and he was trained and sometimes employed as a CPA, a certified public accountant. She even began to think of a scheme where she might pose as the human relations director for a classic car dealership, like Fantasy Junction in Emeryville. Maybe that would lure him out with the story that the firm needed an audit of its books before it was sold. Another long shot which she would only consider after she had talked to the owners of the dealership and see what level of trickery they would tolerate.

Wednesday. Another very ordinary day at the library. A few old books, much the worse for wear and not checked out by anyone for a few years, would now be on their way to the used book sale. In the afternoon she got a response from Doug, the college professor and auto historian. He directed her to a couple of contacts in the U.K. who might be able to tell her where the C-type Jaguars that Max Shepherd might be pursuing could be located.

She also got a response from the job placement office at the community college. They had posted a notice that there was a part-time job for a "researcher" with excellent computer skills. Would anyone respond? Only time would tell, but it seemed a bit unlikely. It was May, and most students would be looking for a full-time job or an internship as the summer break drew near.

Thursday was not going to be humdrum. Oh, there was the usual four hours at the library after which she went to her yoga class at the Seaside Yoga Sanctuary on Grand Avenue. She had been going there the entire eight years they had been in business. She liked the other people in the group and found it a good activity for both her mind and body.

Another surprise awaited her on her computer at home. She had contacted the leading producer of replica C-type Jaguars, Maximum Sports and Racing Cars in Buckinghamshire. They produced exactly ten replicas each year, no more, no less. She had asked if it was possible to have a car replicated without the modern upgrades, such as better brakes. She knew that their motto, "Where Classic Meets Clever" implied that they were clever enough to make the upgrades very hard to detect by the casual or untrained observer.

What she wanted to know was, first, could they take an original XK 120 roadster and use it as the basis for a XK 120 C-type replica? Secondly, had anyone ever given them such a challenge for their cleverness?

Their answer surprised her more than she had expected. Yes, it could be done, but at greater cost than simply using raw materials and new parts to build a replica. They went on to say that she wasn't the first American to propose such an idea. They had been approached by an American named Dred Maxim with such an idea to add to his collection in a proposed museum near Las Vegas, Nevada. They indicated that the idea was unusual in that most customers wanted the look of the original race car, but wanted the enhanced performance and greater safety of the clever upgrades.

Kitty had a feeling, the sort of intuition that Jake had encouraged years ago when he called her his "S-2." Something about the fact that an American was looking for the most difficult to detect replica, was willing to pay an outlandish sum and wanted it to go to a museum which no one had ever heard of just didn't ring true. Then there was that name, Dred Maxim. "No one names a kid Dred, do they," she thought.

As she looked at the name, she began to think that this name was perhaps an anagram. You make an anagram by moving letters in a word around to make a new word, or perhaps add a letter or two. If you take Maximillian Shepherd apart, use the letters at the start of the first name you create the last name Maxim. Take the last letters of the family name, Shepherd, move them around and reverse them and you get "Dre." Now add a letter "d" and you have Dred. Of course, it's a stretch, but could the mysterious Dred Maxim be the missing Max Shepherd? "Oh, Jake," she thought, "wherever you are, do you think this is just insane or could I be on to something?"

Time to think about that over the weekend. On her voice mail she had a message from Angus Mulbrae. He wanted her to know that he would be off-duty this evening, so how about that second date? He'd be free after his shift ended at six in the evening. He gave her his cell phone number and said he hoped he would hear from her.

"Okay," she thought, "he's interested so it's time to go forward in first gear or hit the kill switch." She picked up her phone, dialed the number and heard his voice say, "Hello, this is Mulbrae."

"Hey, Angus, this is Kitty. I got your message and tonight sounds good. Let's say I'll pick you up at work at 6:15this evening. I'll reserve a table for us for 6:30. Will that work for you? Oh, and dress real casual. I'll be wearing jeans and a shirt that I won't mind getting salsa on."

"Okay, I'll meet you out front at 6:15. I'll call you if any emergencies come up."

Kitty had started the day at the library and things had gotten her a little distracted. There was the Shepherd case to mull over, and she would have to get back to Maximum and ask how much, in U.S. dollars, would a project like the one proposed by Dred Maxim cost. How would they want the payment made? It was all a hunt for clues on her part, but if she had a member of law enforcement ask about how Dred handled the financing, under the guise of stopping drug trafficking "Lord," she thought, "I hardly know the guy and I'm trying to drag him into my spider web. A couple of months ago I'd never heard of a C-type Jaguar, and now I'm trying to tie the sale of a replica to international drug trafficking. What am I, a nut case?"

"Yes," she thought, "this may be lunacy, but I remember John DeLorean. He was having the car of his own design built in Belfast, of all places, and was selling them at a loss in the U.S.A. To cover his financial problems, he got involved in cocaine smuggling, sales and distribution. So, it is possible that Max has become so obsessed with his quest that he'll go to any lengths, legal or not."

Now it was time for another challenge. How far and how fast did she want this new ride to go? The first step was easy; make the dinner reservations. Next, check out the movie show times for that evening. Over at the multiplex at Del Monte they were showing what might be the last movie ever starring Robert Redford. "The Old Man with a Gun" was showing at eight that evening. Perfect! Dinner, a dash in the Jaguar over to the Del Monte Center, a movie where the cops win, ice cream, and …well, we'll see.

So, there she was, the middle-aged redhead in her 52-year-old convertible parked in the 20-minute zone in front of the P.G. police station. Right on time Angus joined her and they were off on the short drive to Peppers. Just enough time for her to ask him "Did your colleagues ask about the woman in the Jaguar?"

"They did," he replied. "You surely must know that this car sort of makes you noticeable around town, except maybe in late August when all the car crazies are here."

"So, what did they say about me?"

"Well, they wondered who you were waiting for, and when I said you were my C.I., they all laughed. Then I told them you were telling me about a plot to steal classic cars during 'car week' and that shut them up for a while. They'll keep pestering me for details, so be prepared," he said.

She parked on Forest so that she could keep an eye on Malcolm. They entered and were seated promptly. The crowd was typical for a late spring evening, skewing toward college-age and young professionals. It didn't take Kitty long to make her selection from the menu, telling the waiter she'd have, "Chips and salsa for two to start, and I want a margarita and two enchiladas, one chicken and the other beef."

"I'll have the beef fajitas and a bottle of Lagunitas IPA," Angus told the waiter.

"After dinner," Kitty said, "let's go over to Del Monte. I want to see the new Redford movie. It's about an over-the-hill bank robber. Do you know the famous story about Willie Sutton?"

"Wasn't he some famous bank robber of the 1930s?"

"Yes, and on his way to prison a reporter asked him why he robbed banks, and Sutton replied, 'because that's where the money is.' Then he got out, wrote a book and said that he never made that quote. Today in medical schools they teach Sutton's Law."

"So, what is Sutton's Law?" Angus asked.

"In medical school they teach that when trying to diagnose an illness, you should first consider the obvious. Don't run a bunch of expensive and maybe painful tests until you've checked the obvious. People obviously rob banks because that's where the money is, and that dumb reporter should have known that. I'll bet there's even a version of that law that they teach for investigating a crime."

"So, tell me, my lovely felon," he asked, "what did you do to get a criminal record? Everyone at the station will want to know what qualifies you as a C.I."

"I was apprehended leaving a home in Bel Aire with a bag full of gold jewelry. I had been in the house working for a caterer, knew that the family was on vacation and thought it would be a snap. It wasn't. Copped a plea, did my time, got paroled. Next question."

"Was that your only offense?" he asked.

"Only time I was arrested," she replied, in what she knew was a Jesuitical manner.

"Remember," she thought, "he's a cop and trust only goes so far at this point. He's played for the other team his whole adult life."

They bantered back and forth about trivia like the weather, things that come up at work. Much as she had expected the waiter started to give the bill to Angus before she grabbed it, saying, "This one goes on my credit card." She thought, "Someday they'll learn, maybe even in my lifetime, that women can pay their own way if they get treated like equals."

They were on their way across Monterey to the Del Monte Center in time to catch the eight o'clock show. She loved the movie, as she did all of Redford's films. Angus wasn't so wild about it because the old robber kept the police looking pretty stupid for a long time. Kitty simply told him, "It just goes to prove that old adage about looks being deceiving. The bank robber looks like a harmless old man, he never really tries to scare people so he just gets overlooked. I'm sure people see me in the Jaguar and never think of me as an ex-con. They probably think I'm some gold-digger who married an old man for his money and his snazzy car."

As they walked back to the car after their ice cream Kitty said, "Now, I'm going to drive you back to the station. Since it would be inappropriate for you to be seen exchanging DNA samples with your C.I. in front of the station, we're going to get the kissing out of the way in the car before we leave here." So, there was an amorous embrace, her red lipstick got somewhat smeared, and she knew there would definitely be a next time. She got her breathing under control, her seat belt on and motored back to P.G.

As he climbed out of the car, she said, "Call me when you want to do this again, and next time maybe we'll stay at my place, watch TV and eat popcorn. But do call me. See ya."

She slipped Malcolm into first gear and motored off to home. She definitely wanted to light a candle on her altar in front of the figure of the Goddess.

Chapter 19

The weekend went very quietly for Kitty. Angus gave her a call early on Sunday morning. He wanted her to go scuba diving with him. He had begun to learn how to do this type of diving from a group of firemen stationed in Pacific Grove. They would enter the water of the bay from San Carlos Beach near the Coast Guard Pier. You had to get there early in the day because the parking lot for the beach and dive shop would fill up very fast on a weekend.

Kitty could only laugh at the offer. "Angus," she said, "much as I like your company, this just proves we need to know each other a lot more. I can't swim a stroke, never have, never learned and never will. Just be careful out there and stick with the group. Oh, and don't mess with the otters. I'll talk to you next week."

Next week most of her talking was with Mary Brown at the library. Naturally, "how did your date go?" was the first question of the week. Assured that all had gone to plan, Mary let that subject drop. The next 20 days were massively ordinary. Angus, Kitty decided, wouldn't have a lot of free time, because the last ten days of May and the first ten days of June were always busy in Pacific Grove.

Those 20 days would be when schools were getting ready for end-of-year activities. High schools would be having proms and other festivities related to graduation. This often brought out the "stupid gene" in some young people, especially the young males of the herd. Calls related to loud parties, drunken driving, vandalism of school property and complaints of sexual assault became more frequent. All these took many hours of police work, often overtime.

Then, late in May, Memorial Day arrives, and with it the unofficial start of the vacation season. Not every tourist is a drunken, loud-mouthed reckless driver, but the ten percent who are give the police departments all over the Monterey area plenty of cause for overtime work assignments, plus an abundance of paper work. So, it was not surprising to Kitty that officer Angus Mulbrae was not heard from during that period. Kitty had other things to think about beside her barely existent "love-life."

She had contacted the people from Maximum to see if the Dred Maxim order had been completed, using the guise of wanting to see the finished product before she placed her own order. She learned that the replica C-type would ship out of Southampton within a week on a "roll-on, roll-off" ship, the Marina Maru. Delivery to Corpus Christi, Texas would occur on or about June 15. That type of ship was built for delivery of any automobiles, new or used, because the car can be driven on, protected with a moisture proof cover, tied down and be ready to roll off the ship when it reached port.

She pressed her luck a little bit there, asking how customers usually paid for their C-type? Also, how did the buyer skirt the U.S. rules about car safety and air quality controls? She was informed that the company preferred wire transfers of the payment from banks in Switzerland or the Cayman Islands, with any financing handled strictly by the bank. They required that 50% of the agreed upon price would be in their hands before the work began, and the balance was payable upon delivery of the car to the ship. They also informed her that the shipping company determined the cost of shipping and that the cost of getting the car to the U.S. usually ran from $800 to $1,000.

As regarding the U.S. rules, which made it almost impossible for an individual to import any car made after 1968, they reminded her that the car was based on a scrapped 1954 Jaguar. The "rebodied" car would be admitted to the U.S. as a 1954 Jaguar, and all those rules about safety and pollution controls were not applicable.

Maximum went on to inform her that the U.S. owner had to make all the arrangements to have the car transported to its ultimate location, as well as registering and licensing the car in the state where it would be based. They built the car, but it was all the new owner's concern once they got it to the ship at the port.

Kitty began to see a pattern emerging, if in fact a crime was about to take place. To test her theory, she first had to contact the dealership known as Fantasy Junction In Emeryville, in the San Francisco Bay area. They had advertised a Maximum C-type "re-creation," built in 1966 for sale at just under $140,000.

Had it been sold, and if so would they tell her to whom they had sold it so that she could make the new owner an offer? Her intuition might be paying off.

The new owner, a Mr. Maxim, had paid for the car with a wire transfer from a bank in the Cayman Islands and arranged to have it shipped to Las Vegas, Nevada.

Kitty was working on the theory that the mysterious Dred Maxim was, in fact, the long-lost Maximillian Shepherd. The second part of her theory was that Max was planning to swap the recently ordered Maximum replica for one of the original 50 C-type Jaguars. If that was the case, why did he buy another older replica from Fantasy Junction? That was where her criminal past came into play.

Kitty had learned more than library management skills while serving her sentence, years ago in the prison in Chino. She learned about the oldest scam in the world of crime, which could often be seen used openly on the streets of large cities like New York. It was simply labeled "the shell game." The trickster, and that's what she liked to call the con artist, needed a flat surface like a table top, a small object like a pea and three walnut shells.

The "sucker" is encouraged to guess which of the three shells has the pea hidden under it. The shells are shuffled about and the bet is made. Pick the correct shell and you win, get it wrong and the trickster takes your money. Usually, the pea isn't under any of the shells, because it was scooped off the table when the shells were in motion. To convince the person being "conned" that they had a chance the trickster let them win a time or two.

Kitty's theory was that Dred Maxim was going to work a variation of the shell game. One reason the "game" can be successful is that the three shells look alike. In her theory the "pea" would be the authentic C-type Jaguar, and the older and newer replicas would be in identical transport vehicles. All this was just a crazy scheme in Kitty's mind unless, of course, one of the authentic cars were to be entered into one of the many auctions held during "car week," or entered into one of the very exclusive shows on the Monterey Peninsula during that week. Establishing that part of her wIld and crazy theory would take some heavy-duty research on her part.

Another part of the plot would be to determine if there really was a mystery classic car museum in Las Vegas. If Max was determined to steal an authentic C-type, what was he going to do with it? People who steal works of art from museums, whether public or private, have two courses of action if the theft is a success. They can hang the artwork in a private room in their home and enjoy it in solitude behind closed doors. Doesn't sound like a lot of fun, does it?

Or, like a Nazi official after World War II, you could try to resell the painting to someone in another country and hope that your story of "it's a previously unknown work by the artist," goes unchallenged. But how do you do that with a car?

If you really love classic cars you don't just steal one and lock it in a vault. No, you want to get it out on the road and drive it, show it off to people, leave it to your heirs as a family heirloom to be enjoyed by them or sold after you die.

Or, like the thief at the art museum, you let the insurance company know that you've got it and they can save a lot of money that they'll have to pay out to the owner for the loss of his million-dollar baby by paying you a "fee," what we might call a "ransom," for its return. If Max were going to just try to make a heap of money that way it would be out of character, at least as far as his family knew. They saw him as a man who liked older classic cars, who had an obsession, based upon childhood memories of a long-ago race, of getting his hands on the winner of that race. No, he wouldn't steal the car just to "ransom" it. He'd want to, if only for a short while, enjoy the thrill of the ride.

Kitty figured that her next task would be to find out if there really was a "museum" in Las Vegas where Max might display a car collection. Also, what about Corpus Christi and the Maximum replica arriving there? If Dred Maxim were there to take delivery, and she could identify him as the missing heir Max Shepherd, would she not have solved her case? Her assignment was to find Max Shepherd if he was still alive, not to try to solve a crime which hadn't happened yet.

She could see two long and probably meaningless trips ahead of her. Las Vegas was the shorter of the two so she began to plan how she would get there and find out if Dred Maxim had bought or leased a building large enough to hold a small, exclusive car collection. Would she go alone, or could she persuade a scuba-diving cop to take a road trip with her to "Sin City?"

Now that might prove interesting once the madness of the first ten days of June were over. Time to hit the Shepherd family for some travel money, including a rental car to make the drive. Old Malcolm would definitely not enjoy a hot summer trip across the deserts of Nevada. Her next step would be to plan a trip that might produce some real clues as to the whereabouts of Max Shepherd.

Before she began making any concrete plans for the Vegas expedition she noticed an advertisement in the Sunday edition of the Monterey Herald. Macy's was having a "Get ready for summer sale." It suddenly dawned on her that if she was going to Vegas she might need to expand her wardrobe. Surely there would be time there to lounge around a pool and get a second-degree burn on her pale skin, and to do that she had to purchase a swimsuit. She also thought, "Maybe I should buy a dress. If I'm going to buy things I haven't owned in years, why not go whole-hog. A swimsuit for the girl who can't swim, and a dress to wear if I can ever get Angus to try dancing, and a slip or half-slip to go with the dress." With that she decided that she had been sitting around too long thinking. It was time to clear her mind and take a long run. Within five minutes she was out the door and running to clear her head of old cars and middle-aged men.

Chapter 20

Kitty anticipated a call from Angus once the middle of June arrived, and sure enough on Thursday the 14th her phone rang, and the now familiar voice said, "Kitty, how are you, and what does tomorrow night look like on your calendar?"

"Angus," she responded, "it's good to hear your voice. I guess you must have survived graduation week. How about you come over to my place in the evening and we watch a movie together? I've got popcorn to go with it."

"What's the movie?" he asked.

"I rented one called Mr. Holmes from Netflix. It's supposed to be about Sherlock after he retires to the countryside to keep bees, but he's troubled by the one old case that he never really solved. Does it sound interesting?"

"Yeah, it does, and I want to catch up on all your amateur detective work. How about eight tomorrow night?"

"Okay, eight it is. I'll see you then," she said as she hung up the phone.

Friday dawned cold and drizzly, unusual for early summer on the Monterey Peninsula. Kitty got her grocery shopping out of the way early and put in 45 minutes working out in her garage gym. She had her usual light supper and made sure that the cat, Pyewacket, was comfortable for the night. She hoped that Angus wasn't allergic to cat hair and dander. "First time he's in the house for any length of time, I don't want our relationship to end in a sneezing fit," she thought.

She thought about that word, relationship. She wondered what his colleagues on the police force thought about his "confidential informant" and how long would they swallow that explanation for their being together. Also, what would he think about her wacky ideas relative to Dred Maxim and the plot to steal a very rare and expensive sports car. What if he told her it was a nutty idea and that pursuing it any further would be silly? This evening could be a real test of male chauvinism, or a display of male support.

Angus was, as usual, very punctual, knocking on her door at 7:55 on the dot. Kitty wasted no time after the usual quick kiss of greeting getting to the subject of what she had been thinking, or was it fantasizing, about the case of the missing Max Shepherd.

"Angus, the first thing I want to run by you is what I call you. Angus is a lovely name, but if I'm Kitty to you, would it be all right if I just call you Gus?"

"Ms. D'Literie, I'd be very comfortable with Gus. I mean, most guys at the station just never get beyond Mulbrae, so Gus would be very nice for a change."

"Good. Now let me bring you up to speed on my case." She proceeded to lay out what her intuition, or was it her over-active imagination, had laid out for Max Shepherd, AKA Dred Maxim. She ended up announcing that she was planning to drive to Las Vegas and see what she could learn about a proposed private classic car museum.

"Wow," Gus said, "you really have given this a lot of thought and some research with this English car company, Maximum. But what do you think you'll learn in Vegas?"

"Well," she responded, a little coyly, "here's a thought. Why don't you come with me? I'll contact the Chamber of Commerce, and maybe a realtor or two, to see if there has been any sale or rental of a large warehouse or similar building that could house a collection. You could, if appropriate, check with the Nevada version of the DMV to see if the car sold at

121

Fantasy Junction has been registered in Nevada. What do you think?"

"It's not a bad idea," he said, "but I can't get away until after July 4th. There are always a lot of disturbances then, especially with the Monterey Beer Festival going on over at the fairgrounds. After that, it should be quiet around here until the VW car show comes along here in P.G. on the 22nd. So, I could maybe, and I stress maybe, get a few days off after the Fourth. How long are you planning to devote to this trip?"

"Well," she responded, "I figure it would take me two days to drive there, two days looking around and asking questions and two days to get back. Oh, I know, you're thinking 'Why don't you just fly there?' but if I'm that far south I probably should go on to L.A. to check with people in that area. Plus, I hate flying and all the hassles at the airport."

"You're right about my thoughts," he said. "I could fly from here, meet you there and fly home while you go on to L.A. I'm not wild about you driving alone over those mountains and deserts, especially in the heat of July. What would you do if you found this mystery museum, what would you say to people about your snooping around?"

"Well," she said, "I'm not taking the old Jaguar on a trip like that. I thought I'd rent a new car for a week, and while I'm gone the work the Jaguar needs could be completed."

"If I do find the so-called museum, I'll say that I'm researching an article for the Society of Automotive Historians, and I'll just flash my membership card and say I'm looking into a story about replicas and their role in history. Now, how's that for a cover story?"

"I'm glad to hear that you're thinking about a newer car to make such a long trip," Gus said. "Your cover story sounds believable. Of course, it really won't matter

122

much if it's all part of this elaborate plot you've cooked up in that head of yours. If you find this mystery museum, they might not let you talk to anyone at all. Then you're also planning to go on to the L.A. area. What would you hope to accomplish there?"

"I should really have a face-to-face talk with Napoleon Shepherd if I learn anything at all from the Vegas trip," Kitty responded. "I'm also going to be spending some of their money on this expedition, so a direct conversation seems fair. I've got a young man from the college working on another angle, using his computer skills. He's going to check voter rolls to see if Max Shepherd turns up anywhere as a registered voter. He's also going to finish what I started, looking at death records to see if Max is no longer among the living."

"So maybe one day to get from Vegas to L.A., another day there, and a day to get back here. Is that what you're thinking of in terms of time?"

"Right," Kitty replied. "If all goes well, I'll not only meet with the Shepherd family but also collect some money I'm owed by a business in downtown L.A. I may have to put in one more day there to meet with a lawyer."

"Does this have to do with your felony record?"

"It does," she replied. "There's a firm that says they can get the whole process started and finished in six weeks to maybe six months. It costs about $700 to just get started, and then the fees start to pile up as the paperwork piles up. It's a simple case, one conviction on two charges, one for burglary and one for theft. That's why I want to see the man in L.A. who owes me some money. It should be enough to cover the costs of the court process, at least I hope so."

"So, what do you need done to the old Jaguar?" he asked.

"A big overhaul of the brakes, and parts of the suspension need replacement just because of normal use

123

and age. I'm going to leave it all to the guys at Matteson's Garage," Kitty replied.

"Why not take it to Jaguar Monterey over in Seaside? You know that dealership isn't too far from where I live."

"One thing I've discovered about car repairs," she said, "is that dealers are into sales, but really make their money on the servicing of cars they sell. They really don't want to work on older cars that they weren't trained on, and they don't stock parts for cars that are 40 or 50 years old. So, they end up having to get the parts from the same importer that the local garage would contact, and then tie up space in their shop that could be used to service newer cars. No, I'll stick with Ernie and the guys at Matteson's. I'm glad to find out where you live, however."

"Well, don't think that you'll ever see it," Gus said. "I share an apartment with three other guys. It's got three bedrooms and a kitchen and all that, but it isn't the sort of setting where a guy would want to bring a lady friend. Heck, you probably would think of that old Disney movie about Snow White and the Seven Dwarfs. We're not a quartet of slobs, but housekeeping is not real high on our daily schedule, if you get my drift."

"Since you brought it up, why don't I put the popcorn in the microwave and get the Holmes movie on the TV. Do you want a beer to go with it?"

"That would be great, as long as it's real and not that light stuff."

"No, I've noticed what you like to drink the two times we've been out, so this won't disappoint you."

So, they settled down on Kitty's love seat with their popcorn and brews, and soon she noticed that Gus had his left arm over her shoulder and his left hand just a bit lower than her shoulder. "What the hell," she thought, "so he gets to second base tonight. It's just nice to be snuggled up to him and put my head on his shoulder."

The movie over, and Mr. Holmes having, sadly, sort of solved his last case, there was more exchanging of DNA samples. Gus asked, "And what comes next on our agenda?"

Kitty replied, "Now you head back to Seaside. Mrs. Murphy next door would be appalled if you're seen leaving in the early morning hours, so we have to be a little discreet, lest I become the talk of this very small town."

"Of course," she added, "if we were together at the same hotel in mid-July in Las Vegas who knows what adventures might be had. For now, my brave defender of law, order and feminine virtue, I'll bid you good night and a safe drive home."

Chapter 21

Thursday morning, the fifth of July, dawned bright and sunny, although the reek of the smoke of fireworks lingered in the air over Pacific Grove. Kitty had a busy day planned as she prepared for her trip to Las Vegas.

She intended to be on her way by ten in the morning on Friday. That meant that she had to take Malcolm, her faithful but aging Jaguar E-Type, to the garage where the needed repairs would take place. She had arranged for Enterprise to pick her up at the shop. After the paperwork was completed, she would drive her near-new rental Mustang back home and start her packing.

Her original intent was to drive over to the entrance to Yosemite and follow Highway 120 over Tioga Pass to Mono Lake. She would then head south on Highway 395 and overnight at Bishop. The following day would be the desert challenge; cross Death Valley on Highway 190 and arrive at Las Vegas from the north.

That was the original plan that she had outlined for Gus while they had dinner on Tuesday night at Crabby Jim's on the wharf. His reaction, which at first upset her, made her change her mind. His initial response was, "Are you nuts? Driving all alone, that far from civilization. Plus, you're going north to start a trip that ends up going south. What earthly sense does that make?"

"So, what do you suggest?" she asked, with a bitter tone in her voice. "How would you get to Vegas from here?"

"I would want you on roads patrolled by the CHP. I'd go down Interstate 5 and get a room in Bakersfield for night number one. Then you could go over the Tehachapi Pass and pick up Interstate 1-15 at Barstow. In two more hours, you'd be in Vegas."

"Hey," she said, "I think it's sweet that you're concerned about me being out on some lonely highway by myself. It's just that being on the Interstate doesn't sound adventurous or exciting."

"Okay," he responded, "it's more boring, I'll agree, but getting there and testing your theory about this Maxim guy is the real purpose. The route I'm suggesting is just as quick and there are more services, like gas stations, along the way. Don't discount the presence of the CHP should something go a little sideways on route."

So, she agreed to his plan for her route, and she began making reservations on the Fourth. She would stay at the Marriott in Bakersfield, which was on the route she would follow the next morning. The one hotel she was familiar with in Las Vegas was Bally's, and she hadn't been there for close to 20 years. "Two nights there," she thought, "then a couple more at the good old Biltmore in L.A., and I'll be on my way toward home."

Getting familiar with the rented Mustang was something new to her. In the 12 years since Jake's death, she had become very well acquainted with her inherited 50-year-old Jaguar, not to mention the even older Jeep. To a younger generation, the use of the clutch and the gearshift was an arcane art form. To her, it was simply how you drove a car. Now she had to adjust to the new and mysterious world of 21st century automobiles.

One thing she got used to very easily was the new idea of air conditioning. Oh, it was a familiar thing long ago at Jake's home in Palm Desert, but Jaguars were built for the cold and damp of the United Kingdom, where people didn't think it was necessary in a "motorcar."

The other feature, which was new to her, was the satellite radio system. Now she could drive anywhere; desert, mountain or downtown traffic and listen to several different broadcasts without commercials.

127

She had one other advantage with her rental ride. Unlike Malcolm, the Mustang had more room for her luggage, so she could pack more items of clothing. She might never get to use it on this trip, but she had carried out her plan to buy a swimsuit, just in case the opportunity arose to lounge by a pool. There was somewhat more business-like attire for meeting with lawyers in L.A., not to mention the Shepherd family, and something that might look like what an automotive history journalist would wear for the hoped-for encounter with Dred Maxim.

Before departure she called Angus on Thursday evening. She was all business-like, while he was all concerned for her welfare. She said, "Gus, I'm off tomorrow morning by ten. I'm at the Marriott in Bakersfield tomorrow night, and Saturday at Bally's in Vegas. I've got us two rooms, and do you want me to pick you up at the airport?"

"Please call me as soon as you're checked in at Bakersfield." Gus replied. "I really worry about you out there all alone. I've got a flight out of here on Sunday morning and I'll get my own rental car when I get there. We'll probably be going in two different directions Monday morning, so I'll need my own ride."

"Don't worry about me, babe," she said. "I guess I never told you a wise saying I learned from an old Special Forces soldier named Jake. He learned it from some general when he was in 'Nam. It goes 'Be polite, be professional, but have a plan to kill everybody you meet.' That's going to be me, a nice middle-aged lady who down deep trusts no one and will kill if necessary. Got it?"

"Well, that reassures me a bit," he said, "but I'd be alert at all times. There are a lot of folks out there who shouldn't be out in the world, and that's why I worry about your trip. Plus, where you're going is a place founded by people who would kill just to cover a bet."

"I understand," she said, "so I'll see you on Sunday. When does your flight get in?"

"We should be on the ground there by about two, and I'll be at the hotel by three. Think about where you want to go for dinner, and I'll call your room when I get there."

"Okay, Gus, see you in Sin City on Sunday," Kitty said as she ended the call.

Friday morning, and Kitty was on her way at ten a.m. after giving Mrs. Sanchez a key so that she could take care of the cat. She followed the usual route to join Highway 101 in Salinas and then headed south. Still craving a bit of adventure, she headed for the junction with highway 198 at San Lucas, about an hour south of Salinas. Most folks would have kept going south on 101 to Paso Robles and then take highway 46 east to join Interstate 5. Not Kitty. No, she would take the twisting and little used 198 some 60 miles, passing the state prison at Coalinga, and then pick up the I-5 at Lost Hills.

That route, I-5 southbound, was as safe and boring as possible. She was in Bakersfield by four in the afternoon. If you enjoyed country and western music, Bakersfield was the Nashville of the west. If that was your interest there was the Crystal Palace, owned by a famous singer, Buck Owens.

Kitty's preference was one of the three restaurants with a French Basque heritage, and her choice was the Wool Growers Restaurant on 19th Street. Country music had absolutely no appeal for her.

Saturday morning Kitty checked out of the Marriott Courtyard by nine and after refueling the Mustang was on her way eastward on highway 58. Within two hours she had climbed over Tehachapi Pass and descended into the Mojave Desert. Ninety minutes later she was at Barstow and heading toward Las Vegas on I-15.

As she had passed by such military training sites such as Edwards Air Force Base, China Lake Naval Weapons and Fort Irwin she wondered how many times Jake had trained here during his reservist days. She wondered what her mentor of long ago would think of her theories on Dred Maxim.

Three p.m., and Kitty was pulling up to the Bally's Hotel and Casino. Checked into her room, it was time to try that new emerald green swimsuit and a happy-hour drink by the pool. The pool itself actually scared her. It was 12-feet deep at one end, and for a non-swimmer the very thought of water that deep was a bit of a fright. "Maybe," she thought, "I'll see if Gus can teach me to swim. That would be something else we could do together. I'll trade off swim lessons for ballroom dancing lessons. Yes, that might work."

She wasted little time on such plots. She had researched the name and address of the two top firms in the area that dealt with the sale or rental of commercial property of an industrial warehouse nature. She would hit them early on Monday.

She also thought about contacting existing auto museums to see if anyone there had ever heard of Dred Maxim, Max Shepherd or a planned new museum. When she brought the issue up with the concierge, she learned that the long-established museum at the Imperial Palace Hotel had gone away after over 50 years in business. Ah yes, the ephemeral Las Vegas scene. Hotels it seemed, on a regular basis, were demolished by a huge, controlled explosion, only to be replaced by one of grander and more fanciful design.

The "museum" at the Imperial Palace had been in reality an elaborate used car lot. Every car in the "collection" was for sale at the moment some big winner came out of the casino, saw something flashy and classic and asked, "How much?" The price? Well, how much of your winnings do you wish to leave behind? Sales fell off in 2017 as the "high rollers" went elsewhere on the Strip, so it was time to sell off the remaining cars and shut the operation down. That's Vegas reality, 101. Nothing lasts like excess.

Undeterred, Kitty went to the Hollywood Cars Museum on Dean Martin Drive. The owner believed that people would pay to see cars that had a connection with a movie. It began with the collection of cars owned by Liberace, and now there were over 100 cars that had been in everything from James Bond movies to *Chitty Chitty Bang Bang*.

Kitty went straight for the "soul" of any museum, the curator. Jay had earned a reputation for creating custom cars used in movies, and had insights as to where some of the "relics" of moviedom could be found. Kitty used the Society of Automotive Historians cover story to gain access and quickly got to the point of her visit.

"Jay, I've heard a story, and have some facts to support it, that a man calling himself Dred Maxim is going to open a car museum here in Vegas. Have you any knowledge of this story?"

"Lady, I've never heard that story, and I've never heard of any guy called Maxim. I do know that guys who collect rare or unusual cars often buy or rent a warehouse to store the collection. They like Vegas because the dry atmosphere keeps the cars in better shape, and the tax laws are good if you start selling cars."

Kitty asked, "If someone was buying replicas of famous cars what would they do with them? I think real car guys would steer away from buying one, so why collect them?"

"Listen," Jay responded, "there's a lot of ways to make money besides selling a car at auction. Some buy replicas because they want the look, others are planning a movie or a TV series, or they plan to use the car in advertising."

"Just one last question," Kitty said. "I'm trying to help a family find a relative who they know collects cars. Have you ever seen this guy at any auctions or shows?" she asked as she showed Jay a photo of Max Shepherd.

"Well, I'll tell you," Jay replied, "I think I've seen him at some auctions in California or maybe Arizona. If it's the guy I'm thinking of he often bids on cars with a high reserve. Then, if no one meets that price and the car is unsold, he'll hit the guy selling the car later on and try to make a side deal. He's trying to avoid the commission the auction company gets. But I'm not sure from that photo. Sorry, I couldn't be of more help."

"Thanks, Jay," Kitty concluded. "I'm going to talk to real estate people tomorrow and see if there have been any sales or rentals of space to store a collection."

"Well, if you do that," Jay said, "ask about property out toward North Las Vegas. Anyone with a small collection probably couldn't afford the prices they get around here, even if they were charging folks to take a look at what they had collected."

"Thanks, for the advice, Jay. And good luck with the collection," Kitty said, as she headed for the exit. It was time to get back to Bally's and await the arrival of Angus. Little did she know that a short, five-letter word was going to have a negative effect on her next 24 hours in Las Vegas.

Chapter 22

Kitty came back from the Hollywood Cars Museum in time to get into her swimsuit and be sitting by the pool, drink in hand, when Gus arrived. She didn't mind that he eyed her over with a look of admiration, or was it lust? Nor did she mind when his greeting was "Wow, that suit is really something, and what's in it ain't bad either."

"Well," she responded, "I take it that your flight went well, and you'll be joining me for dinner this evening at the BLT Steakhouse. I booked a table for two for seven thirty. That okay?"

"Sounds great. I just dropped my bag in my room. I'm going to back there and get my swim trunks and take a dip in this pool. I'll be right back, and then you can fill me in on what you've learned. Knowing you, I'm sure you've been out 'researching' as you call it."

"Okay, I'll be here trying to avoid sunburn," she said.

While he was away she began to review what she had and had not learned. She had learned that Max Shepherd may have been spotted at classic car auctions, and people in the business had never heard of Dred Maxim. She planned that tomorrow morning at nine she would be on her way to the offices of Kevin Buckley at First Real Estate. She had learned that the firm was the leader in commercial real estate. She tentatively planned to also check with Logic Commercial Real Estate. They specialized in properties that were in receivership. If you were looking for a low-cost deal on a warehouse, you might do well to talk to the people who were trying to help some poor soul out of bankruptcy by unloading some property.

She also hoped that Gus would go over to downtown Las Vegas while she was talking to realtors. If he would go by the police department on Bonanza Road and ask around about Dred Maxim and Max Shepherd, something useful might be learned. If he had time, he could also check for building permits at city hall on Main Street. If a warehouse was going to be used to store classic cars it might need a better fire protection system, an upgraded electrical and security system, and all of that would require permits. Then they could get together at the Bellagio and have lunch while planning their next move.

Gus was back in a few minutes and promptly into the pool. This was the most unclothed she had seen him in their short time together. She was not at all disappointed in what she saw, but she tried to keep her mind on the reason for the two of them being here in Vegas. She would have to report something to Napoleon Shepherd to justify this trip, and it couldn't be how much she liked the physique of her cop boyfriend. "Come on, Kitty," she thought, "get your mind off his body and back on the job you want his brain and background to do for you."

While Gus sat in a chair by her and dried off he asked, "Have you learned anything at all so far?"

"What I've learned is that one person, the museum curator, thinks that he has seen Max Shepherd at car auctions and no one has heard of Dred Maxim. I'm hoping we can turn up something tomorrow."

"And what exactly do you want me to do?" Gus asked.

"Tomorrow, if you would go to the police headquarters and ask if anyone has heard of Dred, seen anyone like this picture of Max or heard anything about a new car collection it would help. I also hoped you might go to city hall and see if there are any permits issued recently to upgrade a warehouse or similar building. They may have planned to enhance their fire and theft security."

"What do I use as an excuse for asking this sort of information?"

"Your confidential informant thinks that a major theft of classic cars may be planned for August during car week in Monterey by one or both of these men. By the way, aren't I supposed to do some paperwork in order to be a C.I.?"

"Yeah, I'm supposed to get you registered, but no one is pushing that issue since you're not asking for any money to compensate for your services. I suspect that most of the force knows what you really are, but they play along with the cover story."

"Well, that's nice. I'm not sure if I like the term 'services' for what I do. Sounds a bit too racy or illicit."

"Don't worry about it," Gus said as he arose. "I'm going to go change and I'll ring you before seven. I want to talk to you about something you said before you left P.G., but it'll wait until dinner. Now you better get that pale skin of yours out of the sun before you get it damaged."

Kitty decided that dinner would be the appropriate time to show Gus that she didn't always dress the same way. She had followed her plan to take advantage of that summer sale at the Macys in Monterey. She had not only bought herself that emerald green swimsuit but also a basic black dress and the lingerie to go with it. She hadn't worn a dress in several years, not since those days when she would show up at a premiere or awards party on Jake's arm.

Gus was at her door punctually, as always, at a few minutes after seven. He did do a bit of a double take as he surveyed her new wardrobe acquisition, but he reserved comment for later. Once seated, and the menu in hand, he turned more serious in his expression than she had ever seen before. She said, "Gus, you look a little bit bothered about something. Is everything all right?"

He replied, "I've been thinking about something you said before you left P.G. It was that line about being polite and professional but having a plan to kill everyone you meet. You followed that with something like 'deep down you trust no one.' Is that how you really feel?"

"Yes, I guess that's how I really am. That troubles you?"

"It does. Does that mean that you don't really trust me? If that is the case, what are we doing here together?"

"I guess," she said, "that I really do have what the shrinks would call trust issues. I'm really careful around people until I get to know them very, very well. Even then I'm likely to still have a little area of suspicion lurking in some part of my brain."

"So, you don't trust me completely yet?" he asked.

"I trust you more each time we are together," she responded. "I don't know everything about you, and maybe I never will. Trust takes time and familiarity over time, and that's how I feel about it. I assume that you have done things which I don't know about to learn more about me."

"Like what," he asked.

"Come on, Officer Mulbrae. I'd be very surprised if you, as a cop, didn't know some details about me before you ever knocked on my door when I got back from L.A. You would have run the plates on the Jeep, so you knew who the owner was, her name and address.

"Once I told you, out of concern for your job, that I was a felon I'd be surprised if you didn't look me up on some Department of Corrections database. By date number two you knew more about me than anyone else in P.G. Am I right?"

"Okay, I'll admit that I used my job to check you out. Is that all so bad?"

"No, it's not bad. It's just proof that a good cop is a little distrustful of strangers, and trust is something that takes time, especially for a civilian like me."

"So, can we move on and enjoy dinner," he asked.

"Of course," she said. "After dinner I suggest we pretend we're two characters in a James Bond plot and check out the action in the casino. I don't understand a single thing about card games, I think slot machines are moronic, but that roulette wheel might be worth a try. Isn't that what James Bond would try?"

"Yeah, I can see you at that table. The mysterious Kitty D'Literie, the woman in black who only bets on the black and the odd numbers. I assume you're not going for the same table as the high rollers."

"You got that right, officer. This dress-up outfit cost me more than I can really afford on a part-time librarian's salary, and I'm not going to rip off my clients by gambling with their money."

"Okay, I'll watch you play for a while, and then you can watch me lose money when I can't hit 21 at the blackjack table."

Dinner over and an hour spent in the casino and only a few dollars lighter Gus said, "I'm tapped out, so I think it's time for me to test the quality of the mattresses in this fine establishment. What time do you want to get started tomorrow?"

"I'd like to talk to the real estate guy at about ten in the morning. Then, if we have learned anything useful, we can check it out in the afternoon. Are you flying back tomorrow night or Tuesday morning?"

"I'm on a flight to Monterey on Tuesday morning at ten," he replied.

"Okay, let's do breakfast about eight and be on our separate ways by nine thirty," she responded.

137

They parted after a quick kiss at the elevator. Kitty wondered if the trust issue had taken any thought of romance out of the relationship.

"Right now," she thought, "all I hope is that we can find something, anything, that will make this more than a long trip to nothing."

True to form, she was ready to do business early in the morning. The black dress and accessories were hung up for another evening. Today it was black slacks and a dark green jacket over a white blouse for Kitty. Gus looked like a big city detective in a grey suit, with his badge and sidearm located appropriately. They were both playing this one with professional seriousness.

When they got back together at noon at the Bellagio, where Kitty wanted to see the famous fountains, there was much to share. Kitty had learned that a large warehouse in North Las Vegas had indeed been leased for a year by a car collector and paid for in advance. The tenant could not be identified by name, as the leaseholder was known only as a corporation. At last, she had an address to investigate.

Gus had a big grin that told Kitty that his morning had not been a waste of time. The Vegas police had been very cooperative. They had a file on Dred Maxim who, for business security, had applied for and been granted a "concealed carry" permit. He could carry a sidearm under his coat, just like a private investigator. The address given on the application was in North Las Vegas, the same one that Kitty had found. At city hall he discovered that permits for work on climate control, electrical wiring and security measures had been issued. Kitty almost did backflips she was so excited.

Lunch was very tasty, but Kitty could hardly eat. She wanted to get on I-15 and head for North Las Vegas and that warehouse where she could confront the man called Dred Maxim. Gus said, "Let's go in one car and I'll go with you. I'll pose as a photographer, who you've employed to document the collection for your story. That is, if we are allowed to see it. Just let me ditch the suit and dress more casually, as a photographer would." Kitty agreed, and by two in the afternoon they had found the warehouse.

Gus had insisted on driving, and they followed Las Vegas Boulevard north through the entire length of Las Vegas. She would have taken I-15 because there would be less traffic, and they could take advantage of the high-speed limit in Nevada. Gus was assertive, saying he wanted to see the whole of Las Vegas if possible.

After what seemed an eternity to Kitty, they found the warehouse at the junction of Hollywood Boulevard and Azure Way. They approached the building's office door, rang the bell for admission and heard a voice from within demand the reason for their being there. Kitty used the historical journal article as her cover story, and expressed her desire to speak directly to Dred Maxim.

The lock on the door buzzed, and they were admitted. The armed security guard checked their identification and had them both print and sign their names, including addresses. The process reminded Kitty of her trip earlier in the year to the Jewelry Center in L.A. to see. Mr. Sarkisian. Someone was treating this collection with great concern and care. The guard said, "Wait here. Mr. Maxim will join you in a few minutes."

Kitty's heart was racing in anticipation, but it almost fell into her stomach when the man entering the room and said, "How may I help you? I'm Dred Maxim." The man was clearly Black, and he bore no resemblance to Max Shepherd.

Chapter 23

Kitty tried hard to mask her surprise at encountering Dred Maxim. Clearly, her imagination had led her down a false path in her search for Max Shepherd. She now had to make the best of an awkward situation.

"Mr. Maxim," she said, "I'm very glad to have found you. I'm Katherine D'Literie and I'm here to gather some information for an article I'm writing for the Society of Automotive Historians. I'm interested in the growth of replicas and how they fit into automotive history." To herself she thought, "Goodness, what a load of rubbish I'm trying to peddle here."

"Well," said Maxim, "we do have a couple of interesting replicas here, along with a number of vintage or classic cars which we have collected. Would you like to take a look? And may I ask, how did you learn of us?"

"I first got interested in the subject back in 2014 when I saw what looked like the original Benz automobile from the late nineteenth century," Kitty replied. "Then I was interested in the story of Mrs. Benz driving the original over some sixty miles to visit relatives before the car was ever patented. Then, I learned that the factory had actually made about twenty or more replicas, including the one I saw in Carmel. My question is, why did they make them?"

"That's easy," said Maxim. "Back in 2002 Mercedes Benz decided to make about twenty replicas of their original car which was in their museum. They did it solely for display purposes. Copies were loaned to their top dealers around the world. Some ended up being sold by the dealers for huge sums to wealthy collectors."

"I began researching replica builders, which is how I found Maximum in England," Kitty said. "When I asked the company where I could see one in the United States, they told me one was being shipped to you. Then I saw a used one that was for sale in the Bay area which was sold to you. Why that car?" she asked.

"It's what I bought them for that's important," Maxim replied. "I know that some will call them fakes, like they do with some paintings. I'm relying on people who want to rent one for some purpose."

"What purpose would lead someone to rent a replica?" she asked.

"Some just want to drive something unusual for a short while. Others want to incorporate a rare car in a TV ad, or a movie, and they can't find or afford an original. That is my biggest market. A replica is good if there's a chance that the car will get damaged. That way you haven't wrecked a priceless original."

"I notice that you have an assortment of cars of all types and ages. Are they all replicas?" she asked.

"Oh, goodness no. Movies require a wide range of vehicles from many eras. The producers will try to get the owner of an older car to loan it to them, but most owners just say 'no.' They have heard horror stories of the car being damaged and needing expensive repairs. So, it's easier to find a company like mine and just rent the car and then buy special insurance to cover any damage."

"This is my photographer, Gus. Could he take a few pictures to go with my article?"

"Sure," said Maxim, "as long as The Maxim Collection gets a little P.R. out of the story."

While Gus started wandering around taking some pictures, Kitty said, "I have a couple more questions for you."

"Okay, what would you like to know?"

"First, why locate here in North Las Vegas? Why not in the L.A. area closer to the studios," Kitty asked.

"First is the cost. To rent this facility in Southern California would be prohibitive. The second reason is what's right across the road. Over there is one of the best and least used racetracks in America. Once a year, a big NASCAR event, then a few club races. I can set up a customer, whether an individual thrill-seeker or a movie company, with a ready facility to drive, take pictures, shoot an ad, you name it. That's why just over there," as he pointed toward the east, "is the factory Carroll Shelby built to produce his copies of the Fords that won at Le Mans and elsewhere in the 1960's. Customers came and got to test the car before shelling out big dollars."

"Okay," Kitty said. "Are there others in your line of business?"

"Oh yes," said Maxim. "There's another black guy like me down in Irvine, California.

His name is Lance Stander, and his company is called Shelby Legendary Cars. Shelby, when he was making cars over here, registered a bunch of chassis numbers that never got used. Stander got Shelby to sell him the rights to those numbers. Now he has a car built in South Africa, which is where he came from. It's got no engine or gearbox when it's imported. Then his other company, called Hillbank after his father's used car lot in South Africa, tells the buyer in America where they can buy a motor and gearbox, and they help him get it all together."

"So, these cars in Irvine, they're really just fancy replicas?" Kitty asked.

"Oh no, dear lady, never say that. They are 'continuation cars.' They will sell for $170,000 up to $300,000. The originals, built by Shelby here in the U.S. and sold by Ford, sell for $7 to $11 million dollars. The first car Shelby built sold for $13,750,000 at Monterey two years ago. The Walton family insured it for $100 million."

"So, is there anyone else in this business that I should talk to?" Kitty asked.

"Well, there is an outfit in Michigan. They make very good replicas, but not as exacting as the cars from South Africa. The 'continuation' cars are so detailed down to period-correct nuts and bolts that they are worth the most. Near L.A. in Sun Valley there is a company called Ghost Light. They handle Ferraris, Porsches, and all kinds of rare cars for rent to the studios. We're just a small infant in this business, but I hope we grow."

"One last question, and I'll be out of your hair, Mr. Maxim. I've been looking for a man whose family wants him found to settle an inheritance. He's a big fan of the XK120C cars that won at Le Mans in the early 1950's. I thought he might settle for a Maximum replica. Here's a picture of him over ten years ago. I wonder if he has ever contacted you about renting or buying your new Maximum?"

Maxim took the photo and examined it closely. "I haven't seen this man, but his appearance may have changed over the years. Tell you what; give me your card, and if he shows up, I'll give you a call. Would that be okay?"

Gus was signaling that he had all the photos he might want, so Kitty said, "Mr. Maxim, I wish to thank you for allowing me to see what you have here, and especially for all the information about the role of replicas in modern automotive history. You've been a great help to me, and I do hope you'll call me if Max Shepherd comes to your attention."

With handshakes all around she and Gus were out the door. As they drove back to Bally's Kitty said, "Well, that was a massive let-down, but at least I can look elsewhere for Max. I'm sorry you came all this far for such a disappointment. I guess my intuition took a beating there."

Gus responded, "Don't feel so bad. I enjoyed being a detective for a while. Maybe I'll rethink the notion of taking the exam for that promotion. So, what do you have in mind for tonight?"

"Well, I hope you'll enjoy it. I've got us seats for the show with Celine Dion at Caesars Palace. I've always wanted to see and hear her live. They seat people about seven thirty, and then we could get a late dinner at Rao, if you like Italian. Or, we could dine earlier if you need time to pack for tomorrow. Your call."

"I'd prefer an early dinner, if it's okay with you," Gus responded.

So, it was decided. Kitty got back into her black dress, Gus showed up with a very comfortable looking outfit, and they went to dinner. Kitty had a surprise to share.

"Back in my room I got a call from Rudy. He's the college boy I hired to search for Max Shepherd on various databases. He called me with the best news I've had this week. He found that a Maximillian Shepherd was given a license by the state of Arizona three years ago. It's the equivalent of the Class A license in California. What does that classification mean?" she asked.

"What it means is that a Max Shepherd can drive any truck, a commercial bus, just about anything on the highway," Gus said. "It also means that there must be a record of an address, a residence, somewhere in Arizona. It means you now have a hope of finding the missing heir."

They enjoyed dinner and the Dion show. As they strolled back to Bally's, Kitty said, "Gus, on the drive from Monterey I heard an old song on the radio. Rod Stewart was singing songs from the 'Great American Songbook.' There was one I'd like to recite for you. I can't carry a tune or sing a note, but the words might mean a lot to both of us."

"I'm all ears," Gus said.

144

Kitty said, "I can't recall every word, but the song starts like this;

"For all we know
We may never meet again
Before you go
Make this moment sweet again

We won't say goodnight
Until the last minute
I'll hold out my hand
And my heart will be in it"

"There's more that I can't recall, but the last line I really want you to hear," she said, taking both of his hands in hers and looking directly at him. "The song ends like this, and I hope you get the meaning."

"So love me tonight
Tomorrow was made for some
But tomorrow may never come
For all we know,"

"Just one more thought," she said. "There's a quote I recall from a movie. 'Carpe diem,' means 'seize the day.' I want to use another phrase, 'carpe nocturne,' meaning 'seize the night.' So, what do you think of the song's words and 'carpe nocturne'?"

"Well," he responded, "I guess we've resolved the trust issue. Give me a few minutes to pack, and I'll be happy to seize the night with you. I need a six-a.m. wakeup call, however."

"I'll await a knock on my door, "she said as they parted at the elevator. And, as the TV ad might have said, "What happened in Las Vegas stayed in Las Vegas."

Chapter 24

Kitty got a double dose of wakeup at six a.m. The front desk was calling as requested, and her alarm was buzzing. Kitty lay still for a moment, thinking how nice it was, after many years, to feel the warmth of another human being against her back. She rolled over just enough to poke Gus with an elbow and say, "It's time, big guy. Rise and shine. You've got a plane to catch and I'm going back under the covers for another hour."

Gus grunted and stumbled off to the bathroom and soon she heard the shower water running. She dozed fitfully. She, who had been taking their relationship so slowly and cautiously, had just basically said, "Take me, my love." He had, and with enthusiasm, but what, she wondered, would come next.

What came next was Gus, out of the shower and getting dressed. She feigned sleep, but she was watching the man she now, what? Loved? "Oh, my," she thought, "I hope I haven't made a total fool of myself. Last night I acted like I was still that twenty-year-old college girl, giving herself to that law school student at the Biltmore so long ago. Please, let this not be the end of what I hoped would be something good."

Her thoughts were interrupted as Gus, now fully dressed, came to her side of the bed and said, "Sweetie, I've got to go back to my room and get my suitcase, badge and gun. I love you, and I want you to be careful today on the drive to L.A. Promise me you'll call when you get settled down there, okay?"

"I will," she replied. "I loved our night together and I'll be thinking about you. Thank you for understanding my wishes when I told you those words from 'For All We Know,' last evening" she said with a smile.

"Well," he responded, "I want to tell you that last night helped me to solve a mystery I've been interested in since we met."

"Oh," she said, "and pray tell me what that might be."

"From the first day we met, when I came by to warn you about parking in the street, I wondered about your red hair color. I asked myself 'Is that natural, or did it come out of a bottle?' Now, I know. As natural as can be," he concluded with a broad smile.

"Oh, you dirty old man," she said as she started to laugh. "Now get out of here and catch your flight," as she threw a shoe at his retreating figure.

Kitty thought, "Well, I guess we're about as 'involved' as two middle-aged people can get, and he did say he loved me. It's strange having a man in my bed again. Twenty years since I last slept with Alex McEwan before we divorced. Twenty years! Am I ready to hop on that merry-go-round again? Can't worry about it now. I've got things to do in the city of the angels. I have to remember the first law of Wicca, 'And it harm none, do what thou wilt.' I haven't hurt myself, and it looked like Gus was pretty undamaged, so I feel I haven't broken the rules. Time to get dressed, pack up and hit the road."

Kitty had three objectives when she got to L.A. In no particular order of importance, they were: check with Avedis Sarkisian on the sale of the gems, talk to Napoleon Shepherd about the hunt for Max, and confer with the Pickering, Milton and Newlin firm about the hope of expunging her felon status.

She was checked out of Bally's and heading south on I-15 by ten a.m. just as she had planned. A quick pit stop at Barstow for fuel, coffee and a restroom, and by three thirty she was checking into her room at the Biltmore.

The first thing she did was to give Avedis a call. When his familiar voice came on the phone with, "This is Mr. Sarkisian. How may I help you?" Kitty said, "Avedis, this is Kitty. How's the Imperial Valley doing these days?'

"Oh, things in the valley are fine, from El Centro down to Mexicali. That product you were interested in, well, it's on its way to Caracas. If you can come by tomorrow morning I'll have some of the, what can we call it? Oh, residue, that's it. So, about nine thirty tomorrow, will that work for you?"

"Yes, I'll be there bright and early. I'm right over here at the Biltmore and I know the drill for entering the Jewelry Center. See you before ten."

Her next call was to Napoleon Shepherd. She arranged to meet with him and his sister, Josephine, at the family home in La Habra Heights. They would meet in the early afternoon on Wednesday and she could share with them the little she had learned in the last twenty-four hours about their brother, Max.

She would wait until the following morning, Wednesday, the call the lawyer. She had found the Record Gone firm on the Internet. Record Gone was a subsidiary of the Pickering, Milton and Newlin law firm, which had offices in several states. Record Gone could get you started on the road to "expungement" with an online test. She learned that direct expungement might not be an option for her because she had served time in prison. She would have less of a problem if she had been given probation, but that hadn't been the case.

Her best bet might be a "certificate of rehabilitation" under California Penal Code section 4851. There was also the possibility that a judge might, seeing that she was rehabilitated, simply reduce her conviction to a misdemeanor.

She had taken the online test from the Record Gone firm, and she seemed to be eligible for a "1203.4 dismissal." The criteria which she met included; only one

148

arrest on her record, she had completed her three-year sentence, she could show signs of rehabilitation, and her felony was non-violent. The only thing she could not answer was the value of the items she had stolen. It was a grand theft conviction, but if the "grand" part was a sum of less than $950 it could be reduced to a misdemeanor.

With all that in mind, she had paid the $50 fee to start the process. Now she needed to go face to face with an attorney at their office in Glendale and see if her felony could be reduced to a misdemeanor. If the firm decided to take her case and give her a chance at reduction of the felony, she would gladly pay the basic fee of $1350. That fee was the reason why she hoped that Avedis Sarkisian would have some good financial news for her the following morning.

After another extravagant dinner at the Water Grill and a good night's rest, she was off a little after nine to meet with Avedis at the Jewelry Center. She got past the check-in procedure at the lobby of the center and was soon in his office at number 310. After a quick handshake and the usual "How was your trip?" conversation, she got down to the business at hand.

"So," she said, "the emeralds went well once you got them to Mexicali?"

"They did indeed," Avedis answered. "My contact there was impressed and called his contact in Mexico City. Things progressed quickly from there, and as I had guessed there was a ready market for loose gems in Venezuela.

The regime there is in trouble and officials want to have the easily portable wealth of precious stones if they have to flee. They might have their assets in banks seized or frozen, so stones make escape easier."

"How about the opals, mounted in the bracelet?" she asked.

"That is now in the jewelry box of some lovely lady in Vera Cruz. It seems she is the wife of some bureaucrat in Pemex, the national oil company. The little rubies also found a jeweler who will use them in some future creation."

"What did it all come to in U.S. dollars?" she asked.

"You'll remember I quoted you a figure of about $7,000 or more, and I was close. I'm keeping 20% as my fee, so I have a check here for you with the nice round sum of $6,000."

"Fantastic," Kitty exclaimed. "That will pay, I hope, all the legal and court fees I'll be looking at in the coming months. I might actually be able to keep some of this in the bank, plus I might have some other expenses if all the legal stuff works out. I like doing this missing person tracing, and it would be a little easier if I were allowed to be a licensed detective or investigator."

"Well, young lady," Avedis said, "I have a check here for you and I wish you all the best success with your legal problems. I have a strong feeling that this may be the last time I'll ever see you, but it has been a pleasure doing a bit of business with you." With that, they both rose, Avedis gave her a hug, and she was on her way to the nearest branch of the Bank of America on Sixth Street.

With the check safely deposited in her account, she reclaimed her rental Mustang and headed east toward La Habra Heights and her meeting with the Shepherds. Napoleon greeted her at the door of the home on Camino Lane with the great view. Josephine asked, "Have you anything new to tell us about Maximillian?"

"I have," Kitty replied. "The assumption that I made about his living in Las Vegas with a collection of cars proved false. While there I learned from my employee, who has been searching for Max electronically, that he or someone with exactly the same name was given a license to drive trucks by the state of Arizona. I now know that he was alive and able to drive a large vehicle three years ago."

"Where was he living in Arizona?" Napoleon asked.

"That I don't know yet, but we'll continue to search the data bases. We do know that he has not died in any state in the U.S.A., and if we get an old address from Arizona the police may be able to find his employment or banking records. I do have a member of the police force in Pacific Grove who helped me eliminate the false lead that I had."

"Why did you think he was in Las Vegas?" Josephine asked.

"I thought a man who has a car collection there, and whose name might have been an anagram of Max Shepherd, could be Max living under an assumed name to avoid detection. However, the collector, once we found him, proved to be an Black man. So that trail was a dead-end, unless the collector encounters Max at a car show or auction."

"So, what will you try next?" Napoleon asked.

"Next we keep picking at that little thread we found in Arizona. Your brother wouldn't have gotten a truck-driving license unless he intended to work as one or start a trucking business. Also, he had to get training. Nothing in his past prepared him to drive a semi-truck and trailer rig. So, where did he learn? How did he pay for the training? What does his picture look like on the license? We now have one clue and we'll keep pursuing that even if government agencies are reluctant to share information, even with another agency."

Napoleon said, "It sounds a bit encouraging but frustrating. It shows how possible it is for someone to disappear if they want to."

"Yes," Kitty replied, "someone can 'get off the grid' as they say, but not if they want to live somewhere that's not a forest or jungle. Oh, he'll surface somewhere, but it may not be in your desired time span. My hope is that he surfaces in Monterey in August. That's when all the car lovers come out to see what's for sale or display. I'm hoping Max cannot resist the temptation."

"Well," Napoleon said, "I'm glad you came by to brief us, and I wish you luck as your research goes on."

"I'll stay in touch," Kitty promised as she went out the door and headed back to her car and the drive to Los Angeles.

Chapter 25

As soon as Kitty was back in her room at the Biltmore on Wednesday evening, she dialed Gus. He answered, as usual, "This is Officer Mulbrae."

Kitty said, "Hey, Gus, it's Kitty. Just letting you know I'm in L.A., and all went well. The Shepherds aren't thrilled with the lack of progress, but they seem to realize that brother Max is one very elusive character."

"So, what's next for you?" Gus asked.

"Next, I'll call the law firm and confirm my appointment for tomorrow morning, the twelfth. An attorney named Rhyman has been assigned to my case. If all goes well, I'll be on my way back to P.G. by a little after noon and be home by maybe six."

"Okay, good luck with that and we'll talk when you're home again. Have a good drive and be safe my love."

"I'll be okay. Talk to you day after tomorrow."

Now she thought, "It's time for an early dinner. This evening I'm going to try to avoid splurging, so the Water Grill is out. This place called Checkers Downtown got good ratings, so I'll test it." Checkers is the restaurant in the Hilton Hotel on Grand Avenue, so it was only a short walk before she was looking at the menu. She knew that the 14-ounce rib eye steak for $36 was too much, both in price and size. The seared salmon was considered, but the Angelino Quesadilla was her choice. Chicken, two kinds of cheese plus avocado, sounded affordable and not too hard on the calorie count. Since it was pseudo-Mexican cuisine, a beer would be the appropriate beverage.

While she waited for her dinner she thought, "This is funny. Just hours ago, I banked six grand, and here I sit trying to save money on my dinner. I've got to check with Google maps when I'm back in my room and plan a route to Brand Boulevard in Glendale. I just hope these people at Record Gone are as good as they claim in their advertising."

Back in her room she organized her clothes for Thursday morning. She wanted to project an image of total rehabilitation. The gray jacket with flecks of black in the fabric, black slacks, and a very subdued shade of lipstick should project the right picture. If she was about to put a couple of grand into this process, she wanted the start to be very positive. A quick check with maps on Google, and she was set for the morning.

She decided to grab a quick breakfast at the Biltmore before setting off at 9:15 in the morning. Traffic, as usual, was terrible as she made her way back to I-5 and then north to the 134. The Brand Boulevard off-ramp came up quickly, and the Pickering, Milton and Newlin offices were just a couple of blocks south of the freeway. One last check on her appearance in the mirror and then into the office to start, she hoped, one of the major events of her year.

The receptionist contacted Mr. Rhyman, who greeted her and got her seated in a comfortable chair. His office appeared to be well organized, which reassured her. He started the interview with the usual opening monologue; "Did you have any difficulty finding us?" "Where did you park?" and "We'll validate your parking." Then came, "How did you learn of us?"

"I searched the internet," she replied, "and I found that there are many firms that seem to be in the line of legal help that I need. Yours seemed to have a larger range of services and many offices in the western U.S., so here I am."

"Okay, and what services do you want?" he asked.

"I'm tired of living under the cloud of my felony conviction. If possible, I'd like to get it expunged. If not, then I'd like a certificate of rehabilitation, and maybe that could lead to a pardon. What do you think you can do for me?"

"Okay, let's talk about expungement. Did you take our online test?"

"I did, and I think I qualify, but I don't know about the dollar value of the items stolen. That value, if it's over $950, might be what disqualifies me."

Rhyman responded, "That's one of the things we can do first by checking court records and the original arrest report with LAPD. Now, let me ask you some questions about your case. When was the offense, the crime, committed?"

"December 21, 1988," she replied.

"And when were you convicted?"

"January 20, 1989," she replied.

"Well, that went pretty quickly. Was there a trial?"

"No," she answered, "I had no money, no property, no living relatives. Bail was out of the question. I just told the public defender assigned to me to get me the best deal, the shortest time in prison, and I'd take a plea deal. The district attorney's office was eager to process me, so at my plea hearing before a judge I just said 'guilty' and got the three-year minimum sentence."

"So, what were the charges?" Rhyman asked.

"One count of burglary, one count of theft."

"And the sentence received was what?"

"A three-year minimum, with parole for the balance of the five-year maximum," she replied.

"Now the judge, if we were in his courtroom, would ask about your compliance with court obligations. Did you have any fines or restitution to pay?"

"No, the stolen jewelry, three gold chains or necklaces and a gold bracelet or bangle, were all recovered as I left the scene of the crime, and I guess they went back to the owner as soon as my case was settled. My problem is, I have no idea what they were worth, and I know the law says the cut-off for expungement is $950."

"Well, as I said, it will be our job to go into the records and see what, if any, dollar value was set on the jewelry. Were there any other obligations imposed?"

"None, other than serve my parole for two years. My Parole Officer got me a job in Monterey County when I got out. I wanted to be as far away from L.A. as I could at that time. Then I got married, then divorced, then my P.O. got me a job down near Palm Springs. That's when I got a real break," she said.

"So, any other convictions or arrests since 1989?" he asked.

"No, I learned my lesson, and I learned in prison a skill that I now use as a part-time librarian," she answered.

"So, what did you learn in prison?" he asked.

"Well, besides how to run a small library, which is what I did behind bars, I learned about what you might call 'prison etiquette,' the rules for survival."

"Tell me about them."

"Well, because my crime did not involve violence, no one was hurt, no sex or drugs were involved, I was in a slightly more relaxed internment. There were rules, sure, but there are behaviors the other inmates impose."

"The first one is not to listen to other people's conversations. The really big one is to be very careful about personal space. If you've got a cellmate, and you will, be very careful not to be intrusive."

"How about relations with the guards," he asked.

"Some of them hate being called guards. They are 'corrections officers,' and you want to avoid trying to be seen as friendly with them, because the other inmates will think you are an informer. The one thing that is hardest to get used to is the lack of privacy, even when you use the toilet. That would be followed in order by the lack of connection with people on the outside. But hey, that's why they call it prison," she said.

"How did you keep your sanity?" he asked.

"I became something of a fitness freak, working out in the gym. I still do, at my little gym in my garage. I really learned a lot about how a library works, I read everything I could, and I found religion."

"What do you mean by that?" he asked.

"Well, I found a few women who were into the Wiccan religion, you know, witches. I got involved and pursued that area before and after I got out. So, I guess I'm like the semi-official witch of Pacific Grove."

"Okay, I've got a couple more questions about the Certificate of Rehabilitation, the alternative to expungement if you don't qualify for that. Have you lived in California for five years?"

"Yes, I've never lived anywhere else. Born in L.A. about fifty years ago, never left California."

"Okay. After parole, tell me about rehabilitation."

"I got a great job with a man who was loosely tied to the movie industry. I was his researcher, the major-domo for his home and office, and his companion for social events. He died about ten years ago, a suicide. He left me one quarter of his estate, plus two old cars. That gave me enough that when I moved to Pacific Grove I could buy my small condo without getting a loan, which is almost impossible for a felon. I got work part time in the library, plus some work as a hostess at a restaurant, as I had done before. Now I'm helping a family look for a missing relative. I want to get the felony off my record so I can do the things that normal people do."

"Like what?" he asked.

"Well, I like the idea of finding missing persons. I could do that better if I was a licensed private investigator, which felons can't be. I'd like to travel, but I'm denied a passport. I can't vote. Certain jobs are closed to me. For example, I'd like to be an investigator or researcher for a law firm, but I can't as a felon. I'm like that girl in the novel, Hester Prynne, who has the scarlet letter 'A' sewed on her dress. All of that because, at age 21, I broke into a house and stole gold jewelry. I was stupid. I'm not that young girl anymore. I'm a middle-aged woman who dates a cop, if you can believe that."

"Okay, Ms. D'Literie, I've got a pretty good idea of what we should try to do. We are probably going to have to appear, together, in front of a judge in this county. Can you get here on short notice if it comes to that, and it probably will?"

"You call, and as much as I hate flying, I'll be at Burbank airport within 24 hours. I thank you for giving me some hope."

"Thank you for giving Record Gone a shot at helping you. We'll stay in touch during this month, and you'll be invoiced for fees. The receptionist will validate your parking, and I hope you have a safe trip home."

"Thank you and goodbye," Kitty said. The sun felt good as she emerged from the office building, and she headed for the interstate and home.

Chapter 26

The sun was still shining when Kitty got back into Pacific Grove on Thursday evening. While the drive from Los Angeles in the rented Mustang was more comfortable, she missed the sense of adventure and nostalgia she got from driving the old Jaguar.

She found that the cat, Pyewacket, had done an excellent job of maintaining home security, even waking up to watch her unpack. She took the Mustang for a last drive down to the Red House Café for a light supper. Upon returning home she offered a prayer of thanks at her altar and then slipped under the covers for a good night's sleep.

She slept late on Friday, the thirteenth day of the month. Her reluctance to get up had nothing to do with the superstitions attached to that day and date. No, to a Wicca, 13 is a lucky number, not an evil one. There are 13 full moons in a Wiccan year, and the religion has 13 basic beliefs, what some religions would call commandments. No, she was thinking about belief number four. It deals with the relationship of men and women, and makes sexual relations and related pleasure a natural result of that relationship. So, in addition to planning her day, she was also thinking about Gus.

Then she had a moment of enlightenment. If today is July 13, then tomorrow is July 14. That means it will be Bastille Day, the French national holiday. It also marks the beginning of events, which, in time, brought her ancestors to America.

So, she began to plan her day. First, she had to find out if the work on the Jaguar was finished. Second, she had to get an appointment with Karen at Prim to get her hair trimmed and styled. Then she would call Gus to see if he had to work on Saturday. If he were free in the evening, she would get a reservation at Fandango, the restaurant most similar to a French restaurant in P.G.

If he were working the night shift on Saturday, she would propose a midday picnic. After all, that's what people in France would be doing, having a picnic in a park. Then, maybe, she would have a chance to introduce Gus to her religion, with an emphasis on belief number four; sex equals pleasure.

Thus inspired, she got out of bed and hit the shower. While having a week-old bagel for breakfast she added "groceries" to her to do list. As expected, Mrs. Sanchez was at her door at nine, and was paid for her care of Pyewacket.

A call to Prim got an eleven o'clock appointment for her hair trim, and the mechanic at Matteson's told her that the Jaguar would be ready on Saturday morning. She decided to hold off on calling Gus until around eleven, after she got her hair done, then go by the Grove Market and get her food re-supply situation dealt with. The market shared the parking lot with Fandango, so if dinner with Gus on Saturday night was possible, she could pop in at the restaurant and make a reservation.

At eleven she was at Prim, ready to have her red hair shortened a bit. Karen, of course, would want to know all about her activities since her last visit. "What have you been up to recently?" was the opening question. Kitty had decided that her relationship with Gus should remain private, so her answer was carefully worded.

"Oh, I've been to Las Vegas and Los Angeles. That was to check out a theory that I had about the missing family member I'm trying to locate, and to confer with a lawyer," she responded.

"Anything exciting happen in Vegas?" Karen asked.

"Well, I did take in a Celine Dion show, and I lost a few dollars trying out the roulette wheel. The big deal for me was finding this car collector who I thought might be

160

the missing heir. That turned out to be a big balloon buster," Kitty explained.

"So, did you do all this on your own?" Karen asked.

"Well, sort of. I got clues from the Vegas police and a couple of museum employees. It was all a bit of a disappointment for the family down in La Habra Heights, but a clue did surface about the missing man and his driver's license in Arizona."

"So, what happened in L.A.?" Karen inquired.

"Oh, I settled some business affairs that were in need of being put behind me. I met with a lawyer who is going to try to get my felony record wiped out. That would really be a big deal if it can be done."

"I'll bet that will cost you some big bucks."

"It's not all that expensive when you think of what getting the record cleaned up will do for me. For example, did you know that I can't get a license to do what you do?"

"You mean, even if you went to cosmetology school, you can't be a hairdresser?"

"That's right, not in California. So, getting the record cleaned up, proving that I'm rehabilitated, is a very big deal. A lot of doors that are now closed to me would open. That's why it's worth the money."

"So, I didn't see your old Jaguar out front. Is that a new Mustang you're driving?"

"I had to have some work done on the Jaguar, so I thought a rental car from Enterprise was needed for my trip. The old car will be ready tomorrow. I can hardly wait to see the bill," Kitty said sarcastically.

"Yes, but it's a lovely car. Do you enter it in any of the shows during 'car week'?"

"You know, I haven't done that, but I think I will this year. That big show that they have on Friday of that week, the one where they block off six blocks of Lighthouse and get over two hundred cars. After the show, about five p.m., they caravan with police escort all around town and end up with a big spaghetti dinner. I think I'll do that this year." Kitty said.

"Hey, good for you," Karen said. "Do you have any plans for this weekend?"

"Maybe," Kitty said. "After I get to the market I'm going to see if I can get a reservation at Fandango."

"Well, that would be nice if you had someone to share it with," Karen replied.

"You never know, something might turn up, especially now that you've got me looking a bit better. I'll see you in a few weeks," Kitty said as she exited the shop.

Before driving to the market Kitty made the call to Gus. When he answered, the first question was, "How did things go with the lawyer?"

"Gus, I'll fill you in tomorrow if you're free. Do you have duty on the night shift tomorrow?"

"I'm free until midnight, then I'm on duty until eight a.m. What have you planned?"

"It's Bastille Day, which means nothing to you, but it's a French holiday. I'd like to do dinner at Fandango if I can get a reservation. Are you up for that?"

"Sure, if you can set it up. Just don't make it too late because I've got to get ready for work, which means changing into uniform."

"Okay. I've got to get groceries now or starve to death with my cat. I'll call you later this afternoon and let you know what's on for tomorrow night. Bye for now lover."

Kitty's next stop was the Grove Market, but once parked she decided to go across the shared parking lot and go into Fandango and get a reservation. Marietta, who, with her husband, Pierre, was one of the owners, greeted her. Kitty knew that Gus would need time to get

162

to his duty station. She asked for and reserved a table for two at 7:30 on Saturday night. With the restaurant closing at nine she figured that they could have an enjoyable meal and not worry about work.

Last stop on the trip was the Grove Market. She particularly liked their deli section, where she knew that if needed she could order an entire picnic basket. Then it was back in the Mustang and a quick trip to home. She went to her garage gym, put in a thirty-minute workout before another shower and shampoo to get the loose hair clippings off her back. Now it was time to relax and think about tomorrow, when she would reunite with Gus the cop and Malcolm the Jaguar.

Chapter 27

Saturday, July 14, dawned beautifully in Pacific
Grove. Kitty was up before the sun because she knew
that in her Wiccan faith Saturday is a day to build
strength. She first went for a long run. Down Lighthouse
to Point Pinos, past the golf course. A turn to the right
and then the long stretch down Ocean View to the turn-
around at Lovers Point. She noted that the Tinnery
Restaurant, once one of her favorites, was still closed for
renovation.

Then it was up 17th Street to Pacific, and back to
Lighthouse. Thankfully, she completed the circuit before
traffic filled the streets and the hazards of running
became too great.

Then at the appointed hour of eight, it was time to
light a black candle on her altar and offer a prayer to the
goddess for success in her legal affairs. While she
enjoyed breakfast, and the cat made a very brief visit
outdoors to check on the neighbors, she began to figure
out what she had to do before her dinner date at 7:30.

First on the list was to reclaim Malcolm, her faithful
Jaguar. That would also involve a call to Enterprise to
return the rental Mustang. Then she could begin to plan
for "car week." The main events at first, in the 1970's,
included only a vintage car race at Laguna Seca on
Saturday, and the Pebble Beach Concours de Elegance
on Sunday. Now, over 40 years later, there would be a
full ten days of car-related activities. Any one of these
events might prove to be a chance to find Maximillian
Shepherd.

Some of the events she could cross off her list
quickly. Unless a Jaguar XK120C was entered in the
races at Laguna Seca she could check that one off the
list. She could also pay very little attention to the two
shows that would occupy the streets of Pacific Grove.

Max would disdain such events; the cars were too small and too common, even if some were over sixty years old and had cost their owners a small fortune to buy and restore.

The Mecom auction, held over three nights in a big tent at Fishermen's Wharf, very probably would be on his "no interest" list. Cars there were usually "muscle cars," which meant large, loud, and American. No, not Max's cup of tea.

Shows where he might have some interest included the one for Italian sports cars, where Ferraris and their gold-chain-wearing owners were to be seen. That might catch his eye if he were interested as a collector.

Chances are that the events to show German cars, especially Porsche and BMW, were probably of less interest to Max. At least that was her guess, and she realized that a lot of this was purely "feminine intuition" with an added dose of research on what and who usually showed up for these events.

That left three major auctions for her to think about. The one that was the longest running at Monterey had evolved into a purely electronic media event. Oh sure, people could come and look at the cars, for a price. Bidding, however, had moved from the hurly-burly of earlier days when it was a live "show" in the big hotel ballroom to a more "civilized" form. All the bidding would be conducted electronically. The bidders didn't even have to put in an appearance. Ah, the sterility of the world of technology, where one didn't have to rub elbows with some crass movie producer eager to impress his latest starlet discovery. If that attracted Max, and it might, she would never be able to tell where he was.

The auction conducted near the site of the Pebble Beach Concours might very well attract Max. The event, held late on Sunday, would not interfere with people wishing to attend the auction at another hotel in

Monterey that attracted the sportier or racier entrants, both as buyers or sellers.

So, the question, or dilemma, was how could she cover all these events where Max might appear? She knew that the police, including Gus, would be too busy trying to maintain some semblance of order as a half million people descended on Monterey.

There was one show that Kitty felt sure would be attractive to Max if, and that was a big if, he had any kind of criminal intent. That was the very exclusive show held late in the week at the golf course at the Quail Lodge on the Carmel Valley road. It was neither easy nor inexpensive to gain entrance, and the location was so remote from most of the other action that it would be hard to provide law enforcement. That responsibility would fall to the sheriff of Monterey County within whose jurisdiction the golf course was located.

Kitty knew very well that old saying about being unable "to be in two places at the same time." It became obvious that there were two probable scenarios. One, Max would show up just to observe, or maybe buy a collectible car. Or, two, he would be there to steal the car of his dreams if it should show up to compete or to be sold. Either scenario meant that she needed more pairs of eyes.

She knew that she would have to ask young Mr. Bermudes, her "researcher," if he had a half-dozen college friends who would like to attend car shows and auctions and be her "recon patrol," a military term she had learned so long ago from Jake. "And there," she thought, "goes another chunk of money."

She also knew that she would be asking Gus for the names of deputy sheriffs and CHP officers who might be involved in preventing the theft of an extremely expensive collectible car if her suspicions were correct.

166

To her mind it would be better to be prepared to prevent the theft than to try to recover the car after the theft.

Kitty thought, "Enough of this speculating. I've got to hire guys to look for Max at several events. Tonight, I'll ask Gus to tell me with whom to work at the Sheriff's office. With luck, Max will show up at an auction, I'll bring this 'hide and seek' game to an end and tell the Shepherds where to reach dear Max. Now, I've got a dinner date to get ready for."

Kitty's thoughts were interrupted by a phone call. The mechanic, Ernie, was all ready to return her Jaguar to her, and he wanted it done so he could close shop and get to lunch. He had already alerted the Enterprise shop so the return of the Mustang would go smoothly and quickly. Kitty, checkbook in hand, got there before noon, and was happy to see Malcolm again. The amount of the check was another dent in the checking account.

Kitty and Gus met in front of Fandango that evening at 7:25. Gus had left his car at the police station, which was only two blocks away. Pierre had them seated quickly, and as they looked over the menu Gus asked, "Bring me up to date on your legal situation."

"Right now," she responded, "I have a lawyer retained. He's going to get all of my records ready to present to a judge. The big issue is how much was what I stole worth in the 1980's."

"Why does that matter?" he asked.

"It matters if I want the felony record expunged. There's a dollar limit on how bad a girl I was. If that fails, we try for a certificate of rehabilitation and hope for a pardon. That's going to take longer and is a less certain option. Now, enough talk. I had no lunch, and I'm starving."

So, they ordered, starting with an order of calamari to share. Gus went for the Caesar salad and the twelve-ounce N.Y. steak. Kitty chose the filet mignon with scampi and a hearts of palm salad. Gus elected to pass on anything alcoholic since he would be on duty in a few hours, but Kitty went for a glass of Pinot Noir.

While they waited for their meal Kitty brought up the thing that was troubling her. She asked Gus, "I've got to be prepared to find 'Max the Missing' next month if he shows up to look at cars, and why wouldn't he? I hope he just shows up, looks at cars, and maybe bids on one or two, but what if he has come with crime in mind? How do I work with all these police departments?

"If you have any reason to think that he'll steal a car, then you need to work with the sheriff's office. I can give you the name of their detective who works on auto theft."

"Gus, again I'm doing all this on intuition or instinct. I think the strangest thing is the fact that Max has a valid Arizona license to drive a truck. Why does a man who was a professional journalist, and then an accountant, get that kind of license? It makes no sense, unless he plans to do something involving trucks. 'Car week' sure gets a lot of big trucks involved, hauling cars to shows, races and auctions."

"Well, I've got to tell you, kiddo, that you've got a pretty sketchy scenario there. Just because a middle-aged man makes a big career change, that doesn't make him a thief."

"I know, Gus, it's all very far-fetched." Putting both hands to her face she said, "I just wish this whole case was over. I'm in over my head, I know it, but I can't just let it go without some result." A couple of tears of frustration ran down her cheeks.

"Okay," Gus said, "let's get some dessert and let the whole Max business rest for a while. What do you think would be good?"

"You're right, I'm just stressing myself out because the big event is about a month away. Let's get some

Crème Brule and coffee and come back to 'Max the Mysterious' later."

Chapter 28

Desserts were served, and Gus said, "Okay, Miss Franco-American, you told me this date, July 14, had some connection to your ancestors being in America. So, what's the story?"

Kitty put down her cup of tea and asked Gus, "What do you think the ancestors of a man named Farmer might have done for a living six hundred years ago in England?"

"I'd guess that they were farmers. Do I get a prize?"

"No, you don't," she responded. "A man named Cooper probably had an ancestor who made barrels, and a man named Gardener...well, you figure it out. So, take a look at my family name, D'Literie. Now we translate from the French. De means 'of' and Literie means 'bedding.' So, the family name means they had something to do with bedding."

"Okay, so your ancestors were the mattress kings of France?"

"No, according to family history, legend or myth, we were very big in the linen business. I mean the fabric, which was used in clothing, sheets, curtains, and things like that. It's made from flax, a plant that grows in colder climates."

"So how does that get you tied to the French revolution and the U.S.?"

"My ancestors, somehow, around the time of Louis XIV, must have made some really good sheets that the king liked. Louis liked luxury, and he liked to control things. His economy was very closely controlled, so that taxes were easy to collect. When he built the new palace at Versailles, he made my long-ago, many greats grandfather the exclusive supplier of bedding for the palace."

"So, your family was doing pretty well then," Gus said.

"I guess they were, until people turned on Louis XVI in the 1780s. The D'Literie business looked like an enemy of the people. Some family members were executed and some fled to the United Kingdom, especially Northern Ireland where there was a linen industry."

"So how does all that get you to America?"

"Have you ever heard of DuPont?" Kitty asked.

"Well, sure, they're a big company in chemicals and such."

"And," Kitty said, "they were really good friends with Thomas Jefferson. He knew them from before the French revolution when he was ambassador to France."

"So how does this relate to your ancestors?"

"Alexander Hamilton wanted to encourage industry. The DuPonts were big in the gunpowder industry in France. They wanted to open up a branch in America, Jefferson recommended them, Hamilton got them land in Delaware, and 'voila,' another industry was created."

"Let me guess. Jefferson had slept on sheets that your ancestors made, and Hamilton got them a deal like the DuPonts."

"*Exactement, mon cher*. Jefferson thought that growing flax would be a good farm crop, and Hamilton liked the idea of an American linen industry. So, my ancestors came, and members of my family were in the textile business in some way until I came along."

"Was your father in that business?"

"Yes. He was on a business trip selling textiles when he died in a plane crash. And while I like a linen jacket for warm days, I hate the way it gets wrinkled so easily. So, like most Americans I prefer cotton."

"So, the revolution made it a good idea for your ancestors to come to America, and that's why July 14 is a big deal for you, right?"

"Now you've got it, and you know more about my background than you ever wanted."

"And your mother, was she also French ?"

"No, her ancestry was Irish. They came over to North America, actually to Canada, during the famine of the 1840's. Then her great, great grandfather moved south to Michigan and the next generation moved to Ohio, and as a young woman my Mom moved to California where she met my Dad."

Now it was almost nine o'clock, and the staff was looking to close Fandango so Kitty said, "We should be on our way so these people can clean up and go home. I still have something related to my search that I want to run by you. Let's get in my car and go back to my place. I'll get you back to the station by eleven, I promise."

"Okay, that sounds like a plan. I'd like to hear what you've dreamed up this time."

They left Fandango and in five minutes they were back in Kitty's living room. Kitty wanted to explain how she might get more information on Max Shepherd.

"Gus, how would an employer find out if a prospective employee was bondable?"

"Well, they would have to do a background check on the prospective employee."

"I've been looking at the two major companies that transport cars to shows and auctions. Both Dependable and Trusted say they want a driver with three years experience driving big trucks, plus a clean driving record. Now if Max wanted to get a job working for such a company, how would they know if he had a clean record?"

"That's easy," Gus replied. "They would need to contact the DMV in the state, such as Arizona, to see if there was a record of accidents or moving violations. To check criminal records, which their bonding company would expect, they would have to go to the police and ask them to go through records about arrests and convictions. That's what your lawyer in L.A. is going to do about you as you try to get your felony wiped off the record."

"Okay," Kitty said, "if you wanted to find out if a guy had been hired, for example, by a rival firm and what his job reviews were like, what would you do?"

"Well, I'd pose as a potential employer, call up the firm, and ask about his references. If they said that he had never worked there, then you could cross that firm off the list. I think I see what you're working up to."

"This is what I'll do," Kitty said. "I'll pose as a human resource person for a brand-new trucking company. I'll call it Wilshire Trucking. I'll call up Dependable, for example, and ask if Max Shepherd had ever worked there, and if he had, what was his level of experience. If they say he's working there right now, then it's likely he'll be in Monterey sometime in mid-August, and not just to look at cars. If they never heard of him, then I try Trusted, and so on."

"That might work," Gus said, "but your one major problem is that you don't have his Social Security number. If you had that you could make a more realistic pitch to the HR person at the firm you're calling."

"I know, that's why I've been behind in this game all along. I'll give them a number, one which I'll make up, but only if they insist on my identifying my supposed employee by that number. I'd think that the Arizona driver license number would be enough."

"If I give them a fake Social Security number, maybe they'll think I've got some illegal immigrant posing as Max and using a stolen ID."

"You do come up with the wildest schemes, don't you," Gus said. "Now, it's about time for you to take me to work."

As they rose, Gus put his arms around her and gave her a very passionate kiss. She felt his left hand trying to make its way down inside her jeans. She pulled back and with feigned outrage said, "Officer, I know you want to practice your skills at searching a suspect for a concealed weapon, but I don't think your technique is the approved method. Your approach could get you a sexual harassment charge at the very least."

"Hey," he replied, "I read that all witches carry a knife, so I was checking out that story."

"Well, we do, but you wouldn't find it where you were planning to search."

"So why do you have one?" he asked.

"We always keep one handy to carve the letters of our magical script on our talisman. We use a special alphabet, like a code, when communicating or writing out a spell. There are five different Wiccan alphabets, and I prefer the Runic one. The ancient people of northern Europe used it. You carve the letters in a candle before you light it, so a small knife is very handy."

"Well, I can see you've got a lot of secrets that I'll probably never know, so let's get on our way."

Kitty dropped him off at the front of the police station just a few minutes before eleven with a final kiss and a promise. "I'll inscribe your name on a candle tonight with a wish that you're safe all night. Then the god of summer will be watching over you. Get a good sleep tomorrow, and I'll call you on Monday." With that, she slid the Jaguar into first gear and sped off into the night.

Chapter 29

Kitty spent time on Sunday, July 15, thinking about the five weeks that lay ahead. The Pebble Beach Concours had been moved back one week to August 26 because of an amateur golf tournament. That was a lucky break for her because the ten days from August 16 to 26 would be a madhouse of automotive activity. If Max Shepherd were to put in an appearance, this timespan would be her best chance to make contact with him.

Her first concern, as she had mentioned to Gus, was that she was only one pair of eyes searching for an elusive character in a huge mass of people. She knew that she would need to employ up to a dozen young men and women to attend the multitude of events and look for Max. On Monday she would have to contact her lone employee, Rudy Bermudes, to be a recruiter. All she could really afford to offer would be tickets to selected events and hope that her "recruits" could spend time looking at faces as well as exotic automotive coachwork.

Her second and greater concern was that of cost. When she had been working as a parolee at Tarpy's Roadhouse in the early 1990s, one could go and see the cars at Pebble Beach for about $100. She had heard people who claimed that they got in for free back in the 1950s. By 1998 things had changed radically. People who were showing their cars complained about the crowds, which were so large that cars often were damaged by the bumping of people trying to see the cars.

The solution was to raise the price of admission. From $25, it jumped abruptly to $100. The crowds remained far too large. Raise the admission to $200; the crowds thinned but not enough. In 1998, admission went to $375 if the ticket was purchased in advance, or $500 if you just showed up on Sunday. That worked, and another wrinkle was added: The Tour of Elegance.

The competition to win Best in Show, or even Best In Class, is fearsome at Pebble Beach. Why not, if winning means that when your car appears in an auction, the bidding will probably start at one million dollars.

The organizers of the concours came up with an idea that pleased most of the competitors and also thousands of spectators who could not afford the price of Sunday admission. Why not have the cars drive around the area, let the "unwashed masses" have a free look, and give any entrant who participated bonus points on their score when judged on Sunday morning at the eighteenth hole on the Pebble Beach course. And it worked. Roughly 75% to 90% of the entrants would leave the golf course on Thursday morning, drive in a column around various parts of Monterey, go down to Big Sur and end up on Ocean Avenue in Carmel. They would all stop, filling the street completely in both directions for blocks, get out and have a catered lunch in the park. They then had two days to spruce up their car for the show on Sunday morning. Thousands lined the roads to see the passing parade, ticket sales didn't suffer, and the concours now had "the right crowd and no crowding."

More difficult for Kitty to surveil would be the event at Quail Lodge. The show there had its origins in the crowding at Pebble Beach. Starting in 2002 the hotel decided to offer an alternative show with an emphasis on "performance" cars, cars that had, or still might be, raced. They also would have a strict limit on the number of cars, admitting no more than 200. They would also limit the number of spectators to 3,000 people who would only be admitted if they had a ticket, paid for in advance and selected by a lottery. Ticket prices would be $950 to $2,500, with the higher priced tickets reserved for "patrons." The show would be on Saturday, meaning that the car owner could show his car there on Saturday and still be in the show at Pebble Beach on Sunday morning.

In addition to looking at exotic cars, for your $950 you got to partake of an excellent culinary event, with lots of champagne to go with the food. Automotive manufacturers were also encouraged to bring their latest design prototypes to be displayed, and gauge the reactions of automotive experts in attendance. And those $2500 "patrons" would get to drive one of those prototypes on the local roads.

All very exclusive at "The Quail," and Kitty could see no way that she would not be excluded. Her only hope there would be that a catering firm might need an extra employee for the "culinary event." The hope that might happen seemed very slim. Yet this event was the one place she reasoned where a thief might have more luck. The site was more remote than any other that week, and the very rarity of the cars made it more attractive to a thief with a desire for the best and rarest of automotive jewels. "Damn it," she thought, "If I weren't a felon, I might get work as a security person working for the hotel."

The one thing that Kitty could research before the event was the list of entrants at both "The Quail" and at "Pebble." If Max were going to become a thief she knew what he was most interested in acquiring. If there were no C-Type Jaguars entered at either show, then he most likely would only be there as a spectator. If she could find out whether or not he had won a ticket in the lottery at the Quail, she could decide whether or not to concern herself with that event.

Kitty then got on her computer to do a bit of research. If she was to find out if a C-Type was entered at either event, she needed to determine who could give her that bit of information. Pebble Beach was easy. She found the announcement for the event online, posted back in

December. It informed her that anyone interested in entering their car needed to complete an application, with photos, and get it to Sarah Brady by January 2. Very good! Sarah Brady would get a phone call on Monday.

Quail Lodge was a bit trickier. Their online posting, which stressed the point that "This is not Pebble Beach" and the exclusivity of the whole event, told her that, like Pebble Beach, women were in charge. She would start with a call to Mary Mendoza, who managed events at the Quail Lodge. If she were not helpful, then there would be a call to her presumed boss, Courtney Ferrante, the director of "signature events" at the Lodge. One or the other could presumably tell her if a C-Type Jaguar would be in the show. Finding out if a Max Shepherd had won a ticket admitting him to "The Quail" might be a whole lot more difficult.

She also, on what she felt would be a long shot, decided to call someone to see if such a car had been entered in the Rolex-sponsored Motorsports Reunion at Laguna Seca. The event had begun in 1974. A man with money and a taste for Ferraris, rented the track on the Saturday before Pebble Beach and invited some racing buddies to join him in staging an event. Two years later, he saw that this could become a business and started a company to organize the event. By 2009, he was staging races for hundreds of car owners at Monterey in August, and at Sonoma in the spring. He decided to keep the Sonoma event and turned over what had become known as the Monterey Historics to a new business organization, The Historic Motorsports Association (HMSA).

Thus, the Monterey Historics became the Motorsports Reunion. Given the type of people who competed there, HMSA felt the need for a sponsor, and

178

Rolex looked like a logical choice for competitors with a high level of income.

The Reunion, like Pebble Beach, had become so popular that there needed to be some limits. Not on the number of spectators; there was ample space around a 2½-mile track for many thousands. The number to control was that of the entrants. Thousands of entries are submitted every January, and a committee of 11 men with expertise in old race cars selected the 550 cars that would race over the two days in August.

Kitty knew that there were many hands in the pot of money that the Rolex Motorsports Reunion produced. There was SCRAMP, the Sports Car Racing Association of the Monterey Peninsula; the group that built the track in 1957 on land donated by the U.S. Army at Fort Ord. SCRAMP was a huge charitable operation supporting youth groups like Boy Scouts, Veterans organizations, church groups and so on all over Monterey County. Of course, there was HMSA, which actually staged the event, and the business organizations which over the years had either sponsored the event, or paid a great deal of money for "naming rights." All this made it hard for Kitty to figure out who could answer a simple question: had a C-type Jaguar owner sent in an entry, and had it been accepted?

She decided that early in the coming week she would simply contact people at the track and ask if anyone was available to answer her question, and if not, then connect her with someone who could. With that decided, she put her "to do" list aside and said to Pyewacket, her resident cat, "Pye, I'm exhausted, and I've done nothing. It's time for me to go for a run out 17 Mile Drive to Pebble Beach. When I get back we'll have some lunch. Keep an eye on things while I'm gone." And with that she was out the door.

Chapter 30

As the last half of July began, Kitty's life became somewhat mundane. She liked to use that term because it meant "belonging to the world," and not something heavenly. There was nothing heavenly about her routine that week as she put in her time at the library cleaning, repairing or salvaging books. Each day began with her exercise routine, then time at the library, and after lunch came phone calls or emails to various people. Mundane.

Young Mr. Bermudes promised a campaign to find young men or women to go to events during "car week" and look for Max Shepherd. She had a long and promising conversation with Mr. Rhyman, the attorney working for Pickering, Milton and Newlin firm and their Record Gone program. He informed her that he had in hand all of her arrest records and court proceedings, plus records from her time in prison and parole reports.

He told her one thing that got her hopes up. He had found that there had been no claim filed with the company insuring the property she had stolen. That meant that there was no specific data about the dollar value of the items she had stolen. This implied that the prosecutor assigned to her plea and sentencing hearing had simply made a judgment that the property was worth over $950, and was therefore a felony. Rhyman figured that a judge could be convinced that there had been another "miscarriage of justice" since there was no evidence establishing a dollar value. That news made Kitty's day a little brighter and a little less mundane.

The best was yet to come. On Wednesday, while she was fixing lunch for herself and her cat, she answered the phone. She heard a voice that she had only heard once before during her visit to Las Vegas. The male voice said, " Ms. D'Literie, I hope you remember me. This is Dred Maxim from Las Vegas."

"Mr. Maxim, what a pleasant surprise. How are things going with the collection?"

"That's why I'm calling," he said. "You may recall that I was having a Maximum delivered from England. Well, it arrived, and that's why I'm calling."

"This is the new one coming into port at Corpus Christi, if my memory is correct."

"That's the one, and it came by Trusted Transport just yesterday afternoon, and I remembered your search for a long-lost heir to a family inheritance."

"What was it about this delivery that made you remember me?"

"The driver, that's what. He had driven the truck carrying the car from the customs impound directly to our shop here, and I'll swear that he's your man."

Kitty had to grab a chair as her heart began to pound and her blood pressure to rise.

"Oh, my goodness," she gasped. "What makes you think it was him?"

"Well, the first thing was that he had a slight beard, not a full beard but enough facial hair to indicate he hadn't shaved in a week. But the shape of his face and head looked like the picture you showed me. Then there were his questions."

"What did he ask about?" Kitty inquired.

"He asked a lot about the Maximum. How closely did it resemble a real C-type? Did I know where a real C-type could be found; did I know any C-type owners? I mean, he had no interest in any of the other cars in the shop, only what did I know about C-type Jaguars. So, since he seemed about the right age and physical appearance, your visit came to mind."

"Did he look like a full-time employee of Trusted?"

"Oh yes, he had on one of the company shirts, and he certainly knew how to unload the car and drive that big rig."

"Did he say anything about future assignments," Kitty asked.

"No, he didn't. He just indicated that his next job was to get the rig back to the company headquarters in St. Louis."

"Mr. Maxim," Kitty said, "I can't thank you enough for this information. I knew that Max had obtained a license to drive those kinds of trucks about three years ago in Arizona, but I had no idea what he had been doing since then. This really helps my search a lot. So, thank you again, and I hope you have luck with your business there in North Las Vegas."

"Well, I'm glad I could be of some help," Maxim said. "I know that if I was in line to inherit something, I'd like to think that someone was looking for me. I'll let you know if that same driver shows up here again."

"Thank you, Mr. Maxim, and do stay in touch," Kitty concluded.

Kitty had to take a deep breath and think about what to do next. If Max Shepherd were employed by Trusted as a driver, the chances are that he would be involved with "car week" in Monterey. But in what capacity, she wondered? Because of the time differential she decided to wait until the following day to make a call to Trusted.

Instead, she decided to call Sarah Brady the woman in charge of organizing the concours at Pebble Beach. She also decided to use the "auto historian" cover story, and when she got through to Ms. Brady's office she said, "I'm writing a history of British sports cars that have been winners at the concours. I'm curious to know if one of the Le Mans winning Jaguars will be entered in the concours this year?"

Brady replied, "We would be thrilled to have one in the event, but no entries for either a C- or D-Type Jaguar were submitted for consideration. Maybe next year,

182

when we will have a class just for race cars of the post-war era."

Kitty thanked her and thought, "Well, I'll still need eyes on the crowd that will be there, even if he is just spectating, and there's no way to tell in advance if he will be there."

Her next call was to the Quail Lodge to pose the same question to Mary Mendoza. She encountered more reluctance to give a simple "yes" or "no" to the question about whether such a car was to be in the show. After much pleading and encouragement to "help automotive historical research along" she finally got "No, nothing like that has been entered," in response.

"Great," she thought, "now should I try to get a pair of eyes on the crowd there? I know some people are good at 'gate crashing' but will it be worth my while to have someone try it and probably get thrown out on his or her ear? I'll have to think about this some more."

About three in the afternoon, she decided on trying the "long shot," a call to the number listed for the Motorsports Reunion. She used the same cover story; automotive historian researching an article about Jaguars competing at Monterey. She finally was connected to a representative of the track, whose response was, "You should have been here in 2011. We had four C-type Jaguars entered that year. Jaguar was the featured marque, and there was another one that showed up just to be on display. This year? It looks like we do have one entered. It's being flown in from England to Oakland the week before the race. That's when the entrants can take their cars out on the track and get familiar with the circuit. So, yes, there will be one in the class for 1947-1955 cars with engines over two liters."

Kitty knew then that she had done a good days work. If Max were doing the same kind of research, he would know that if he really wanted to see a XK120C Jaguar, he had to be at the Motorsports Reunion. He might spend time at the other events, but the odds favored the race setting as the place he would most likely be found.

Kitty decided to make one last call. This time, on Thursday morning, she called the office of the company, Trusted, which might employ Max Shepherd. This time the cover story was very different when she reached the personnel office of the company.

"Good morning. I'm Katherine Vanguard, and I have a classic Jaguar that I'm planning to ship from Monterey, California to an auction in Florida. A friend in Las Vegas, Nevada, just had a car delivered by one of your drivers, and he spoke very highly of him. I was wondering if a Max Shepherd is still employed by you, and if he would be available to deliver my car during the week ending on August 26?"

"Ms. Vanguard, we do have a driver employed by that name, and we are glad that he is getting good references. Unfortunately, Mr. Shepherd has asked to take his vacation right at that time. Apparently he wants to take in some of the events in Monterey that week. He did say he would be available as a substitute or relief driver should someone became ill and would check with us periodically to see if he were needed in an emergency."

"Thank you very much," Kitty responded. "I'll get back to you next week when my plans are finalized for the trip to Fort Lauderdale. If Mr. Shepherd should contact you, would you let him know of my request?"

"We'd be happy to do so, Ms. Vanguard, and we look forward to helping you with your transportation needs. Thank you for calling Trusted."

Kitty felt as if a great load was off her shoulders. Max planned to be in the area "taking in some events." The search was narrowing, but the haystack in which this needle called Max might be hiding was still going to be pretty large. She could hardly wait to call Gus and tell him the news, maybe one evening this weekend. Now it was time to go do some yoga and let the tension just slip away.

Chapter 31

Kitty waited until ten on Friday morning before she called Gus. He answered promptly, and she made it short and sweet.

"Sweetie, really quick, when are you free to go to dinner this weekend?"

"Wow," he responded, "no opening gambit like how am I feeling or how has my week been going. I wonder if that's how husbands and wives might open a conversation?"

"Okay, look, I didn't want to waste your time on the job. I've got a lot to tell you about, and I thought a nice dinner out on the wharf would be good. So, when are you free?"

"Well, it just so happens that I've got no duty after end of shift at four, so I could pick you up about four-thirty or a quarter to five. Will that be okay?"

"Let's make it four-thirty," she responded. "Have a good day and I'll see you then."

Her social, or was it her love life, arranged for the evening, her next call was to Napoleon Shepherd.

"Mr. Shepherd, this is Ms. D'Literie calling to give you an update on my search for your brother Maximillian."

"I hope you have something positive for me," he responded.

"Oh, I've got a lot to tell you about," she replied. "The first thing is that I know he is alive and working as a driver for a company called Trusted."

"What kind of company is that?" he asked.

"They are one of two major companies that deliver cars to various events, such as shows or races. He was seen making such a delivery in Las Vegas. The customer there remembered my search and called me."

"And have you determined where he is living?" Napoleon asked.

"No, I haven't, but I contacted the company employing him and learned that he plans to be here in the Monterey area in August."

"So, I take it that you'll try to contact him then?"

"I will, but that's where we get into some difficulty. There will be so many car related events between August 16 and 26 that I'm going to have to get help in trying to spot him."

"And how are you going to do that?" Napoleon asked.

"I'm going to employ some young men and women to go to these events and watch those who attend. That is going to take some funds, and I don't have the bankroll to cover paying these people, plus the cost of admission to some of these events."

"If you feel you're that close to locating him, send me an estimate of the projected costs on Monday, and I'll see that you get the funds."

"That's great, but I have another concern. If he is definitely identified, I can try to strike up a conversation with him and advise him of the situation with the estate. If he wants nothing to do with me, or your family, the best I can do is to get details on where he can be reached."

"That sounds fine, but I sense that you have some other concern," Napoleon said.

"Yes, I do. His behavior, when he delivered a car to my contact in Las Vegas, makes me think he may truly be obsessed with getting his hands on that one model of 1950s era Jaguar. I've learned that only one such car will be in the area in that time frame. My concern is: what if he tries something truly dangerous, like theft?"

"I can't believe that my brother is so far gone that he would try something that crazy, but then anyone can be lured into crime if their desires become great enough. What do you propose to do if that scenario plays out?"

"Well, I've become very friendly with one of the police officers here, and he is going to have me talk with a detective from the Monterey County Sheriff who would deal with that. I know it sounds far-fetched, but what if a crime could be prevented before anyone got hurt?"

"I agree with that point of view, and I'm sure that Max can be trusted to do the right thing if you can just talk to him. I do really appreciate that you've gotten this far in the search, and please call me as soon as you make any contact with my brother."

"I'll do that," Kitty replied. "I'll stay in touch, maybe as often as weekly, to let you know what develops here. And I'll hope that Max wants nothing more than to get a picture of his dream car with him standing next to it. My fear is that he has something more daring in mind. Goodbye for now, Mr. Shepherd."

That bit of her day done, Kitty turned back to the humdrum details of life, like getting her groceries bought for the week ahead before the crowds of shoppers hit the stores on the weekend. She also began again to think about where things were going with Gus.

When she had said to Napoleon Shepherd, "I've become very friendly with one of the police officers here," she knew she was minimizing the relationship. "Friendly" didn't really do justice to what they had become in just a few months. They could continue as they had, seeing each other once a week or so, or they could move to something more involved, like living under the same roof, sharing the same bed. And what was he thinking during their brief conversation this morning when he said something about husbands and wives having conversations. They certainly would have more to talk about tonight than the Max Shepherd case.

She also realized, for perhaps the first time in a long while, that she didn't have any real female friends to talk to about such relationships here in Pacific Grove. She knew women who worked at the library but she didn't really socialize with them. It was the same way with the women at the yoga group or the hair salon. She knew them, but didn't really interact socially with them. "Good grief," she thought, "I've become some sort of hermit. Does that word even apply to a woman?"

That sent her scurrying to her computer to ask Google "What do you call a female hermit?" She learned that the term was hermitess, and that it came from the Greek word (didn't everything?) "Eremos," which meant solitary. People chose the life style because of their religious beliefs, as she had, or just because they liked solitude. She also saw that a synonym to solitary was recluse. Another term suggested was loner or lone wolf, as used by some people who thought of it as a derogatory term. The references then got into all kinds of pseudo-psycho analysis about whether being a loner was a good or a bad thing.

What would be said about a hermitess? The question that arose was "If a man's solitude is a thing of nobility, then what's left for a woman?" She came across an essay by Rhian Sasseen, a writer who lives in Massachusetts. Sasseen had found that even people like Thoreau, who spent two years living alone, could not conceive of a woman living alone.

Her research had led Sasseen to write that society felt that a woman who lived alone must have something wrong with her. She put it in one short sentence: "We don't burn witches; we just shame them." Kitty could relate to that.

Sasseen went on to write "not all women can be alone." She gave an example from American history, that of Sarah Bishop. During the American Revolution the British burned down her father's house in Connecticut, and she was raped. She lived out the rest of her life in a cave and became known as the "nun of the mountain." Her motto, if she had one, probably would have been, "Don't tread on me."

The author concluded that the last hermitess was movie actress Gretta Garbo. She is always associated with the quote "I want to be alone." Garbo, many years later, said that she had been misquoted. What she really said was "I want to be let alone." Then she just disappeared and became a modern myth.

As she shut down her computer, Kitty felt better. She thought, "I can live with someone calling me a hermitess. I chose to be a solitary when I became a Wiccan. I chose not to be part of a coven, even if I could have found a dozen other witches in Monterey County to form one. And being compared to Greta Garbo, that's really cool. I do interact with other people, I just live alone. Maybe I won't live this way forever, but I like being able to 'paddle my own canoe' as the saying goes. If men find it hard to believe that I can make it on my own, well, that's their big mistake."

She also felt that the quote about "We don't burn witches, we just shame them" was very interesting, since that guy down in L.A. had been talking about her being a witch consultant on a TV show. She hadn't even thought of Mel Goldfarb for at least a month. "Tomorrow, no make that next week," she thought, "I've got to give that guy a call. I wonder if having a man in my life, even if it's a part-time role, is distracting me from things like getting back into the entertainment world, if only as a consultant."

With that she began to think about the man in her life again. Dinner tonight, on the wharf at Albonetti's, would be nice, but she needed help. She would bring up the developments in the search for Max, and press him for a connection to the Sheriff. Then they could talk about where their lives were going; together, or just crossing in some random pattern. The solitary Wiccan knew things might get strange in the next thirty days.

Chapter 32

Gus was his usual punctual self when he knocked on her door at four-thirty on Friday evening. Kitty had dressed for what she figured might be a cool July evening on the wharf. When Gus asked, "Where did you have in mind for this evening?" She replied, "I've booked a table for two at five-fifteen at Albonetti's. It's way out at the far end of the pier, so we've got a bit of a walk from the parking lot."

They chatted about the trivia of the day as they drove to the wharf area. Traffic was heavy but nothing like it would be when 'car week' arrived in August. Kitty always liked the walk down the pier, past all the restaurants and the little shops selling post cards of Monterey and the sweat shirts designed for tourists. They would suddenly realize that the waterfront was chilly in the evening, even in July. The shirts always had "Monterey" or "Carmel" emblazoned across the chest. "Who buys that stuff?" she wondered. She was glad someone did, because it meant that there were tourists, and that's what Monterey lived on now that Fort Ord was gone and mostly forgotten.

Once at Albonetti's the question was "inside or outside" seating. Kitty voted for the fresh air, even if it did smell a bit of harbor seal. The seal was prowling around under the wharf, hoping that some chef would toss him the head of a salmon if he was lucky.

The first thing on the menu was the extensive antipasto bar. Kitty asked, "Do you want to split a full order of calamari?"

Gus replied, "No, I'm going to try an order of the buffalo calamari; it sounds strange and in need of my research."

"Okay, you do that and I'll get a glass of Pinot Griego to drink, unless you want to split a bottle."

"No, I'm going for a pint of North Coast Stellar IPA. That way I'll get a beer in a glass, not be handed some bottle I'm supposed to drink out of. One thing that serving in the Army in Germany taught me was how beer is supposed to be served and consumed. It seems that many Americans think this stuff is supposed to be drunk straight out of a bottle like a soda. You'll never see that at a German Octoberfest."

"Okay," Kitty responded "now that we've got that important cultural point clarified, what are you going for on the dinner menu?"

"Since it's seldom available, I'm going to try the swordfish steak," Gus replied.

"Good, and I'm going to have the grilled salmon," Kitty said, "and I'm going to tell you where my investigation is at this point and ask for your help."

"What's the latest on the fugitive?" Gus asked.

"What I've learned from that guy in Vegas, Dred Maxim, is that Max is working as a driver for Trusted. I posed as a potential customer and learned that Trusted does employ Max and that he'll be in Monterey for car week as part of his yearly vacation. He also told them that if needed he could step in as a substitute, should something happen to one of the other drivers on duty."

"So, how are you going to find him in the big crowds that week?"

"I've got my assistant, Rudy, lining up what I'm going to call my Bow Street runners, college men and some women who can help me."

"Whoa, what's a Bow Street runner?" Gus asked.

"Back in the 1750's there was a lot of crime in London, especially in an area called Bow Street. A man named Henry Fielding, the author of Tom Jones, recruited some young men to investigate crime, track down suspects, and generally keep an eye on things. His brother, John, managed to get him some government support and the Runners became the first London police force. In 1850 Robert Peel got the government to finance a larger police force for the entire metropolitan area of London. My guys and gals are like that, sort of amateur detectives helping me look for Max."

"And what happens if you or your Runners actually find him?"

"His brother, Napoleon, wants me to talk to Max about the inheritance in the hope he'll, at least, make contact with his family. I'm still suspicious that he will really be here for more than looking at cars. That's why I want to talk to someone in the county sheriff's department."

"What do you think he might do?" Gus asked.

"I've learned that one, and only one, of the 1950 era Jaguars that Max is fascinated by will be at the races at Laguna Seca. If my suspicions are correct, he'll try to take that car."

"He may have a very nice inheritance coming, but it won't be the millions he would need to buy the car. I think he may be planning a robbery."

"Let me guess," said Gus. "You want me to introduce you and your suspicions to Joe Bumgarner, the detective who works all the auto theft cases in the county."

"Right. I know he'll think I'm insane, but all I want to know is how do I proceed if I want to prevent this theft which I think might happen. I've got no proof that it will, just a hunch, an intuition. Jake, my boss of long ago, often trusted me to act on my intuitions. All I know for sure is that Max has worked himself into a position where he just might be able to pull off this theft."

"Okay, on Monday I'll call over to the sheriff's office in Salinas and see if Joe can meet with you this coming week. I'll let him know you're my C.I., my 'confidential informant,' and that you've been working to find this guy Max for months. His recent behavior makes you

194

think he's planning to steal a particular car coming in for the races. No guarantee that Joe will even want to hear your theory, but we'll give it a try."

"Good, now let's eat, drink and talk about something else," Kitty said.

As they finished their dinner and some casual chat about the weather and the like, Gus said, "I have the impression that you wanted to talk about something beyond your criminal conspiracy instincts."

"Yes," Kitty replied, "I'd like to talk about us."

"What about us?" he asked.

"About where this relationship between us might be going, and where it might take us. When I called you this morning to set up this dinner, you said something like 'Is that how husbands and wives open a conversation?' That got me thinking about our relationship. We've become something more than a cop and his C.I., don't you think?"

"Well, you're right. After that weekend in Las Vegas I think we are more than a cop and a C.I. I know guys at the station wonder about us. I doubt that many are stilled fooled by the 'informant' label. We've never really kept it a secret that something is going on with us, and I do think we should decide where this is all going."

"Okay," she responded. "I more than 'like' you, I think I'm in love with you. After our conversation earlier I did some serious thinking, not about us but about me. I've spent the last few years, pretty much since Jake took his own life in 2006, in what is almost a hermit-like existence. I've not joined any groups, haven't developed any real friendships. Then one day you came knocking on my door to tell me to stop parking the Jaguar in the street. That changed my life, at least I think so. Or am I just kidding myself? Could it be that the lone she-wolf is looking for a mate?"

"I don't know about the 'lone wolf' bit," Gus said, "but I know that I enjoy whatever we do together, and I'd like to keep doing things with you. I'm not sure how ready you are to change your way of life." Gus paused, looked at Kitty, and continued. "You had an interesting life before you came to Pacific Grove, and then you settled down, or so it seems. Are you really ready to make some changes at this point in your life?"

"I think so," she said, "but before I do, I want to make the big change that could lead to a lot more."

"And that would be...?" he asked.

"To get the word 'felon' off my name. You know I'm pursuing that in court. Then, just think, I could try to get other investigative jobs, maybe get a private investigators license, work for a law firm, heck, I could even get a passport and travel. I'd like you with me if we did that. So, would you be up to traveling the world with the woman who was once your C.I.?"

"Of course," he replied. "Now what about dessert?"

"Okay," she said. "I'll get the check, and we can get ice cream cones back down the wharf at Carousel Candies. Then let's go back to my place for Friday night TV watching. We could watch reruns of *Hawaii Five-0* and *Blue Bloods*, and you can tell me what mistakes the writers made about police procedures. And then we can see if you can tolerate my religion."

"What does that mean?" he asked.

"Oh, you'll see. You may have noticed there's a full moon this weekend, and we witches are supposed to dance in celebration. And let's just say it's a 'clothing optional' ceremony."

Chapter 33

Monday, the 23rd day of July, was unusually warm for the Monterey peninsula. The weather seer on TV told Kitty that the high temperature might reach 90 degrees, thanks to high pressure over Nevada. Kitty began to feel enough of her own high pressure when she looked on her calendar and saw that "car week" was exactly 24 days away.

The mundane always wins out over personal concerns. Kitty got to the library before the 9:30 A.M. opening and spent the next five hours ensuring that the library patrons would have freshly covered books to check out. She also arranged to have the group meeting room available to her and her "Bow Street runners" for a meeting on Saturday afternoon. She also arranged another hair care session at Prim for Thursday afternoon.

After work there was time for a quick run out 17 Mile Drive toward the Inn at Spanish Bay. "Maybe," she thought, "if I drop some subtle hints, I can get Gus to take me there for my birthday. Surely, the whole Max Shepherd case will be a memory by mid-September."

Once she was home, she noticed the flashing light on her answering machine; a message awaited her. She played the message to hear the familiar voice of Gus Mulbrae.

"I'll call you after my shift," he said, "because I've got you an appointment with Detective Bumgarner on Thursday. I'll call you about six. Bye for now tootsie."

Sure enough, the phone rang at six as Gus called, just as promised. "Can I come by now and give you the details?" he asked.

"Of course," she replied. "I'll have two of my best TV dinners warming up in the microwave. Now you'll get to see my real culinary skills."

She wasn't kidding. Given limited choice, Gus picked something labeled "Beef Merlot," which at some time at the ConAgra plant was probably in the same room with a bottle of Merlot. Kitty selected one of her favorites, a spicy Chinese chicken meal allegedly inspired by some general of the Imperial Army. "That's probably why they lost Hong Kong to the English," she thought.

"What's the good news on the auto theft front?" she asked. "It sounds like the detective will meet with me."

"He will, Thursday morning at ten o'clock. He'll be at the Sheriff's substation. That's over near the courthouse on Aguajito. It's his weekly visit, and he probably has an appearance to testify in the court, so you might not have a lot of time with him."

"That's okay," she responded. "I'm just happy that I get a chance to share my wacky idea with someone besides you. How did he react to the idea of my keeping Max under observation, assuming I can find him at all?"

"Well, Bumgarner is skeptical, because we're not talking about a known felon as our suspect. On the other hand, I know he has worked with the Highway Patrol and even the FBI on cases involving race cars. Never something like a vintage or classic race car."

"So, he didn't seem completely skeptical about my theory?" Kitty asked.

"Well, he may have been skeptical, but like a good cop he isn't going to ignore a tip from a local citizen. You're going to have to be pretty organized about how this crime could, at least in theory, take place. Like all experienced police personnel, he'll want to know what events have led you to believe that a crime may be going to occur. He'll ask you about motives, both Max's and yours. Let's face it; right now, you come across more like Nancy Drew than Miss Marple. You must be prepared to meet a lot of 'why should we expend

198

resources on your theories?' questions, so be prepared for that."

"Okay," Kitty responded. "I had Thursday afternoon all set up to get my hair done. I'll have to call the shop and see if I can move my appointment to another day. Is there anything else I should know before I meet Mr. Bumgarner?"

"Yeah, if you want to flatter him, ask if he ever drove a Pontiac Firebird or GTO. He'll ask why you asked that, and you come back with 'because you look like a TV star I used to see often, and that's what he drove."

"How's that supposed to flatter him?" she asked.

"Because he is very distantly related to a TV star of long ago, and he likes to think that people see the resemblance. It's all a bunch of baloney, but like all guys he likes to think that the woman he's talking to thinks that he's something special. Oh, and make sure he sees the Jaguar."

"Why?" she asked.

"Because he'll figure that any woman who drives a car like that just might know someone who would steal a car like that. It'll enhance your credibility, shall we say."

"Okay, officer, I'll do my best to be a credible felon and confidential informant. Want to stay for dessert?"

"Not tonight, but let's get together this weekend so you can let me know how the interview went. Oh, and maybe another dance recital?"

"Not likely," she replied. "That's a full moon event, and we won't have another one of those until about the middle of car week."

On Thursday, July 26th, Kitty was at the Sheriff's substation before ten in the morning. Detective Bumgarner was right on time and showed her to a small office used by the Homicide and Robbery Unit when they had a case on this side of the county. He wasted no time getting to the point, announcing, "I've got to be ready to go into court today, so we might get interrupted at any time."

"I understand," she replied, "and I'm glad you could see me today." She then went into the whole narrative about why she was involved with looking for Max Shepherd, and why she thought he could very well be planning the 'grand theft auto' event of the year.

"So, you think this guy, Max, is going to try to steal a car during 'car week,' and that would most likely take place out at Laguna Seca. Is that correct?"

"Yes, because that is the only place the car, that he has wanted since childhood, will be here in the U.S.A. It is going to be transported from and returned to Oakland airport by the company he works for. He also has arranged to be here in Monterey at that time."

"How are you going to find him in all the crowds that week?"

"I'll have about 20 young people watching for him at all the various events: shows, auctions, and the races. I know he may be here just to take some pictures, but I've also got to let him know that he's an heir in order to complete my basic assignment. And, if I'm right, to stop him from stealing that one rare race car."

"Well," Bumgarner said, "we can help you out a little bit if you think that the races on Saturday and Sunday are a potential crime scene. It is going to involve what we police call a 'stakeout' for those two days, and the nights as well."

"What would my role be?" she asked.

"We have had occasions in the past when it was necessary to do some surveillance of cars and crews at the track. So, we have a spot where someone can watch the whole paddock area and the comings and goings of all the cars."

"Why would the Sheriff's Department have such a spot, and where is it?" she asked.

"Well, there is an organization of professional racers who still have events at the track. They go by the acronym IMSA. A few bad apples in the bunch gave the group the nickname 'International Marijuana Smugglers Association.' This was back before 'pot' became sort-of legal in California."

"Some racers were smuggling drugs using their race car or transporter?"

"Yeah, there were at least three cases we worked on with DEA and other Federal agencies to try to stop the trafficking. For example, there were two brothers, Don and Bill Whittington, who made so much money smuggling dope that they bought a Porsche to race at Le Mans with a duffle bag full of cash. It was in 1979, right at the track in France."

"Did they ever get caught?" she asked.

"Well, not here," he replied, "but one of them got caught for tax evasion in 1986, sort of like Mickey Cohen in the 1920's."

"Were there others doing the same sort of thing?"

"Well, in 1988 a racer named Lanier was caught and convicted of smuggling 300 tons of marijuana. Randy was a good driver, rookie of the year at Indy in 1986. He got out of prison about four years ago."

"So, you had a spot to watch these guys out at the track?"

"Yeah, I'll show you where it is, probably next week. One last story, if I may. The wildest case was a father and son team. John Paul, Sr. and Jr., both suspected of drug running. Daddy killed a Federal witness, went to prison, got paroled in 1999 and promptly disappeared. Or got rubbed out. Junior got five years for racketeering, and I have no idea what became of him. I do think these vintage racers are pretty clean, but they've all got lots of money somewhere. We don't always know how."

"So, what are you going to do about my theory?" Kitty asked.

"Not much, right now," Bumgarner replied. "You've got a theory, a hunch, based on the unusual behavior of a guy you've never met face-to-face. Your intuition may be right, so I'm going to show you a place where you can keep an eye on things at the track on the 25th and 26th of next month. You may find this guy you're looking for, tell him he's an heir to a small fortune, and he'll give you a big hug and a lovely dinner. Or, he may not show until the cars are at the track and try something there. If that's the scenario you'll call me and let me decide what we do. Remember, you're just an interested civilian informant. Keep us informed and stay the hell out of our way. That okay, Ms. D'Literie?"

"It's very okay," she replied. "I hope I'm wrong, that I can find Max, give him the good news and watch him leave for L.A. If that fails, I hope he doesn't try anything foolish."

At that moment the phone on the desk rang. It was the court bailiff letting the detective know he was the next witness after a ten-minute recess. She shook hands with Bumgarner and said, "I'll see you next week. Just tell me where and we'll meet at the track. Good luck with the trial."

"Funny," she thought, "who would have thought in 1992 that a parolee named Kitty would be wishing some cop 'good luck' as he went to court to put some person in prison. Life sure takes some strange twists."

She climbed into the Jaguar and headed for the library.

Chapter 34

On Saturday afternoon, July 29, Kitty held her first "get acquainted" meeting with the young men and women that Rudy Bermudes had recruited for the Max Shepherd search. She kept it brief. She told them she was "employed," to use the term loosely, to find a long-lost family member who would be an heir to part of a sizeable estate. She distributed copies of a photo of Max taken over a decade earlier, plus copies of the small photo on his Arizona driver's license. She explained that it appeared he would be on vacation in Monterey during "car week" and that their task would involve attending several events during that ten-day period.

Rudy had managed to recruit 22 people who could be of help looking for Max at some point during the ten-day period. Kitty pointed out that even if they had 100 people it would be almost impossible to cover all the events that Max, or any car lover, would be able to attend. So, she had eliminated some events. One example was the "Concours de lemons," a fun event on Sunday morning, August 26. People could display some of the worst looking, least reliable cars which they had ever owned at a park in Seaside. Fun, amusing, but not likely to attract Max.

She also decided they would skip the opening event on August 16. The "Concours on the Avenue" might have 350 cars on display at Carmel, but she didn't expect Max to show up for the opening event. It was a popular event because most of the cars entered were American "muscle cars" and the show was completely free to spectators.

Although she personally enjoyed the "Little Car Show" in Pacific Grove on Wednesday, August 15, she was gambling that Max would not care about cars with small, under 1500 c.c. engines which would be on display. What really concerned her during the opening week was a new feature of "car week."

Since some of the over 500 entrants for the "Motorsports Reunion" may have never driven on the track at Laguna Seca, the promoters had decided to allow those who could fit it into their schedule and budget to come a week earlier and get in some practice. Kitty's problem was not knowing exactly when the XK120C Jaguar would arrive from England and be delivered to the track. She decided that one or two of her "runners" should be out there to see if it did arrive, and where it would be located in the infield paddock.

Fortunately for her budget, the promoters were not going to charge those dedicated enthusiasts who wanted to come out and watch this practice at the track.

She asked for volunteers from the group to go to the track on Saturday and Sunday, August 18-19. Two young men from the group, Tom and Jack, agreed to go on those days. Kitty gave them pictures of the type of car they would be looking for, as well as the Trusted Transportation which would be used. Their instructions from her were simple: "Just look for the man in the pictures and the car if it arrives. If you see him do not approach, but try to get a picture with your camera. If the Jaguar shows up, get a picture of it and make note of where it will be in the infield." She also said, "There's no cost to get in, but get yourselves some lunch while you're out there. Just try to keep it under $20 per day; money is tight for this operation."

Next, she decided she had to deal with the auctions. She asked if anyone would like to attend one, either alone or with a friend. There were three auctions to cover on the evening of Wednesday, August 22, and she particularly wanted eyes at the Gooding auction at the Monterey Conference Center. This was where the highest level of bidding would take place, the sort of action most likely to attract Max.

She had no trouble getting three young men, Patrick, Shawn and Mike, who would be eager to go and bring a date. "Impress the girls with the big spenders, right guys?" she said. "Just be sure to look for faces in the crowd, and if you see our target, again, do not make contact, but try to see where he goes when he leaves, if, in fact, he shows up. I'll have tickets for you the day before the event."

"Now," she said, "we turn to a big crowd event, the Tour of Elegance on Thursday. All the cars, well, most of them that are in the big event at Pebble Beach on Sunday will be in the tour. They stop for lunch at the park on Ocean Avenue in Carmel. I know from experience that thousands of people will show up to look at the cars up close when they park along Ocean. I need eight, no, make that ten people to mix and mingle in the crowd, looking at faces. It's free, no admission charge, but if you have to pay for parking bring me the receipts and you'll be reimbursed."

She had no trouble getting seven of the young men, as well as three young women who said they would go together. "The girls will probably spend more time looking at clothes at Carmel Plaza or jewelry at Tiffany's," she thought, "but who knows, they might see Max."

"Again," she said, "same rules. If you see our target, don't approach. If possible, see where he goes. If he gets in a car try to let me know the license numbers, and what make it is. Call me right away if you see him and I'll get there as quickly as I can."

Kitty had something else planned for Friday afternoon. That would be the day of the Pacific Grove Concours and Rally. She had two reasons for wanting to be there. She had seen in the past the great variety of cars that ordinary citizens brought to the show. They would fill Lighthouse Avenue from the Post Office down the street to the movie theater. Money from the entries went to various charitable causes, including a fund for injured police, firemen and EMTs. She wanted people to see and admire old Malcolm, her venerable Jaguar E-Type.

There was another reason for her to attend. Each year she had noticed a gentleman who entered a perfectly restored World War II era Jeep. She knew it was time for her to sell Eugene, the Jeep which had been willed to her by Jake. She loved the old beast, even though she seldom drove it these days, and she wanted it to go to a "good home." She wanted to ask the Jeep entrant for information on any club for such collectors. People like that often flock together, and someone in the group might know of a potential buyer who had expressed an interest in buying such an old vehicle.

She now had to get her "runners" into the remaining events. Since Rudy had done so much for her it seemed only right and logical that he should be the one to get the ticket for himself and a companion to the Pebble Beach Concours. She knew that if Max had no criminal intent, he could be at the concours and be gone before nightfall. Or, he could be at the event, leave before the final awards presentation and be at the track for the last two races of Sunday afternoon.

She had no ready answer for the question, "How do we know if he's at the Quail Lodge event?" She had mulled that over in her mind because access to this event was so limited and exclusive. The event would be on both Friday and Saturday afternoons. Some cars would leave the races at Laguna Seca on Saturday and be escorted over to the Quail and make a dramatic entrance there. She had to accept the fact that the Jaguar might be one of the race cars selected to be in that small group making the trip about midday, and would be out of her sight for some period of time.

Her request to the remaining "runners" was essentially, "Has anyone here ever crashed an Oscars show or a fancy wedding?" One young man, Antonio, said that he loved the thrill of such an adventure. "After all," he said, "what's the worst they are going to do? They'll have the police they are paying to work on their day off as security escort me to the gate and kick me off the property. I'll come up with a cover story, like 'I'm looking for my Uncle Max. He said he'd be here. Isn't he on your list of ticket holders?'"

"Okay, Tony, you've got the job, and have fun," Kitty said. "Now, I need a couple of guys to be in the paddock at the track on Saturday and Sunday of race weekend, one guy each day. The assignment will be to get there early on Saturday, find the Jaguar in the paddock, and keep an eye on anyone showing a great deal of interest in it. I'll be there also. I'll have a place, arranged by the Sheriff's Department, where I can observe the entire paddock from afar after the spectators have left for the day. So, who's up for a day at the races?"

Two guys, Bob and Ray, indicated an interest, and Ray asked, "Could both of us go on both days? That way we could cover more ground and have a second set of eyes looking for Max." Kitty sighed, as the budget began to overrun, and reluctantly said, "Okay, mostly because this is probably our last chance during car week." And with that she said, "Let's all meet again next Saturday for 30 minutes to make sure everyone is still with the program and understands their assignment. I'll see you here at 1:30 next Saturday, August 4, which gives us just two weeks before the events begin."

As everyone cleared out, and she tidied up the room, she quickly placed a call to Gus.

Getting his voice mail, she said, "Honey, call me as soon as you're free. I've got a lot to tell you, and I need a dinner and a stiff drink. Call me back when you're free." Then she was on her way to home and a quick workout.

Chapter 35

Gus called her as soon as his Saturday shift ended. "How about I pick you up around seven and we go to dinner at Max's Grill over on Forest," he said.

"Okay," she responded, "but I do think it's weird that we eat at a place with the name Max on it. I've spent all afternoon planning how my 'runners' can spot him, and now his namesake is going to serve me dinner?"

"Well, he's been here for about 15 years, so he must be doing something right. I've only eaten there once, but it's a nice place with good food," Gus said.

"Okay, but he better have a bar. I wasn't kidding about that stiff drink I mentioned earlier."

"Well, you'll be disappointed then. Max only serves really nice wine with dinner and dessert. Must be something about his learning to cook in Paris. Anyway, you know there's only a few places that serve anything stronger than beer or wine in town. The city is against it because of its history."

"Okay, okay, I'll settle for a good dinner. I'll be ready at seven," she said as she ended the call.

Gus was at her door at 6:45 p.m., and as he drove them over to Forest Avenue and Max's Grill she said, "I've often wondered why there are so few bars in Pacific Grove."

"Two reasons," Gus said. "First, the city council and mayor don't want to have too many, so very few requests ever get as far as the Alcohol Beverage Control offices in Sacramento. The city knows that we live off the tourists, but they want the 'right kind' of tourists."

"And what's the second?" she asked.

"That would be history. Methodist Church groups founded this place as a summer resort for their members. Families could buy a small lot; come here any time and set up a tent and camp out. After a while they would decide to build a house and live here permanently, but they didn't want their town getting like Monterey, or, even worse, like San Francisco, which was a place of sin and debauchery. It has stayed pretty much like that to the present."

"Yeah, and then somebody slipped up and let people like me buy a place here," Kitty said with a chuckle. "So, I guess I'll have to settle for a glass of wine, or maybe a carafe, or... no, a whole bottle would be debauchery, so that's out."

Once inside and comfortably seated, Kitty settled for an appetizer of stuffed ravioli with brie. Gus asked for the tempura ahi tuna roll. She asked Gus, "Do you want to split a bottle of prosecco?"

He declined, saying he preferred a glass of pinot noir from the Scheid Winery. Kitty advised the waiter, "Don't let the bottle get warm; I'll be back for seconds."

Gus then asked her, "How did things go with Detective Bumgarner? Did he seem at all interested in your hunch?"

"He didn't laugh at me, anyway," she responded. "I'm meeting him again next week out at the track, and he'll show me a spot where I can do a stakeout."

"That's interesting. I'll bet it's a location in the campground that the county controls. You'll need something other than the Jaguar if you're going to spend time at night trying to keep an eye on things."

"I hadn't thought about that," she replied. "What do you think I should do?"

"You know I've been reading some of the stories about that fictional detective down in L.A., Harry Bosch. When he retired from LAPD in the novels, he tried the private eye role. He was used to stakeouts in an LAPD unmarked car, but that option was out. He ended up getting a Mercedes Benz SUV. I think it was the GLE

210

model. You could check it out at the dealer over on Fremont."

"Oh, sure. They'll want me to buy one, which I can't afford, and they won't rent me one just for a long weekend."

"So, contact Hertz or Avis out at the airport. Maybe they have one, or something like it, that you could rent. Hertz, I know, has a luxury car supply in San Francisco. It's worth taking a look at least. What else did you do this week?"

They ordered their entrees, a baby spinach salad and grilled salmon for Kitty, Caesar salad with anchovies followed by a 12-ounce rib-eye steak for Gus. Kitty said, "I'll tell you about today after I get that second glass of prosecco."

She then went into the details of the meeting with her 'Bow Street runners,' concluding with, "This is getting so complex. It's all just a gamble that one of us will spot Max, and the expenses are just way out of line."

When their entrees arrived, she chided Gus saying, "12 ounces of red meat, plus potatoes! Not exactly the South Beach or Atkins Diet."

"Relax, sweetie, and finish your wine. You're not exactly the women's temperance movement tonight. What's most troubling to you about the case?"

"I'm trying to figure out what he would do if he did get his hands on that Jaguar. I thought he might just steal it for a 'joy ride,' like a kid who steals a Corvette and abandons it ten miles later after he's ruined the tires."

"Well, he wouldn't get far then, because Fort Ord closed and became Cal State Monterey Bay. Much of the land there became a national monument, and most of the old roads on the base are closed off. He wouldn't get much of a ride for his efforts."

"Right. So, if he did get the car before it went on a plane back to England, what could he do with it?"

"Well, what happens when guys steal art from a museum?" Gus asked. "This car, to a car lover, must be like a piece of sculpture in a museum. What are the options for the thief?"

"Well," she replied, "he couldn't drive it around much. Maybe rent a race track like Willow Springs in Kern County for a day and drive it around, put it back in a locked garage and hope no one called the police."

"Doesn't sound like much fun for all the risks he'd taken."

"I agree," Kitty said. "That would be like the art collector who built a window-less room under his house so he could sit and look at his stolen art collection. I can't see Max doing that after all this time, since he first sort of 'dropped off the grid' as they say."

"So, what are the other options?" Gus asked.

"The one that many would think of would be to wait for the search to cool off. Maybe make that trip to the rented track, have a film crew record that day for future enjoyment, and then sell the car."

"But where?", Gus asked. "The car couldn't be sold in North America or Europe, probably not in Asia to 'Crazy Rich Asians.' That leaves rich crooks in Latin America or Arab oil sheiks. Doesn't sound promising."

"The last option is what most art thieves do. They stash the stolen art work for a few years. There must be a statute of limitations for grand theft, even for autos. By then the rightful owner will have been paid off by his insurance company and moved on with his life. Then, our thief contacts the insurance company and promises to return the art work, undamaged, for a fraction of the real market value."

"Okay," Gus said, "he gets the car, stashes it for maybe five years, contacts Lloyds of London or whoever insured the car, and his profit is what Lloyds gives him to get it back?"

"That's the only option which makes a lot of sense to me. It reminds me of a comment from earlier this year when I went to the Petersen Museum in L.A. and met with the curator."

"What did he say?" Gus asked.

"I asked him if anyone had stolen, or tried to steal, one of their rare cars. He said, 'No, and any attempt would have to be like the movie called 'The Thomas Crown Affair.' I think he was recalling the first version of the movie, where Steve McQueen organizes a theft of money from a bank. This case could be more like the second, later movie, where art's what the thief is after. In both movies the insurance company pays off the client after a police investigation, but the company keeps looking for the insured object in the hope of reducing the loss to their business."

"So, what will you actually do if you think a theft is taking place?" Gus asked.

"Bumgarner made it really clear that I should stay out of his way. I'll be at the track, there will be eyes on the car, and if something takes place, I'll follow the car. Oh, and keep Bumgarner informed by phone."

"That's good advice from the detective," Gus said. "Now, do you want some dessert?"

"I saw they had French vanilla ice cream on the menu, so I'll have a scoop of that," Kitty replied. "And what are you going to have?"

"Hey, after those 12 ounces of steak, I think I'll back off a little and just have a cup of coffee. I'd also like to know what else has been going on with you?"

"Nothing yet, but I think I'll call the lawyer in L.A. to see if anything is going on with my case. I'd really like to appear before a judge and hope that my conviction can be reduced from a felony, or just completely wiped out."

"What about that bit about you being as consultant on a movie? Something about a witch and a private eye?"

"Well, that's another call I could make, but it's pretty far down on my 'to do' list. If it happens it might be fun, but the chance for my day in court is a bit more important. I spent enough time working with Jake O'Malley back in the day to know that most of the ideas people come up with never, ever, get in front of a camera."

"So, no big Hollywood comeback plans for the red-haired witch?"

"No, Hollywood is called a dream factory, which it is. Sometimes your dream comes at least partly true, but most of the time you get disappointed. Better to find a job outside the industry," she said.

"Well, on that sobering note, why don't we get on our way. I can't say 'my place or yours' because you know my place is like a college dorm room."

"Let's drive down to Lover's Point and watch the moon come up," she said. "Maybe we can talk about the two of us, and what happens after I live through 'car week.'" Turning to the waiter, she said, "Put a stopper in what's left of the prosecco; I'll take it with me. I know a cop who won't ticket me for drinking in public."

Chapter 36

On Tuesday, the last day of July, Kitty was back at work at the library when her cell phone rang. It was Detective Bumgarner. "Can you meet me out at the Laguna Seca campground tomorrow at noon?" he asked.

"Yes," Kitty responded, "I can be there at noon. Where should I meet you?"

"I'll be parked just past the booth where you're supposed to check in as a camper, but no one's ever there. They had to let people go because the county is so short on revenue. Anyway, there are things I need to show you and some questions I need to ask. See you tomorrow," he said, ending the call.

Kitty was at the library on Wednesday before it was open for patrons. She figured on getting in an hour or more of work before heading for the Laguna Seca Recreation Area. She decided that since she was probably going to sell her ancient Jeep, Eugene, she would drive him out there to make sure he was still roadworthy. She calculated that if this Korean War "veteran" could make it up that very steep hill to the campground then he was ready for a new owner.

Eugene may have been a bit "steamed" when he got to the campground entrance, but he had made it. She had no difficulty spotting Bumgarner's car. It was the typical car issued to detectives in police forces across the nation. It was a Ford Crown Victoria, unmarked, but with two clues which told any knowledgeable viewer that it was a "cop car."

"Really," she thought, "what car sold to the public comes with two spotlights mounted on the 'A pillar' on both sides of the windshield." She knew that those two spotlights, which could swivel to light up a large area, were valuable when examining a crime scene on the darkest night. She also knew that Ford had given these police cars the most powerful engine in their catalog, the better to catch those who try to outrun the long arm of the law.

Bumgarner gestured for her to follow his car down the road to a campsite which was just above turn five of the race track. She could see instantly why law enforcement would keep a grip on this one site.

Across the track, the paddock was empty, except for a few employees who appeared to be marking off spaces for individual racers. She knew that in a couple of weeks there would be somewhere between 500 and 650 cars parked in those spaces. Some would be supported by an enormous trailer which functioned as a machine shop and tool storage area. Once she knew exactly where the Jaguar would be parked, she could easily see what was happening around it.

"I see why you think that this is a good spot for a stakeout," Kitty said. "What happens to the trucks which have transported the race cars once they are unloaded?"

"They'll all be parked over there," he replied, gesturing toward a fenced area at the base of the hill which formed the north end of the paddock. "That way they can be brought in on Sunday after the races without getting in the way of all the spectators who are leaving."

"So, when will I have access to this site?" she asked.

"You can move in any time. The site is yours for this event, and you'll be able to come and go as you please, but frankly I'd say move in here on Friday evening, August 24. The person working at the gate, and there will be one at that time, will know that you've got site number 21. Oh, and that building to the right? That's a restroom which is available to other campers around this part of the campground, so expect some civilians passing by and wondering what you're doing."

"So, what do you think I should say if asked that question?"

216

"I'd come up with a cover story, such as 'I'm a reporter for the Carmel Pine Cone.' Face it, most folks camping here that weekend are in town for the races. I hope you'll have some vehicle other than that antique Jeep, or that flashy old Jaguar I saw you driving last week."

"Yes," she responded, "I intend to rent something like an SUV where I can at least recline during the night. I assume most people here will be in a camper or trailer."

"That's correct. It'll be 100% out-of-towners, mostly from California, but a few from other western states. Most will just ignore you, but some may try to be the usual friendly and annoying neighbor that we get on just about every stakeout. That's why you might need a story explaining why you're not the usual camper."

"You said over the phone that you had some questions you would like to ask," Kitty said.

"Yes, pardon me, but I've done a little background check on you. I know you're a local property owner, pay your taxes, haven't even gotten a traffic ticket, and work part time for the city. You've lived in Pacific Grove for a few years. I know you have a felony conviction on your record, and I suspect that the 'confidential informant' title is a convenient cover for the relationship you have with Officer Mulbrae of the Pacific Grove police. How am I doing so far?"

"You're very well informed and very accurate. Is there anything else you'd like to ask me?"

"Yes, there is. How did you get involved with this character, Max, who you suspect might be a thief?"

"Well," Kitty said, "I'd really like to be a licensed investigator, but that's barred to me unless I can get my felony conviction reduced to a misdemeanor or expunged. So, I advertise myself as a researcher and a 'finder' of missing persons," she said as she handed him one of her cards. "That got me involved with this family

217

in L.A. County who wanted a long-lost family member found so they can settle and close out an estate. Max, the missing family member, could be an heir to a good-sized sum of money, so I agreed to try to find him. Basically, about all I get out of this is expenses, and the family is a bit too conservative when it comes to handing out money."

"What are you doing about your record?" Bumgarner asked.

"I've retained a lawyer in L.A. He is trying to get me in front of a judge so we can try to get that black mark removed from my record. If I can get that record changed or wiped out, then a whole lot of jobs will open for me, jobs a felon can't get."

"Okay, I wish you good luck finding this guy, and I hope you're wrong about his plans."

"Thank you," Kitty said, "but here's a question I have. What if I'm right and a car gets stolen, and I follow the stolen car out of the area. What do I do then?"

"I'm going to give you a phone number where you can reach me anytime. You give me your number as well. While the car is in Monterey County any suspicious activity is the responsibility of the Sheriff's Department."

"I understand that," she said, "but what if he transports the car out of the county? I mean, should he end up driving the Trusted rig, I could end up following him all the way to Oakland."

"If he's out of the county, and you see something that looks wrong, give me a call and give me details. Once he's out of Monterey County what I can do is pass the information to the Highway Patrol. So, you better have something solid, as I don't want to embarrass myself or the Sheriff by wasting the CHP's time."

"Okay, I get the picture," Kitty said. "Unless you have more questions, I've got to get back to work. You have my business card, and you can see my phone number is on there."

Bumgarner gave her the phone number at the Sheriff's Detective Bureau where she could reach him if anything criminal were to occur. As they parted, he said, "If you call that number, just ask for Joe. And I wish you success, however your search turns out."

"And everybody just calls me Kitty," she said. "Easier to remember and pronounce than my full name."

"Got it. Take care of yourself, Kitty, and call me if you see anything suspicious." With that, the detective was off, down the hill and onto the highway toward Salinas.

Kitty decided to spend a few more minutes on the site, taking a look at where cars would be located, and how entry and exit points would be accessed. After a quick tour of the paddock area, she headed for the "official souvenir store." She needed to buy three-day tickets for herself and the young men who would help her keep an eye on the Jaguar. While there, she asked the clerk, "I'm particularly interested in one car that is coming for the event. Can you tell me which race the Jaguar C-Type will be in, and about where I can find it in the paddock?"

"Sure," the clerk told her as he got the tickets scanned. "The Jaguar will be in race 5B on Sunday. That's the one for 1947 to 1955 Sports Racing and GT cars. If you want to wait a few minutes outside the store, I'll have one of the guys take you over to the row in the pits where most of the cars in that race will be parked. Just look for the guy in the Raceway shirt driving a golf cart."

A few minutes later, Kitty was back in the Jeep heading back to Pacific Grove. "This was good," she thought. "Now I have specifics to tell the guys who are going to be in the paddock about where to find the Jaguar and when it will be racing." Within thirty minutes she was back at her condo for a quick workout, and to wait for things to really get busy on "car week."

Chapter 37

After Kitty's meeting with Detective Bumgarner on the first of the month, she devoted her free time to details for "car week." Having had a good experience with the Enterprise people when she had rented a car from them for her trip to Las Vegas, she gave them a call. "Yes, they could have an Infiniti QX60 available for her from August 21 to 28. No, they didn't have a comparable Mercedes available." They had concluded, in comparing the two, most customers found the higher rental cost for the Mercedes made the Infiniti much more appealing. She went out to the Infiniti dealer in Seaside and found the car would more than meet her short-term needs.

With that out of the way, she turned her attention to communication. She bought for herself a second cell phone. This would be the one which the "Bow Street Runners" could call her on while on their assignments from August 18 to 26. Now, she was all prepared for her Saturday afternoon meeting with the group on the fourth of August.

The meeting was short, yet encouraging. Kitty was pleased that everyone in the group not only showed up, but were on time. They all demonstrated that they knew their individual assignments and what to do if they spotted their elusive target. She said, "Now, this is the phone number you're to use to reach me while on assignment. It will be turned on all the time from Wednesday the 15th through Monday the 27th. I know many of you have my regular number, but don't try to reach me at that number during that time span. I want the number free for any calls not related to our search. Now, each of you give me your number so I can program it into this phone."

That task completed, she began the distribution of tickets to events which required one for entry, and wished her group, "happy hunting." She told them to plan on one last meeting for debriefing on September 1.

Now there was nothing more to do except to wait for people to begin flowing into Monterey County in the second half of the month. A call to Gus seemed in order.

"This is Officer Mulbrae," he answered the call.

"My goodness, you sound so authoritative," she said. "Didn't your phone show that it was me calling?"

"It did, Ms. D'Literie, but as I'm on duty here at the front desk I thought it more appropriate to be a little more formal."

"Ah," she said, "wouldn't want anyone to think you were, shall we say, conducting personal business on the taxpayer's dime. Okay, your confidential informant would like to take you to dinner. Are you free this evening officer?"

"I will be. Can you come by the station and pick me up at seven?"

"I'd love to, and then I want to go to Il Fornaio over in Carmel. I guess I'm just ready for some lasagna and a glass of Chianti. Sound good?"

"Sure, if you can get a reservation. I've seen a lot more tourists this week due to the golf event over at Pebble Beach that pushed the car events back by a week."

"Good point," she said. "I'll call over there right now, and I'll pick you up in front of the station at seven."

"Okay, see you then, good lookin'."

She was in luck, getting a table for two on a Saturday night in Carmel. "Maybe," she thought, "it's an omen from the gods, and things will go well until the end of the month."

Another omen, or just dumb luck, was the fact that she was able to find a parking space on Ocean Avenue within a half block of the restaurant. As they got seated, she asked Gus, "Do you have to work tomorrow?"

"I do," he said, "but not until four p.m. This coming week will be the last quiet one in the month. I've already seen a lot of 'No Vacancy' signs going up around town."

"Well, it looks like it will be a quiet one for me as well," she said.

"So, how are things going with Bumgarner?" he asked.

"Great, so far. I've seen the spot where I'll spend time camping out at Laguna Seca. I now know how to reach him if something that looks suspicious takes place, and what to do if the case goes outside of the county."

"And how about your staff, your, what do you call them?"

"My Bow Street Runners? They each have assignments at places most likely to attract Max, and have a number to reach me if they spot him. And those who need one have a ticket to the event they're covering."

"Sounds like you've got it all covered. Did you do anything about getting another car for your stakeout?"

"I did. Enterprise is going to rent me an Infiniti that looks comfy. The dealer let me look one over. I know he thought I'd buy one if I spent some time in one. Maybe, someday, if I can afford it."

"Okay, sounds like your ready for your next adventure, so let's both try that lasagna and chianti feast you were planning on."

After dinner, as it was still a warm and pleasant evening, they left the Jaguar where it was parked and walked the five blocks down the hill to the Carmel Beach. Kitty just wanted to watch the sun go down over the ocean, but their conversation inevitably turned to "what comes next."

"What do you see coming over the horizon at you?" Gus asked.

"Next week, before things get hectic," she replied, "I've got to talk to Rhyman, the lawyer in L.A. By now he should have managed to get a date on some judge's calendar to present my case. No matter what happens, I've got to talk to Napoleon Shepherd about Max. And lurking deep in some part of my brain is the fact that Felix Morris is near death at the prison in San Luis Obispo. I just hope he lives until, oh, let's say, August 29. Then I can wrap up his life story and send him off to the UCLA Med. School to be the 'cadaver in residence.' Then, if all goes well, I'll get involved with the masters in library science program at San Jose State."

"So, I guess I'll be seeing less of you as the year goes on," Gus said.

"No, I don't think that's accurate," she replied. "In fact, I think we should both start thinking about how we can spend more time together. The way I see that happening is we either live under the same roof, or you get a place of your own. This arrangement you've got with two firemen and a cop from Seaside isn't doing much for our love life, is it?"

"Well, I agree with that last bit, but have you looked at the price of real estate around this county?"

"I know, it's overpriced, and as the university attracts more students, the demand for rental units is going to go up. I just think we should spend some time looking for either a place for the two of us, or a place for you where I could at least leave a spare tooth brush."

"Why don't we try looking for something before Christmas?" she said. "Maybe things will be different after the kids, including college types, are back in school in the fall."

"Okay, I could go for that. Does that mean you'd be willing to give up your place in P.G.?"

"Well, I'd rather not, but you've been there. You know it was never built for two people. Great location, lovely neighborhood, excellent police protection," she added with a laugh. "I just think it wouldn't do us any harm to spend a couple of weekends looking around to see what's available and affordable."

"Okay, that would be nice. I'd like to spend more time with you and not just at dinner at some restaurant. So, let's do some house hunting in the fall and early winter and see what we find," he concluded.

"Sounds great," she said, "but it's getting dark here on the beach. Time to hike back to the car. Want to get some dessert?"

"What do you have in mind?" Gus asked.

"I think I'll drive us back up to Highway 1 and go over to the Del Monte Center. We could get some ice cream at Cold Stone Creamery."

"Okay, but it's a shame you can't get an ice cream cone in Carmel. Well, you can at the little bakery, but they closed at five p.m."

"Do you remember the story about ice cream cones in Carmel?" she asked.

"I've just heard that it was a big issue once, but why?"

"Back in 1929 the city banned ice cream cones. Said it would lead to littering and other immoral behavior. You could buy a dish of ice cream if the restaurant sold it. Clint Eastwood, the actor, was mad at the city because he lived here, and they wouldn't let him build an office building near his restaurant. So, in '86 he ran for mayor and won. He made ice cream cones his big campaign issue."

"So, he won and cones became legal?"

"Well, the City Council voted to repeal the 1929 ordinance. The four guys on the Planning Commission then vetoed the repeal. Don't ask me how they could do that. Clint fired the Planning Commission, appointed replacements, and cones were legal, at least for a while."

"Most of the city leaders don't like the idea because it did lead to really trashy souvenirs being sold by some shops. Anyway, Clint was busy making movies, so he didn't run again in 1990, and ice cream cones seem to be as hard to find as back in the 80s."

"Okay," Gus said, "so let's do the Del Monte run. I'd like a couple of big scoops of chocolate."

Without any hesitation, Kitty fired up the Jaguar and headed up Ocean Avenue toward Highway 1 and the Del Monte.

Chapter 38

It was the first full week of August, and Kitty decided that it was time to take care of two details. The first was a phone call to the Glendale office of Record Gone and her lawyer, Mark Rhyman, a partner of the Pickering firm.

"Mr. Rhyman," she said, when the switchboard put her through, "this is Kitty D'Literie calling from Pacific Grove. I was hoping that you might have some news for me. Do we have a date and time to be in court?"

"I'm glad you called," Rhyman responded. "We have a date for Thursday, October 4. The time is undecided, but I suspect it will either be early before any scheduled trial, or late in the afternoon when any trial would be adjourned. Is the date okay with you?"

"It certainly is," Kitty replied. "Beyond getting myself there on the third of the month, is there anything else I should budget time for?"

"Oh yes. I want you in my office on the afternoon of the third so we can go over exactly what I'm going to present to the judge, and prep you for questions the judge will probably ask of you."

"I understand. I'll arrange to be in Los Angeles no later than the morning of the third of October, and I'll give you a call as soon as I'm in town. I do have one question. What do you know about the judge I'll be facing?"

"Unless there is a change in the court calendar, which is always possible, it will be Judge Morgan. He has a background in the district attorney's office, so as a former prosecutor he may or may not be sympathetic to your appeal."

"Okay, I understand. I'll be on my best behavior, and please call me if anything changes. I'm also going to be very involved in events up here for the next two weeks.

Things could be pretty hectic, so you might not be able to reach me at times."

"Okay, I understand," Rhyman replied. "I'll be in touch before October first, just to be sure that everything is still okay with you. I'll talk to you then."

"Good," Kitty said. "I'll talk to you then, and thanks for the good news."

That detail finished, she concentrated on the mundane part of her life, especially her job at the library. She felt that she had better get in as many of her 20 hours per week on the job as she could, lest she lose the position while the pursuit of Max consumed all of her time. There was also the other detail, the issue of Felix.

She had given him very little thought since her visit to the prison in San Luis Obispo in April. She decided to give the warden, Josie Gastelo, a phone call just to see where things stood with Felix's health.

"Good morning, Warden," Kitty began the conversation. "I've been wondering about the health of my mentee, Felix Morris?" She thought to herself, "I hate that word. But I can't call Felix my 'protégé.' People would think that I taught him how to be a successful murderer for hire."

"Oh, good morning, Ms. D'Literie, it's good to hear from you. Mr. Morris is still clinging to life, but we don't know for how much longer. I suspect he'll be in hospice care within about a month. There's no hope of any reversal on his terminal colon cancer."

"Thank you for that bit of information. I still haven't received anything like a will from him, but I have made the arrangements for the donation of his remains."

"What are those arrangements? Has a medical school agreed to take his body?"

"Yes, he'll be going to UCLA. I know that they will pay for 75 miles of the trip, and I guess I'll be the one to pick up the mileage costs for the balance of the journey."

"I believe, if our records are correct," the Warden added, "that he has no living relatives to pick up any of the costs."

"That's right," Kitty responded. "I'll try to make another trip to see him, but not before the end of this month. Things are getting hectic for me here, at least until the 29th."

"Don't worry about the details of his final journey," the warden said. "Simply send me a contact name and extension number at UCLA, and I can make the arrangements if you're unavailable. The local mortuary we use is familiar with such problems, and the monetary details tend to work themselves out."

"Thank you," Kitty responded. "I'll try to see him in September if he is still alive, but I'm sure your office can take care of those final details. I'll stay in touch, and goodbye for now."

With that done, Kitty had one more bit of research to do, and decided to use one of the library computers while she was there. She knew from past 'car week' events that someone would show up with a carefully restored Jeep from the World War II era. She hoped to meet that person at the show held on Lighthouse Avenue during the week. She also knew vehicles of that type and age were not likely to be at any of the other shows. No, those events drew the Italian exotics or the British classics, but never a Jeep which might have transported the wounded on the battlefield.

Her computer search on Wednesday was successful. She learned there was a large, well-organized group called the Military Vehicle Collectors of California, and there was a national society to preserve such vehicles.

She was intrigued by what she saw displayed on their website.

She found photos of Jeeps in various permutations. Most popular seemed to be a recreation of vehicles used to fight the Germans in the deserts of North Africa. Some had the look of transportation for some general, like George Patton, in Europe. Others had been made to recreate the Jeeps used in Korea, as portrayed in the *MASH* TV show. The group was so inclusive that one could join with a wartime motorcycle, even bicycles used by the British after delivery by parachute to join their airborne units.

She learned that the group held a show each month somewhere in California, from the Central Valley to the Oregon border. The highlight of the year seemed to be a show around Veterans Day in November near Fisherman's Wharf in San Francisco. Kitty felt sure now that she could find a good "home" for Eugene, the Jeep she had inherited from Jake O'Malley years ago. She would try to connect with any MVCC members who were in town for 'car week,' and learn how to let club members know that her Jeep was looking for a new owner.

The balance of her week was so routine that it was boring. She hesitated to call Gus, fearing that he would be too busy getting ready for the ten days between August 16 and 26.

She was prepared for her role, at least that was what she kept telling herself. Then, she had a thought that made her pick up the phone and call Gus. She realized that "camping" was something she had never really done before. Even when she and Jake had been out scouting filming locations, they always found some sort of lodging with two rooms.

When Gus answered, she said, "Gus, if I can get us a table at the Victorian Corner for dinner, can you join me this evening?"

"I can," he replied, "but I have to be back at eight tonight. You sound a bit stressed; is everything okay?"

"Oh, I'm okay, I just need some advice on a stakeout, and after this weekend we're both going to be too busy."

"Okay, make it for six this evening, and I'll meet you there."

"Got it. See you later."

When they were seated at the restaurant, she gave Gus a quick review of her week. Then she got straight to the point of her concern. She said, "I've never been on one of these overnight stakeouts. I want to know what should I take with me for food and drink?"

"Yeah, I can see what you're getting at. You'll be alone, and even if someone was with you the location is such that you can't just go and get a cup of coffee and a doughnut."

"So, what do I bring with me?" she asked.

"I'd suggest that you get some of the stuff they call 'trail mix.' It's intended to give you some energy without a lot of sugar. Have you got a thermos bottle?"

"No, but I can buy one. So, I should have a container of coffee. What else?"

"Do you have a small ice chest or cooler?"

"No, but I can buy one. So, I get a cooler and I put in ice and a six-pack of Coke?"

"I'd suggest you get several small bottles of water, like Dasani or Arrowhead. You'll get enough caffeine with the coffee. What you want is not to get dehydrated, so the water is better."

"I'll be able to get food and drink during the day just by going down to the paddock to take a look at the car. It was the night time I was worried about," she said.

"Now, another thing you'll need out there is a light. I suggest you go to the Home Depot store over in Seaside and get yourself a flashlight. Get a big one, about six or seven inches long. Energizer, the battery people, makes one which is LED and good for stumbling around in the dark while trying to get to the restroom at two A.M. Actually, while you're there, get two. You'll need them at home when the power goes out."

"Okay, big flashlight. Anything else?"

"Well, Home Depot has smaller flashlights, about two to three inches long. The brand is Defiant. They're very compact, intended for construction workers to put in a pocket on cargo pants. You could get a couple of those just in case you need one when you're not near your car. Again, they can be put anywhere around the house that you can reach easily when the power goes out."

"Anything else?" she asked.

"Make sure you've got a phone charger you can plug in to the car's dashboard. Remember, when cops do this, they have radios to call for help. All you're going to have is a cell phone, which better be charged up when you need Detective Baumgarner or the CHP. Are you really sure you want to do this, all by yourself?'

"I hope I won't have to do this. I hope we find Max, and he is thrilled to learn he's an heir, and he goes away on Sunday afternoon. But I don't think he will, so I've got to play out this crazy hunch about him stealing that Jaguar until I can get law enforcement help."

"Okay," Gus said, "let's turn our attention to the menu. I know this place makes a great meatloaf, and I need some before I go back to work."

"Okay," she said, "I'm going for the fish side of the menu. And tomorrow I'll be at Home Depot; not the usual place I spend a Saturday morning. Thanks for all the pointers, and we'll have a fancier feast when all this is over."

Chapter 39

When Kitty woke up on Thursday, August 16, she knew the time for action had arrived. This was the unofficial start of what had come to be known in Monterey County as "car week." A week that now stretched to eleven full days, all organized around the desires and interests of automotive enthusiasts. The opening event would be "The Concours on the Avenue." Ocean Avenue in Carmel would be closed to traffic, and the proud owners of American "muscle cars" and "hot-rods" would put their prize possessions on display. Kitty knew Max would probably not show up there, but it was worth going just to take a look.

She was right, as far as she could tell. No sighting of Max, the quarry in this pursuit, which had taken her over much of the state and even east to Las Vegas. Her next opportunity would possibly be on Saturday or Sunday, the days that cars would begin to arrive by transport.

Hundreds of cars would be delivered to the golf course at Pebble Beach for the concours on August 26. Maybe half of the roughly 600 cars competing in the races at Laguna Seca would arrive then so drivers could get some practice on the course, as well as go through the mandatory technical inspection. Others would arrive later, as individual owner-drivers towed their cars on a trailer behind the family truck.

She decided to give Tom and Jack, her two "observers" at the track for the weekend, a call to see if they were still organized to spend two days at the track. She got Tom on the phone on late Friday afternoon. She said, "Tom, this is Kitty. I'm just calling to be sure you're all set for Saturday."

"Oh, hi Kitty. Yeah, Jack and I talked yesterday, and we're all ready. Any last-minute instructions?"

"Yes, I do have one. If, and it may not happen, the Trusted rig carrying the Jaguar arrives either day, try to get a picture of the driver."

"Okay, but why? Will that be Max, the guy you're looking for? I thought he'd show up later, on vacation."

"No, it shouldn't be Max, but if I'm right Max will approach him then or later. My theory is that Max is going to arrange to take his place and be the driver of the truck on Sunday."

"Okay, that makes sense. I'll pass the request for pictures on to Jack, and we'll let you know what we saw on Sunday evening."

"Great," Kitty said. "Don't forget to keep track of your expenses. If Max's family can't afford a couple of lunches as part of our search, then his inheritance can't be too big. We'll talk later, and have a good weekend."

Kitty felt that things were going as smoothly as she could hope for. She had, as Gus suggested, gone to a sporting goods store and purchased a small ice chest and a good thermos. Then she went to Home Depot and bought some flashlights, and then made sure she had charger for her cell phone so she could use it in the Infiniti SUV she would collect from Enterprise on Tuesday. Now, there was nothing more to be done until the Tour d'Elegance on Thursday the 23rd.

Kitty concentrated her time on trying to keep her nerves under control. She thought she had, as the saying goes, "covered all the bases." She decided it would be good to go out to the race track and see for herself if the Jaguar had been delivered, which was what she did on Saturday afternoon, joining a small crowd of drivers, mechanics and race officials.

She was looking for Tom and Jack, as well as the Trusted rig which would deliver the Jaguar. Her timing was excellent. The transport arrived just a few minutes after one p.m. and began unloading four cars which had shared the flight from the United Kingdom. The Jaguar was the first off the enclosed trailer, to be joined on the ground by a pre-war BMW 328 and two Bugatti model 35's. All four would be in the same race on Sunday, and would be leaving for the airport in Oakland that day in the early evening.

She did not approach the driver of the Trusted truck, but she took a couple of pictures so that she might later identify him. She also took pictures of the cars as they came out of the trailer so that she could prove that there had been four arriving at the track. The question for her was how many would make the return trip to Oakland airport.

She made note of where the Jaguar was deposited in the paddock area, and about that time she encountered Tom and Jack. She asked if they had taken pictures, and was assured they had. "Don't worry Kitty. We've got this covered," said Jack. "We'll stick around until about four this afternoon and be back here tomorrow morning."

"That's good," Kitty replied. "I didn't come out to check on you guys. I just wanted to see for myself what all the fuss and worry I've been into for months was about. Now that I've seen the car, I'm going to go look at some of the other cars and leave here before too long. I'll talk to you guys on Monday after this event is all over."

Kitty did notice that a small motor home had pulled in behind where the Jaguar was parked. She guessed that the people inside would be the driver of the Jaguar, and either a mechanic who had come with the car from England or someone who had been hired here in California for the week.

Never hesitant to do a little snooping, she spent some time looking over the old race car, noticing decals indicating the car had been inspected for races in England at places like Goodwood. Sixty-five years old, and the ancient beast was going to go racing at least one more time. As she looked at the car, she was approached by a gentleman who was probably the same age as the Jaguar.

"Have you seen one of these before?" he asked, with an accent that confirmed he was probably a loyal supporter of the Conservative Party in England, and most likely a "lord of the manor" somewhere in the counties south of London.

"Yes, I have. A couple of C-Types were here about two years ago," Kitty responded.

"Oh, my," he said, "an American woman who recognizes, by name, a very old Jaguar. This is my first time here, and I do wish to learn the ups and downs of this track."

"I think you'll find the turns seven and eight to be very challenging. Americans refer to them as 'the corkscrew,' and it involves a very steep downhill drop."

"I say, have you driven it yourself?" he asked.

"Oh, no," she responded, "but I've watched several races here, some of them from up under the shade of the oaks at the corkscrew."

"Allow me to introduce myself," he said. "I'm Nigel Dalglish."

"Pleased to meet you," she replied. "I'm Katherine Theresa D'Literie, but most people just shorten all of that to Kitty."

"And are you here with one of the race teams?" he asked.

"Oh, no," she replied. "I'm covering the events for one of the small, local papers, and doing an article which I hope to get published in the SAH Journal," she said, slipping easily into her "car week" cover story. She thought to herself, "No sense getting him all worried that someone might try to steal his beloved Jaguar."

"And the SAH Journal, what exactly is that?"

"It's the monthly publication of the Society of Automotive Historians, which is sort of an international group of automotive enthusiasts. Some members in the U.S. and Europe are academics, others are just people who love old cars."

"And will you focus on any particular part of the event?" he asked.

"Well, I'm partial to Jaguars, since I inherited an early model E-Type, so your car may well be the focus of the story when I write it. I'm also interested in the cars that came with yours from the U.K. Must be a big insurance bill for those four cars collectively."

"Yes," he responded. "I don't know the value of the three other cars, all of which are older than mine. I can say that insuring a car for around 14 million pounds sterling does come to a very large sum every year."

"Yikes," she said, "that would come up to something like 18 or 19 million dollars. Does your insurer know what you plan to do here with this car?"

"Yes, and they tack on a surcharge for racing it. I only do that once or twice a year, and at my age this year may be the last time we put the old girl at risk."

"I see from the inspection decal that she was run at Goodwood recently," she said.

"Yes, we were there last year, and may do that one more time. I'll probably employ some competent professional to drive her if we do it again."

"Well, I hope you have a good week here, and do try to get out and see some other things. The Pebble Beach event will conflict with your race, but if you can get over to Carmel on Thursday, you can see almost all the concours cars as they tour the area in the morning."

"Thank you for the suggestion," he said. "I'd like to do that if it doesn't conflict with the other things which we have to do. It has been a pleasure talking to you, but my mechanic is signaling that it's time to get the old girl ready to prove to the technical inspectors that she is fit to race. Goodbye, and good luck with your story."

"Goodbye, and good luck to you. We may see each other again," Kitty said, as she set off to explore the paddock.

"Nice guy," she thought. "I wonder what he does to afford not only the car but the insurance on it? There's the cost of getting here for just this race and getting the old Jaguar back home. Wonder how he got the car, and when? Family heirloom? Bought at an auction? I should have asked him more, but then I'd come across as a nosy Yank. Better to leave it, but maybe I'll chat with him more next weekend."

Kitty spent another 45 minutes or so cruising the paddock, not only looking at the cars but watching the interaction of the competitors. Since its beginning, this event has been purely a show. There are no cash prizes or a championship to race for. These people were like members of a loose fraternity, who get together a couple of times per year to renew old ties and recollect past exploits. The fans in the stands may see it as real racing, but for most of the participants it was more like a homecoming event. Thus, the name "Motorsports Reunion" seemed very appropriate.

With that in mind, Kitty decided it was time for her to head for home and leave the car watching to Tom and Jack. However, as she reached her Jaguar, she thought, "I should come back tomorrow and talk to Nigel some more. After all, I've got questions, and getting the answers would be part of the 'I'm a reporter' cover story." With that, she fired up Malcolm and headed down South Boundary Road for Pacific Grove.

Chapter 40

Kitty awoke on Sunday morning thinking about something Jake O'Malley, or maybe it was his murderous wartime colleague, Felix Morris, had told her about hunting. No, not hunting for a deer or a buffalo, but hunting for a predator, like a wolf, mountain lion or Viet Cong guerrilla.

What they had told her was that the hardest thing to master in such hunting was patience. You pick a place where some clues have led you to believe that the prey would pass by, and then you must wait. And wait. And wait. That was what Kitty had to do now in the remaining days before "car week" came to a close.

Her "prey" was Maximillian Shepherd. Her clues were that he was licensed and employed to deliver cars to events like the Concours at Pebble Beach or the "Motorsports Reunion." She also knew that he had arranged his vacation time so that he could be in Monterey this week

What Jake would have done in Vietnam or Laos would have been to send small patrols out from his likely ambush site to give him advance warning that the prey was approaching. She had done that with 20 young men and women sent to be her "eyes" at different times and locations. Now, frustrating as it might be, patience had to be her watchword.

Jake had also taught her that it was a good idea to have some support that you could call upon if the "prey" proved to be more numerous or clever than you had originally thought. She had done that with Detective Bumgarner of the Monterey County Sheriff's office. She knew that this week, before she took up her post at Laguna Seca, she should touch bases with him to be sure he hadn't forgotten her plan. She decided to hold off on that contact until she had some sort of sighting or contact with the elusive Max.

"Okay," she thought, "I've got a plan, now I've just got to let things unfold. I think I'll do what I was contemplating yesterday. I may come across as nosey, but I think I'll go back to the track and chat with Nigel Dalglish. I'll let him know that my editor thinks it would be a good idea to have the story about the event focus on one person. Play up the human-interest angle. Readers of the Carmel Pine Cone don't want a lot of detail about who won race number seven."

"They would like to make it more personal. So, that's it. I'll go out to the track and try to learn more about him. It's all a 'cover story,' but I can sell it. I'll also tell him the SAH readers want to know more about the history of the car, such things as where it raced and how did the design remain competitive for so long?"

As she motored out to Laguna Seca, she found herself thinking about Jake and Felix. Jake had used his military experience as an ingress to the movie industry, first as an advisor to writers and directors who wanted to know "what's it like out there?" and then as a locations arranger. And Felix? Well, he put those skills of "hunting prey" to use as well, although not in a respectable or legal way. Although convicted for one "murder for hire," Kitty knew from his comments before his arrest that he had used those skills a few more times than that.

His prey? Well, although not what anyone would call an educated man, Felix could drop hints, often couched in Shakespearean quotes. One that he particularly liked to use was from Henry VI. There, in scene two, Act IV, you meet the character, "Dick the butcher." Dick has a line quoted by many people, including Felix. It was the character's, or maybe the playwright's, criticism of how lawyers kept wealthy people in a condition of privilege. It could also be a criticism of bureaucrats and government. When Felix would say, "The first thing we do, let's kill all the lawyers," Kitty knew that he took it literally.

It wasn't difficult, when he was working as an "extra" on a movie, to hear some actor, writer or director complain about some lawyer for the studio, or some agent for a work rival, and then wish that the lawyer or agent mentioned could be dead. And Felix, for a price, knew just how to make that happen. In a short time, the person would have "disappeared," and somewhere off of Bouquet Canyon Road there would be some freshly turned desert soil. Kitty could only hope that Max did not share Felix's interest in removing obstacles to a successful "hunt." She believed that Max, if he was in Monterey, would be hunting his "prey," much as the wolf who is hunted by a man is, in turn, hunting an elk for dinner.

Once at the track it only took her minutes to find the C-Type Jaguar and Nigel Dalglish. She greeted him with a quick question. "Nigel, would it be all right if I hung around with you today? My editors have decided that you and the car should be the focus this weekend. You know, the human-interest angle."

"That would be fine," he replied, "but I really don't think anyone would find my efforts of any great interest. My laps this morning show that there is little chance that I'll cross the finish line first on Sunday."

"That's just the point," she responded. "Readers in Carmel aren't much into motorsports. They do like to know about individuals, their backgrounds, how they came to be involved in racing and what their life is like away from the track. And SAH readers don't seem to care as much about the human-interest angle as they do about the history of the car involved. Topics like: how it came into being, why it was built, what different owners it has had? I'm writing for two different audiences - the

241

small local paper and the journal read by members of a small group of car lovers. And I promise to stay out of your way as you get ready for next Sunday. So, how about it?"

"Oh, very well," Nigel responded. "Can't see that it will do any harm as long as we can keep it short. I do have another practice session in about an hour, so we can chat until then."

"Thank you," Kitty responded. "Let's first do some of the human-interest part of the story. Where do you live in the U.K.? I'm guessing from your speech pattern that it is somewhere south of London."

"Very good," Nigel replied. "My home is in the small, seaside town of Lyme Regis, in Dorset near Devon. About 4,000 people live there, and we do get a fair number of tourists."

"I've never been to England," she said. "Is it near Dorchester?"

"Yes, it's about 25 miles west of Dorchester. You probably know of that town from the work of Thomas Hardy. I don't think he ever came to Lyme Regis, but the grain harvested in 'Tess of the D'Urbervilles' would have, as part of the brewery product."

"Did anyone else we might have ever read about live or work there?"

"Most certainly. There was a famous hotel, the Three Cups, which had a lot of famous visitors. Jane Austen wrote 'Northanger Abbey' there, and the hotel register shows the names of Tennyson, Longfellow, and that hobbit chap, Tolkien. In 1944, General Eisenhower took over the whole hotel for one weekend to meet with all the generals who would invade France in June."

"You used the past tense, was, when referring to the hotel. Is it gone?"

"Well, not entirely. You see, the biggest business in the entire county is tourism now, not farming. And the biggest and oldest business in town is the Palmer Brewery. There's been a brewery there since the 1790's. The Palmer brothers got involved about 100 years later. Their sister was my great-grandmother. In the 1990's the heirs wanted to modernize, and as a distant relative I got the assignment to tear down most of the old hotel and create modern accommodations, plus a modern pub and a wine shop. I'd already built my house near the golf course and planned to build more."

"So, what do you call yourself, what's your line of work?"

"I'm what people call a property developer. That's why I got all the work on the Three Cups project, that and the fact I'm a distant cousin of the Palmers. If my great-grandmother had been a male, I guess I would be a brewer."

"So, Granny didn't get to inherit?"

"Oh no. Back in the 1890's women couldn't vote, hold office or inherit, except from a husband who died with no other heirs. So great-grandma was wed off to a man from Scotland named Dalglish, who was educated in engineering of steam engines. My branch of the family got into engineering, not brewing."

"Now, let's turn to the car. How and why did you acquire it?" Kitty asked.

"I wanted one for some time. My father had been a mechanical engineer and inventor. His principal work was in automobile transmissions. He liked to go to races and started taking me along. I must have seen a Jaguar race at an early age, but the details are hazy. I do recall getting interested very much in 2012. I went to a re-creation of the 24 hours of Le Mans in France and got interested in racing these older machines."

"So that's when you really got the idea which finds you here today?"

243

"Correct. I started watching for Jaguars at auctions. I wanted one of the Le Mans winners from 1953, but they are the most desirable and thus the rarest. So, I settled for one of the 1951 models. It had the drum brakes and a less, shall we say, distinguished racing history, but it was one of only 53 that ever existed. It may be one that raced here in California back in the 1950's, but the records of American races are more difficult to analyze than the ones kept in Europe. So, I made a bid on this car and won it."

"I'm no engineer," Kitty said, "but I can tell those aren't the original brakes."

"You're correct, and you have done some research. It wasn't a massive job of engineering for me to upgrade the braking system. Makes the purists mad, but it's my life coming down that 'corkscrew' turn you warned me about. Speaking of which, I can see that my mechanic, Eddie, is signaling that we should cut this short."

"Okay, one last question, and it's personal. Married?"

"Yes, for almost 40 years."

"Does she come to these events?"

"Seldom, but this was a one-time trip to California, so she is with me."

"Okay," Kitty said. "I'll wrap up with two bits of advice. Take your wife on the 17-mile drive, and before it gets too crowded here, try some of our great restaurants. Thanks for all the information for my story, and I wish you luck on Sunday next week."

"Thank you," Nigel replied, "and enjoy your time covering the event. Now, I must go and get in some more practice. Goodbye."

With that he was back in racer mode, and Kitty felt she had a good start on "car week." So, it was back to her Jaguar, and then a call to see how Gus was doing. "Might be the last chance to talk before the week begins," she thought, as she headed for Pacific Grove.

As she drove homeward, she thought, "Life is strange. I've just talked with a man who makes money developing homes around a golf course. My home now was paid for by selling Jake's property in Palm Desert to someone who was going to develop homes around a golf course. Stories overlapping, like the bit about ships passing in the night."

As she entered the limits of Monterey, she drove past Tarpy's Roadhouse. She hadn't been in it since she had worked there while on parole and married. She thought, "After this week is over, Gus and I are going there, just to see how things have changed. Wonder if anyone there was around when I worked there?" And with that she began dodging the traffic going to the wharf, and headed into the tunnel leading to Lighthouse and home.

Chapter 41

Kitty called Gus late on Sunday afternoon. He sounded stressed, and car week was only getting started. They agreed to meet for a quick dinner at the golf course club house. Gus figured that at five p.m. most of the out-of-town golfers would be on their way home or back to their hotel, and the locals would be few in number then. He was correct.

As they got seated Gus asked, "How is the search for Max going?"

Kitty replied, "Right now it's in the quiet phase. I've been out to the track and checked with my two scouts. No sign of Max. I did meet and talk with the owner of the Jaguar that I think Max may target."

"So how did that go? Did you scare him with your theory?"

"Of course not," she responded. "I stuck with my phony journalist story. Never brought up why I'm really out there, never a word about Max. The owner is a really nice guy, and I hope my theory is all just nonsense."

"So, what do you do next?"

"I wait. Wednesday afternoon I'm going to the Little Car Show on Lighthouse. I'm supposed to meet the guy who may buy the Jeep there. That'll be one less thing to worry about."

"I hope that works out. I guess on Thursday you'll be going over the hill to Carmel for the Tour of Elegance?"

"Yeah, but I also have to get the Infiniti SUV rental taken care of. If Max shows up in Carmel, I've got a bunch of my 'Bow Street Runners' over there watching for him."

"What'll you do if one of them spots him?"

"If he is sighted, I'll try to, very politely and all innocence, let him know that I represent his family, and that they want him to know about his inheritance. From there it's all improvisation."

"What do you mean?"

"Hell, I don't know how he'll react. Logically, he will be a bit surprised and skeptical. I mean, how would you act if a perfect stranger walked up to you and said, 'Hi there. Your brother says, 'Hello', and how would you like a million bucks?'"

"I get it," Gus said, "but be cautious. You've never met this guy, but you think he might be planning the biggest crime of the week in Monterey history."

"I know," she responded. "That's why I'll try to play Little Miss Innocent. I just hope he gets all excited by the news and says something like, 'I've got to get packed and on my way to La Habra Heights. Thanks for the news, and who did you say you were again?'"

"And then on Friday, what have you got planned?"

"Well, that's the day of the big concours and auto rally in Pacific Grove, and I do plan to be there and display the Jaguar."

"Good," said Gus, "because I drew the duty of being the guy who leads the cars around the rally route, driving the old police car from the 1940's that the city keeps just for such events. After that, why don't you and I get some dinner. It'll be the last chance we have until all this car week activity is over on Monday."

"It's a date," Kitty said, "and I've got to check in with Bumgarner from the Sheriff's office on Wednesday. Now, let's finish dinner and go back to my place for dessert."

"What do you have in mind?"

"Don't get hopeful, big guy. We can go by the little ice cream shop next to Toasties and get us some ice cream. After that, who knows?"

Monday and Tuesday were about as normal as Kitty could expect. Gus was back on police duty, and she was putting in her hours at the library. She put in two long days, knowing that she would be gone most of the balance of the week.

As she expected, on Wednesday the man from Pacifica, who was a Jeep collector and restorer, met her just as she had planned in front of the Chase Bank on Lighthouse while the Little Car Show was going on.

"Excuse me," he said. "I'm Ralph Castelo, and I hope you're the lady with a Jeep to sell."

"Glad to meet you, Mr. Castelo. I'm Ms. D'Literie, and yes, I have a nice old Jeep I want to sell. I've got it parked just a couple of blocks down Lighthouse. Shall we go take a look?"

"Sounds fine," Castelo replied. "This is an interesting car show you folks have here."

"Yes, it's a charity event to support a few things that could use the money, like the city library where I work."

"How long has this been going on?"

"About ten years now, when 'car week' began to be more than just Pebble Beach and the historic car races."

They had reached the site where Eugene the Jeep was parked, and Castelo took an immediate interest in the old machine. "How long have you had this vehicle, and how does a woman end up with an old Jeep?" he asked with a puzzled look.

"It's been mine for a little over ten years," she answered. "I got it as part of an inheritance from my boss. We used it a lot when we were looking for a spot in the desert or a hard-to-reach place in the mountains."

"And how did your boss come to own it? It's unusual to find such an old model, and you wonder why it would attract anyone."

"Jake, who was my employer, had used Jeeps at times in Vietnam, and he liked them. As that war wound down the Army began to sell the older models off at bargain prices, and he saw that he could use it in his work."

"Well," Castelo said, "it looks like it hasn't been abused too much in its old age. Let me drive it around a bit and I'll let you know what I think."

"Okay, but I go with you. There's a lot of great memories of days long gone that I have with this old beast. I want one last ride in good old Eugene."

"Eugene the Jeep. That's cute," he said as he started the old Korean war veteran. "Okay, what kind of use did this vehicle get before you owned it?"

"A couple of times a year it would be used in the Mojave or Sonoran Desert. The search would be for a site for westerns. Once we used it to find a Buddhist monastery in the mountains above Big Sur. The producers decided it was easier to use a more urban monastery in L.A. County."

"So, your employer had Hollywood connections?"

"That's right. I did research for him and sort of managed his property."

"Interesting," he said. "I think I've driven old Eugene enough to know that I'll take him. What do you want for him?"

"Well, I use Hagerty insurance, and I asked them for an evaluation. Now, even if I can prove that Steve McQueen once sat in this Jeep, it isn't worth the $130,000 his Jeep sold for. I figure Eugene is in good condition, and Hagerty says around $12,500 would be right."

"Sounds good to me," Castelo said. "I'll go with that price if you're ready to part with your old friend today."

"Good. I've got the pink slip in my pocket, so let's drive him up to the parking lot near the bank. We can make the transfer in the bank, and I can deposit the check right away. Then Eugene is all yours."

"Okay," Castelo said. "I left my son with our car in that parking lot, so this will be fine."

Within a few minutes the legal and financial parts of the sale were completed. Kitty walked Castelo back to where Eugene was parked and said, "I have one bit of advice."

"What's that," he asked.

"Eugene got pretty warm when I drove him up the hill at Laguna Seca, so get the radiator checked soon. And let me take a picture of you and Eugene, just for the memory."

"Not a problem, and thanks for the advice. The trip up Highway 1 is very level, so it'll be fine. Goodbye, and it's been nice doing business with you."

Kitty got her picture, and Eugene the Jeep left up Forest Drive heading for his new home. Kitty shed a tear and thought, "Well, Jake, wherever you are, there goes another bit of both our lives." With that, she got into the Jaguar and headed for Asilomar for an early dinner at the Fishwife.

Chapter 42

Thursday, August 23, dawned like a typical Monterey morning; cloudy and damp. Kitty couldn't be a lay-about, not this morning. Oh, she couldn't have gone to work anyway. The phone company would have technical people all over the library. They were to install all new phones, computer routers and recording equipment, plus an enhanced security system. They claimed that they would be gone by 11:30 at the latest, if you could believe that. Kitty had other demands on her time.

The first was the Enterprise rental of the Infiniti SUV. The Enterprise agent was there, as promised, right at nine. A quick trip to the office in Seaside, paperwork completed, insurance purchased, and Kitty was given a quick course in driving the biggest mechanical beast she had ever been in. Then it was time to go over the hill and down Ocean Avenue into Carmel.

In the early hours of the morning, on the greens of the Pebble Beach golf course, the roughly 200 cars entered in Sunday's concours would be lined up for the tour. The California Highway Patrol officers on motorcycles would escort the long parade on a tour of most of the peninsula.

The 17 Mile Drive would lead them to Highway 1, then north to the Monterey-Salinas Highway, Route 68. A quick left onto Sgt. York Road, then a quick right onto South Boundary Road, and they were on land once part of Fort Ord. A short lap around Laguna Seca Raceway, and they were back to Highway 68. Then came the most challenging part of the tour; the Los Laureles Grade. The steep twisting climb of about ten miles to the Carmel River Valley would be most challenging for cars like the 1911-1914 Simplex's.

Then there was a nice 15 mile drive down the River Valley Road to rejoin Highway 1. A left turn onto

Highway 1 would take them down to the south and the lighthouse at Big Sur. Coming back toward the north, Highway 1 would lead to the Carmel Mission and the narrow streets of Carmel. By then the cars would be well spread out over about 26 miles of road, and their motorcycle escorts would herd them toward Ocean Avenue and Devendorf Park.

Once parked, curb to curb, on Ocean Avenue from Mission Drive to Lincoln Street, the drivers and their guests would go have a catered lunch in the park and let the thousands of spectators look over the cars for a couple of hours, no charge.

Why would the concours entrants do this tour? Well, not for the catered lunch. The tour is all part of a very serious contest between some very rich and very serious car enthusiasts. Pebble Beach is now not just about who has the most unique and beautiful car. It is also about which car can actually function like a car. Finish the tour, and you get bonus points on your Sunday scorecard. Get enough points from the judges and the tour, and you win your class, one of 18. Be one of the 18 class winners, and you might be the proud owner of the "Best in Show" car, now worth more than the ton of money used to buy and restore it.

Kitty was able to get to Carmel in time to get a parking spot in the lot on Eighth Avenue near the Sunset Cultural Center. It would be about two hours before the tour began to arrive, but the town was already crowded with people eager to get a spot where they might be able to photograph the cars before they were parked. Kitty got a copy of the tour program and looked through it to see if anyone she knew was entered. Sure enough, there was Stan, a long-time SAH member. She also spotted the name of Jerry, of the Vintage Auto Racing Association, who would be judging at Pebble Beach. However, meeting old acquaintances again was not her reason to be there that day.

Kitty made her way down Ocean Avenue. Usually she would be window shopping, or just looking to see what new business had replaced one where she liked to actually make a purchase. One stop would always be the old drug store on Ocean. She remembered Jake telling her that the old store was the place to pick up on local gossip, and to get a copy of the Pine Cone, the local newspaper. There was always a couple of jewelry stores to visit, and to cap it off a visit to the Tiffany shop near Carmel Plaza. Oh my, if her parole officer had ever seen that, back in the old days. Now those old temptations were merely a thing of reverie.

Eleven in the morning, and the first cars on the tour came trickling in. These were mostly older cars that had cut the tour short after Laguna Seca. Yes, better to give up some points than risk overheating or brake failure on the Laureles Grade. From then until noon, it was one group after another of 12 to 20 cars with motorcycle escort arriving at Ocean Avenue.

It was time for Kitty to begin checking with her "scouts" to make sure they were all on duty and watchful. Of course, much as she might have expected, some didn't answer their phone promptly. And she was right about one group, the three girls who would work as a "wolf pack" in the hunt. They were found around the Tiffany shop, and promised they would circulate once they finished their "shopping." Amber, Tiffany and Siobhan. "Why," Kitty wondered, "didn't parents give girls 'normal' names like Katherine, Mary or Margaret? Oh well, to them I'm just some middle-aged woman from the land of the ancients. I just hope they keep their eyes on people and not on baubles they can't afford yet."

By two in the afternoon Kitty's feet were beginning to hurt from walking between and around all the cars parked on Ocean, while dodging people as well. She had spotted a few more of her crew of "scouts," but not a sight of Max. Then her phone rang. It was Tiffany.

"Kitty," she said, sounding very excited. "Siobhan thinks we've spotted him. He and another old guy are having lunch at Jack London's, over near Dolores Street."

"I'll be right there," Kitty said. "Don't go near them, and if they should leave before I get there, just follow at a safe distance."

It was only two blocks to Dolores, and then across to the north side of Ocean. The restaurant was about mid-block after she reached Sixth Avenue. She found the girls waiting across the narrow Su Vecino court in front of the Windy Oaks shop.

"Are they still in there?" she asked, breathless after her dash through the crowded streets.

"They haven't come out yet," Amber assured her. "We think the guy you're looking for is wearing a red long-sleeved tee shirt and blue pants. The other guy is wearing something that looks like a truck driver's uniform."

Kitty brought up the pictures she had taken on Saturday at the track as the Jaguar was being unloaded. "Does this look like the guy in the uniform?" she asked.

"I'm pretty sure that's the guy," Siobhan responded.

"Okay," Kitty said. "Good work. Now, you three go down to the other end of the court where it joins Lincoln, near the Da Giovanni restaurant, in case they go that way. I'm going to wait here until they come out. If you get bored, stroll around the area here. This whole block is art galleries, all featuring the work of local artists. If they leave that way just try to follow and see where they go."

"Got it," the three young women said in unison as they headed westward down the court. Kitty waited, knowing this was all she could do now that the "prey" had been sighted.

It was almost two-thirty when the two men that Amber had described emerged from the restaurant and headed toward Dolores Street. Kitty took a deep breath and crossed the court to greet them.

"Pardon me, sir," she said, "but are you by any chance Max Shepherd?"

"Maybe," the man in the red shirt replied. "Who wants to know?"

"Well, I was visiting your brother and sister at their home in La Habra Heights this spring. They asked me to look for you if I was here this week."

"And why would they want you to do that?" he asked.

"Well, they didn't know if you knew that your parents were dead, and they want to settle the estate. Napoleon is the executor, and he said he didn't know if you were alive or not."

"And why would they ask you? I've never seen you before."

"They were just playing a hunch. They recalled that you liked older, classic cars and knew from our conversation that I'd be here this week since I live in this area."

"So, what are you, some sort of private investigator?"

"Heavens no. I just work in the library and do some writing about automotive history, so it was logical that I'd be here and might encounter you."

"So, what happens next?" he asked.

"That's up to you," she responded. "I'll let Napoleon know that I met you, told you that they wanted to get word to you about your inheritance, and the next move is yours."

"Okay," he said. "I'll probably get in touch sometime next week. What did you say your name was?"

"I didn't, but it's D'Literie, and I'm going to get on my way now. Glad I met you, Mr. Shepherd. Have a nice evening."

With that Kitty was off down the court toward Lincoln, where she rejoined the three young ladies, who were waiting near the Carmel Heritage Society. They, of course, had one question, "Was it really him?"

"You know," she replied, "I'm only 90% sure. He never came out with a direct answer, but he never denied it either, even when I called him Mr. Shepherd. He sure looked like the picture we had, so I'm going to call the family and say that I've met him."

"So, what's next?" Tiffany asked.

"Well, for you three, the hunt is over. As we arranged last week, I'll meet with you all at the library on Monday and pay you for your time. And you all have my thanks. Now, I've got to go and rest my aching feet. I'll also call the other members of the group and pass on the news."

"See you next week," the girls said in unison as they headed back to wherever they had left their car.

Kitty headed back to the parking lot on 8th Avenue. As she walked, she thought, "I've got to call Gus. When Max, if it was Max, turned away from me and headed toward 6th Avenue, I swear it looked like he had a gun holstered over his right hip under his shirt. I wonder if it's legal to carry a gun that way in California?"

Chapter 43

Kitty decided to wait until Friday afternoon to tell Gus about her suspicion that Max Shepherd was armed. "No sense getting anyone more upset over what might be just a big wallet in his hip pocket," she thought.

Once back in her home with her aching feet elevated, she placed a call to the Shepherd residence in La Habra Heights. When Napoleon came on the phone, he put it on speaker so that Josephine and Augustus could hear what she had to say. "I have very important news," she said. "Tell us," Napoleon said, "You've located our brother?"

"I have," she replied. "I met him this afternoon in Carmel. At least I'm 90% sure it was him. He never responded in any positive way to my question, but he never denied he was Max."

"What was he doing?" Napoleon asked.

"He had just finished lunch with what I assume was a co-worker from the trucking company. I told him you wanted to get in touch, and the reason why. He indicated he would do so. He never asked for a phone number, just said he would get in touch sometime next week. He seemed to know exactly what I was talking about when I mentioned your name and La Habra Heights."

"This is all very encouraging," Napoleon said. "Do you think you'll encounter him again?"

"Maybe," she replied. "I'll be out at the races at Laguna Seca all this weekend, so I might see him there. Also, I've got young people looking for him at Pebble Beach and the auctions in town. If he shows up at these venues, we may have a chance to meet again. I'll be in touch with you early next week to give you a final report, and you can tell me if he reached out to you as promised."

"That will be fine, and prepare for me a statement of your expenses and time spent on this investigation. I want to be sure that you are compensated properly for all the time and effort spent on finding Max. I look forward to your call next week."

"Okay, Mr. Shepherd. I'll call you no later than, let's say, Tuesday evening of next week. Goodbye for now," Kitty said as she ended the call.

On Friday morning Kitty turned her attention to the big car show on Lighthouse Avenue that afternoon. She was hoping to get a spot near the front of the group so that she could see Gus before he got all wrapped up in leading the tour after the show.

The show is just that, a show. There is very limited judging, no elaborate ceremony with trophies or ribbons for different classes. It was just a chance for people who loved cars to see a wide array of different makes and models. But first, she wanted to get Malcolm the Jaguar all tidied up. She had an appointment for 9 a.m. at Joe's Auto Detailing on Congress Avenue. Nothing major, just making sure the old Jaguar was clean and waxed and looking younger than his fifty years.

The detailing took longer than she had planned, so the front row spot in the show wasn't hers after all. She still enjoyed sitting in a beach chair next to the car and watching people's reactions and answering their questions. As the show began to wind down about five p.m., she caught Gus before he started up the 1940's era patrol car, which would lead the tour.

"Hi there," she said. "What do you want to do about dinner?"

"We probably should go to the barbeque after the tour," he said, "at least for a few minutes."

"Are you in uniform the rest of the evening?" she asked.

"Yeah, I'm afraid so," he replied. "I want to know how things went yesterday with your search."

"Okay, I don't really have a burning desire for barbeque, but I'll go along so we can have a few minutes together. I have a question to ask about a person carrying a gun, and I need to know the answer tonight."

"Sounds serious. Do the tour, and I'll see you at the dinner. How's the show going so far?"

"Great," she responded. "I've had three low-ball offers on the car, and three futile attempts at seduction. Maybe if I'm seen dining with a cop in uniform the 'wolves' will go hunt somewhere else."

"All right, I'll see you after the tour for dinner. Be a safe driver, okay?"

"Of course, officer. I'll be a good little girl, so don't worry," she said, with a touch of sarcasm in her voice.

The Rotary Club officials who organized the event were urging people into their cars so the tour could begin. Kitty knew that not all 200 cars would stick with the tour, as some would have other plans for the evening. She wondered how Gus would react to her, "I think Max has a gun" story. He always seemed to be in a protective mode with her. She knew he meant well, but she wondered how much protection he thought she really needed.

The tour was pleasant as they drove in single file out along Ocean Boulevard to Sunset Drive, then followed the shoreline to Asilomar and the Fishwife Restaurant. She thought, "That's where Gus and I had our first dinner. I wonder if he still passes me off as his 'confidential informant' to the other cops?"

At 17 Mile Drive the tour turned south past Spanish Bay, then looped around and returned to the museum on Central Avenue for the barbeque dinner. Kitty parked the Jaguar and went looking for her "date." That took a while, because Gus got hung up answering questions about the ancient patrol car.

When they finally got their food, they grabbed a table where they hoped for some privacy. Kitty began to realize a little bit more of what it might be like to be the wife of a cop. Before this they had always been just a couple having dinner. Now, it was a "public servant" and "who's that he's with?" for some citizens of Pacific Grove to stare at.

"What's this about a gun?" Gus asked once they were seated.

"Well, I encountered Max yesterday in Carmel. He was pretty surly about identifying himself, but he didn't deny his name. As he walked away, I saw what I thought was a holster on his hip."

"Did you actually see a gun?" Gus asked.

"No, but whatever it was he didn't have it in his pocket. It hung from his belt and was partially covered by his shirt tail. What I want to know is whether a person can carry a gun like that?"

"Not unless he has a permit in California. He is licensed to drive in Arizona and probably lives there. Their rules, on what is called 'concealed carry,' are looser than ours."

"Why would he need a gun anyway?" Kitty asked.

"Oh, I can think of valid reasons. He drives from state to state carrying expensive cargo. He and his employer may be concerned about hijacking, so they expect him to be armed in some way."

"Can we find out if he is armed?"

"Not without arresting him, and we have no probable cause to do that. We can check a state database to see if he has a California permit, but, come on, it's Friday night. I don't see that happening before he leaves here. What kind of gun do you think he had?"

"Well, it would have to be small, like those short handguns that you would see in old movies, where a detective had a small gun with a really short barrel."

"Okay, that makes sense, what used to be called a 'detective special,' useful only for close-up situations like self-defense."

"Well," Kitty said, "I'm going to be on the lookout for him this weekend at the track. I'd feel safer if my suspicions could be confirmed."

"Okay, I'll try to check the Arizona database tomorrow, just to see if he has a permit there. I might get something from Sacramento, but their problems with computers don't make me optimistic. If I find anything I'll call you. My final word on this is just be careful around this guy."

"Trust me," Kitty said, "I intend to just be watchful for the Jaguar of Nigel Dalglish. If I see Max around it, I'll be prepared to follow it. I've let the Shepherds know that I've told him they want to hear from him, so my basic job is done. Now, it's just my hunch I'm following."

"Okay," Gus said, "I've got to get back on duty, but first I must take the old patrol car back to storage until the next big event in town. Oh, one more thing. Did you ever update Sergeant Bumgarner on your encounter with Max?"

"No, I got so involved in just trying to enjoy the show today that I completely forgot him. I'll leave him a message later, and call him tomorrow when I'm at Laguna Seca."

"That's good, and I'll see you on Monday. Maybe we can find a place that's open for dinner. Again, be careful this weekend."

"Don't worry, I'm more likely to die of boredom during the stakeout at the track."

With that, they both cleared their table and headed for their cars. Kitty spent some time, after the Jaguar was garaged, preparing for that stakeout. She put some soft drinks and ice in her new ice-chest, checked to see that her flashlights were functional and plugged her phone into its charger. "Now," she thought, "I wonder what Max is doing. I'll feel like a fool if I've spent money renting an SUV so I can camp out and keep an eye on things at the track. Even if I knew where he was, I can't just go following him around town. For all I know he'd call the police and accuse me of stalking him."

She decided to spend some of the evening preparing herself for protection. Her Wiccan beliefs held that she should do three things. First, she should wear her pentagram pendant prominently, outside her blouse. If she didn't dislike the idea of tattoos, she would have had the pentagram inked into a forearm.

Secondly, she would use rosemary shower gel at her morning shower. Rosemary scent is believed by Wiccans to be good for protection. And finally, she would wear a small lapel pin with a mirror in the center. Every Wiccan knew that a mirror, facing outward, would deter evil, which, if she was correct, Max personified. And if she were at home on Sunday morning, she would burn a yellow-gold candle for protection, but that would be impossible while camping at the track. The last thing she wanted would be to start a brush fire, so the pendant, rosemary and the mirror would have to suffice. That, and staying clear of Max ,until she had cause to phone the Sheriff.

Chapter 44

Saturday, the 25th of August, started as a typically cool and damp morning in Monterey. Kitty knew that by one p.m. the sun would be warming the Laguna Seca race track to a very comfortable degree. She was on her way to the track by nine in the morning to secure her spot in the campground overlooking turn five and the entire paddock area.

She wanted to have a brief talk with Nigel Dalglish to assure herself about the departure of the C-Type Jaguar for its return to England. After having parked the Infiniti SUV in the reserved camping spot, she walked down to the paddock area. Cars were already out on track for their final practice for the Saturday races.

She found the Jaguar all covered up, which was not unexpected as it would not be raced until Sunday. As she approached the car, she was greeted by the mechanic. "Good morning," he said, "Nigel isn't here right now, probably won't show up until afternoon, if at all."

"That's okay," Kitty replied. "I bet he's enjoying some time away from here with his wife. I just wanted to ask him a question, and you'll be able to help me just as well. Pardon me, but I never learned your name."

"I'm Art Kahn, and I was recommended to Nigel by Hollywood Sports Cars. I've worked on a lot of the older Jaguars being restored there, and caring for this one is pretty easy. The factory didn't make it much more complicated than the cars they built to go on the streets in the '50s. So, what do you want to know?"

"This may seem strange," she said, "but if I show you a picture of two guys, can you tell me if either one has been around or asking about the car?"

"Okay, I'll take a look," he said.

Kitty proceeded to show Kahn a picture of Max and his lunch companion of Thursday. He took a look and said, "Well, the one guy is the driver for Trusted who drove the rig that brought four cars down from Oakland. The other guy, I don't know about. He might have been around, but so have a few dozen others, and maybe a few hundred today."

"Do you know the name of the guy who drove the truck delivering the Jaguar?"

"Yeah, it's something like Bubba Brown or Bo Brown. I'm not sure if that's a real name or a nickname, but his last name is Brown, I'm sure. Why are you asking?"

"Well, I'm supposed to write a story about the event, and I've decided to make Nigel and the C-Type the center of it. I just might include you, and Bubba, or whatever his name is, as figures mentioned in the story. Who knows how I'll write it tomorrow afternoon, but I want to get my facts straight before I start writing."

"And what about the other guy in the picture?" Kahn asked.

"I think he's another truck driver who arranged to be here to see all the cars this week. These events sure draw a lot of people to Monterey each summer."

"Okay, it's been nice talking to you," Kahn said. "I've got to check a couple of things on the car, but I'll be sure to tell Nigel that you were by if he shows up later."

"Thanks, I might be back later today," she said as she walked away.

Kitty had an important call to make. She thought that getting to the highest point on the course, the area near the "corkscrew corner," might give her the best cellphone connection. She needed to talk to Sergeant Bumgarner of the Monterey County Sheriff's Office.

"Detective Bumgarner," she said when he answered her call, "I want to let you know a couple of things."

"I wondered when I'd hear from you, Ms. D'Literie," he responded. "Did you get settled in all right out at the campground?"

"I did, and I've also made contact with the man I've been looking for. I've talked with the owner of the car in question, as well as his mechanic, so now it's a matter of watching and waiting."

"So, you've met your 'suspect,' and how did he react?"

"That's hard to say. He didn't seem to be thrilled to meet me, or to hear that he had an inheritance, but then I took him by surprise. I do need to ask about another subject. I think he was carrying a concealed handgun."

"Did you tell anyone about your suspicion?"

"I did tell Officer Mulbrae in Pacific Grove. He was going to check the database to see if Max Shepherd had a permit to carry a weapon, and I'm not even sure if what I saw was a holstered gun."

"Okay, give me his full name, spelled accurately, and I'll try to find out about a gun. But you haven't seen him around the car in question, have you?"

"No, the mechanic hasn't seen him, so I may be wasting my time here, but I'll play my hunch out until the car is on its way back to England. His full name is Maximillian Shepherd, and I'll send you a text message after this call with the correct spelling."

"Okay, I'll see what I can find out about Max Shepherd and a gun permit. If he has one, and does nothing criminal, there's not much that I can do. You, on the other hand, need to stay alert and be watchful, just in case you're right. And stay in touch with me even if nothing major happens."

"Got it," Kitty said, "and if you find anything about a gun permit, give me a call. Bye for now."

That bit of business taken care of, Kitty decided to return to the paddock area, look at some more cars and get some lunch. She realized that her "camping" efforts didn't include much in the way of meal planning or preparation. On the other hand, if it was something edible, then someone would be preparing it in the paddock. She could choose from Thai, Mexican or Chinese cuisine, or her preference, a tri-tip steak sandwich. She knew, however, that after dark it would be a dull and lonely night on stakeout. "Oh, well," she thought, "if I ever do get to be a real licensed investigator, there'll probably be a lot more of those boring nights."

After lunch, she went to get a seat in the grandstand near the exit of the final turn, number eleven, to watch the Saturday races. She noted that the three cars from the U.K. that had arrived by transport with the Jaguar were in the early races. Therefore, they would be ready to load for the trip to Oakland early Sunday afternoon.

As the day wore on, and the cars in each race grew increasingly louder, she decided that the walk back to her SUV was an attractive option. That all changed very quickly after the ninth and final race of the day as a relative quiet fell over the entire area. The 60,000 or more fans quickly departed for home, hotel, or dinner engagement. Mechanics, drivers, and course workers were almost all gone an hour before sunset. Then it was just the camping crowd, each in their own designated spot, roasting hot dogs or whatever they had brought for the evening. Some even left the area, perhaps for dinner, or even for home, having seen what they wanted of the action for the weekend. Then Kitty settled down to keep watch for the night.

Much as Kitty had hoped, absolutely nothing happened. Oh, some campers stumbled by, bumping into the SUV, but her night could not have been quieter or more boring. "One more night," she thought, "unless Max tries something tomorrow." As surely as the sun rises in the east, it rose about six a.m., and Kitty prepared herself for another day of watchful waiting.

Nine a.m., and the cars for Sunday's race number one were out on the track for their final practice. Their lap times would decide where in the group they would start at one p.m. Kitty saw the Jaguar on track, and Nigel seemed to have learned his way around Laguna Seca. Then she got a phone call.

It was Detective Bumgarner. He said, "I've got a news item which may be related to your hunch. Does the name Brown mean anything to you?"

"Well," she replied, "I learned yesterday that the Trusted driver who delivered the four cars from the U.K. for the races this weekend was named Brown, maybe Bo or Bubba. Why do you ask?"

"A driver named Beauregard Brown was admitted to the hospital yesterday with a bullet wound. Nothing serious, but it looks like someone mishandled a handgun, maybe dropped it. Anyway, it went off, and Mr. Brown won't be driving for a while. That's what a bullet through your buttocks will do for you."

"Any report on who the shooter was?" she asked.

"No! Mr. Brown had been out drinking with friends, was pretty much under the influence. One of his friends drove him back to his motel in Seaside and left him. Someone called 911 and left the area without leaving a name. We tried tracing the call, but the phone was one with pre-paid minutes on it, so it wasn't registered to anyone. It could be something deliberate, could be just an accident, and the caller wanted to remain anonymous."

"So, should I be worried?" Kitty asked. "And have you found anything about Max Shepherd and a gun he might be carrying?"

"We do know now that he does have a concealed weapon permit in Arizona, but we can't determine if he has one that's valid in California. My advice to you is to be extra alert and careful today. It may be nothing, but someone is going to be taking over Mr. Brown's driving chores today."

"Thanks, Detective. I'll be extra alert, and I may very well follow the truck transporting the Jaguar which I think is the target. Will you be available this evening if I need assistance?"

"I'll be on duty until midnight, so give me a call if you see anything even remotely suspicious."

"I'll stay in contact with you, and just hope that nothing happens here," Kitty said as she concluded the call.

As she put her phone aside, Kitty thought, "Now, as someone once said, 'the cat's among the pigeons.' Bumgarner may be withholding judgement, but my instincts, my intuition, tells me that Max has arranged things so that he is driving the truck taking the Jaguar to the airport. How he plans to take the car I can't guess, but he is a suspect to me. I'm not going to tell Nigel Dalglish any of this; why get him alarmed at this time."

She also decided to stay away from the paddock. She could observe the Jaguar with her binoculars and see if Max turned up as the replacement Trusted driver. After that, it was just a long drive to see that the car got to the airport as arranged.

"All I can do now," she thought, "is, as they say on TV, 'stay tuned for our next episode.'"

Chapter 45

Kitty decided that she wouldn't make any contact with Nigel Dalglish after his race. She did observe what was happening to the other cars that had arrived on the same day as the Jaguar from England. Although the crowd of spectators was smaller than it had been on Saturday, there were still many who took the time to wander through the paddock and take photos of cars that they might never see elsewhere.

Five p.m., and the only noise was the traffic of spectators leaving, the mechanics putting away their tools, and the announcements about who had won awards. Unlike other races, there was no trophy for winning. After each race a committee had selected someone to be given a trophy, based not on order of finish but on the appearance of the car and crew, and the long-term involvement of the driver in the sport. There would be special awards for things like having the best display of your car in the paddock, outstanding craftsmanship in car preparation, or having the best car made by the company being honored that weekend, such as Ford or Maserati.

The top award was the Spirit Award. The winner had "best embodied the vintage spirit" by how the car was presented and driven competitively. The recipient got a Rolex watch specially engraved with the date of the event. There will be no other exactly like it in the world.

Kitty went down to the paddock to observe all of this and to also watch what happened to the Dalglish Jaguar after the activities were over. She noted that Art Kahn, the mechanic, had packed up all his tools and was just watching for Nigel so that he could begin his trip back to Los Angeles. His last responsibility was to drive the Jaguar to the area where the transporters were being loaded. She noticed that the two Bugattis and the BMW had already been loaded, so when the Jaguar was loaded the transporter would be on its way to the Oakland airport for a pre-dawn flight to England.

Kitty decided she didn't need to watch the loading details, so she went back to her rented Infiniti SUV and prepared to follow the transporter as it left Laguna Seca. She knew the trip would be a very simple one; Highway 68 to Salinas, north on Highway 101 to the junction with Interstate 880. The 880 would be the route to Highway 61, just north of San Leandro, where the driver would turn west for the airport. It was only about 120 total miles, and Kitty was determined to follow that truck to the airport gates.

Kitty was familiar enough with the route to the north that would take her beyond Monterey County. First would be San Benito, then, at Gilroy, into Santa Clara County. She decided that it was time to check in with Detective Bumgarner.

He answered promptly. "What's your status now, Kitty?" he inquired.

"I'm still at Laguna Seca. The car is being loaded into the transporter as we speak, and I see that Max is the replacement driver. I'm prepared to follow it to Oakland, but what happens when I leave Monterey County?"

"Let me know when you reach Gilroy. That puts you in Santa Clara County, and I know who to contact there."

"What if Max, who is the replacement driver on this trip, stops along the way? He might pull over to get dinner."

"Just keep an eye on him without confronting him. I've confirmed that he is armed and has no permit in California. I'm also convinced that he may be our lead suspect, or 'person of interest,' in the shooting of Brown, the other driver. I don't believe in coincidences. He has a gun and someone shot Brown, so he couldn't make the trip to Oakland. But until he does something that would cause law enforcement to stop him, we can't look at his gun. So lay back and keep an eye on him at a safe distance."

"I've got it," Kitty replied. "I'll call you when he gets into Santa Clara County, and we'll see what happens then. Talk to you later, because the truck is moving out now."

"And so," she thought, "the last segment of the search for Max Shepherd begins. I'll be glad when this is over, and I can go back to my hours at the library or my yoga class." With that, she put the Infiniti into drive and set off down the hill from Laguna Seca toward Highway 68.

Following the truck was no problem, thanks to its size and comparatively slow movement. It was about 6:30 in the evening when they reached Salinas and the on-ramp to Highway 101 northbound. Kitty knew that unless Max got off that highway for some reason there wouldn't be another traffic light until they reached the turnoff for the Oakland airport.

By 7:30 they had passed the small mission town of San Juan Bautista in San Benito County. The terrain was hillier here, and the transporter was often slowed below the 55 miles per hour speed limit for trucks. Kitty knew to not only stay behind the transporter but, if possible, to put another car or two between her car and the big rig. "No sense giving Max anything to worry about," she thought.

They came out of the hills and approached Gilroy, the so-called "Garlic Capitol of the world." Even if the light were fading you could tell by the smell that you were approaching the unique farming community. Now she was in Santa Clara County, an area with which she had only limited familiarity. It was time to call Detective Bumgarner again, as they had agreed.

"Hello Kitty," Bumgarner said. "Where are you and the transporter now?"

"We've passed Gilroy, and in a few minutes we'll be in Morgan Hill." There was a pause, then she continued, "It looks like he's getting off 101 at Cochrane Road. He could be going to the Morgan Hill Shopping Center for dinner, or…. No, he's signaling for a left turn on Cochrane."

"There's a smaller shopping center on the west side of 101. Call me back if he pulls in there."

"Okay, that's what he's doing. Sunday night, it looks like most of the shops are closed. Wait…he's pulling into the parking area near the MacDonald's."

"He's probably going to get himself some dinner, seeing as how it's about 7:30. Stay out of sight, don't go in there after him or he'll recognize you and get suspicious."

"Got it. I'm going to the Pieology shop that's a good distance from the MacDonald's. I'll get something to eat and keep an eye on the transporter."

"Okay, Kitty, that's good. I'm going to get a bite to eat now also, but keep me informed of what happens next," Bumgarner said.

Kitty began to feel a bit silly. What if she was just wasting her time while Max Shepherd was just taking a dinner break from the job he was getting paid to do? "No," she thought, as she settled back in her SUV to eat her small pizza, "I've got to see this through. My intuition tells me something illegal is going to happen."

A little after 8 p.m., and the sun was definitely setting when Max reentered the transporter and started the motor. "Okay," Kitty thought, "he'll get back on 101 and head for Oakland now that the dinner break is over." But that is not what happened.

The transporter did not head for the highway to the north, but instead to the huge parking lot of the Wal-Mart

Supercenter across Cochrane road. "Now what the hell is he doing? This is making no sense," Kitty thought.

The transporter didn't park close to the Wal-Mart, but far back in the almost deserted lot. Kitty followed, but stayed a good fifty yards away from her target. She observed Max alight from the rig and not go toward Wal-Mart. Instead, he went to a non-descript pickup truck which had an enclosed trailer attached. He got in the pickup and moved it closer to the transporter. Now, she decided, it was time to get Bumgarner back on the phone.

He came on promptly, and Kitty quickly explained what had happened since the stop for dinner. Bumgarner advised, "Keep watching and stay with me on this line. What's he doing?"

"He has opened up the back of the transporter, and it looks like he is doing something with the tie-downs for the Jaguar."

"That could be nothing except that he fears the load might have shifted, and he's making sure it's secure."

"Yeah," Kitty said, "except he just lowered the Jaguar out of the transporter."

"Still nothing criminal there," the detective said. "That could be just more checking the stability of the load."

"Okay, now he's opening up the enclosed trailer hooked to the pickup truck. Oh, dear God, I know what he's doing!"

"What?" Bumgarner asked.

"He's unloading a very perfect replica of the original Jaguar. It looks just like the Dalglish Jaguar: same color, same numbers on the body. If you were busy loading it on a plane with three other cars in the dark, you would never notice the subtle differences."

"All right, stay cool," the detective said. "He hasn't broken the law until he puts the real Jaguar into his trailer. There must be an actual swapping of real for fake."

"Well, now he's loading the replica into the transporter," Kitty practically yelled. "We've got to do something quick or he'll get away"

"I am," came back the reply. "All this is being sent to the Santa Clara County Sheriff and the CHP. Once he puts the real car into his trailer, they'll be on the scene. Just stay calm. I've given them your description, as well as the description of your SUV and its location. They will want to interview you as an eye witness. They know you're a C.I. for the Pacific Grove P.D., and that you can tell the real car from the replica. What is he doing now?"

"He is driving the real Jaguar into his trailer. Now, he's out of the trailer and closing up the transporter. He has completed the switch. Time for the posse to arrive, I think."

"Hang in there and stay calm," Bumgarner said. "CHP is two minutes out; Santa Clara S.D. is three out at the most."

"Okay, it looks like he's going to leave the transporter and get in the pickup. He must be taking the Jaguar somewhere that we don't know about. Oh, thank God, I see the CHP car pulling into the parking lot."

"See, I told you we would handle this. Now, stay exactly where you are until a uniformed officer approaches you for a statement. And, Ms. D'Literie, congratulations on what looks like your first big case. I'll stay on duty here for another hour, so call me when things settle down there."

"I'll call you later," Kitty said, as a second CHP car arrived, followed by one from the sheriff. Max was immediately ordered out of the pickup truck and searched for a weapon. She saw the CHP officer remove what looked like a handgun and put handcuffs on Max. A deputy sheriff approached her SUV.

274

"Good evening, ma'am," he said to Kitty. "Would you be the lady who has been in contact with Sergeant Bumgarner of the Monterey Sheriff?"

"Yes, I am," Kitty replied. "You guys got here just in time. I was afraid he'd get away with the theft."

"And how do you know this suspect?" the deputy asked.

"I've been looking for him for several months at the request of his family. He's entitled to a good inheritance, but some of his actions made me suspect he might have the theft of a rare car in mind. My contacts in Pacific Grove told me to explain my suspicions to Detective Bumgarner."

"Okay, so you followed the tractor-trailer rig from Monterey to here this evening?"

"That's right, and I kept Detective Bumgarner informed as I followed Max to this place."

"Max, that's the name of our suspect?"

"Yes, Max Shepherd. His family, his siblings, live in Los Angeles County. They know that I've located him and told him of his inheritance. What happens next?"

"Well, our suspect had a weapon which, thank goodness, he didn't try to use. He is also a person of interest in a shooting involving another truck driver in Monterey County, so at some time he'll be returned to that jurisdiction. But the real property crime took place here, so Santa Clara County is involved in prosecuting that case. I need two things from you first."

"What do you need?" Kitty asked.

"I'll need you to come to our Morgan Hill substation and make a written statement for the record. Also, right now, I need you to tell me and the CHP officers how to tell the real car from the substitute. They look the same to me here in the dark."

"Okay, but I don't want the suspect to see me until I have to appear in court. He's seen me once, when I told him of his inheritance, but I've avoided contact with him since. Frankly, I fear him a little."

"No problem. Let me get a CHP officer over here, and you tell us what to look for on the two cars."

When both officers were present, Kitty explained how to tell the original from the replica. "Look at the dashboard area of both cars. The real one will have a sticker there saying 'Goodwood', meaning it passed tech inspection there in England. It will have a similar sticker from the Monterey Reunion , and the replica will have neither of these. Also, look at the tires. The real car raced today at Laguna Seca. The tires will be scuffed, they'll look more worn than the ones on the replica."

"And if you need to, the owner, Mr. Dalglish, will have details on things like the engine number and chassis numbers, which should also be in the paperwork in the transporter. Go look and tell me what you see."

The two officers went, and with their flashlights were able to see the subtle differences that Kitty had explained. They came back to her and said, "Thanks, ma'am, we've got the suspect on his way to a lockup, and tomorrow his gun will go to Monterey for the sheriff to do a ballistics check. If you'll just follow us back to the substation, we'll get your statement and you can be on your way back to Pacific Grove."

"I'll follow the sheriff, and thanks for getting here when you did. I've met the owner of the authentic Jaguar, and I'm glad he didn't lose his wonderful old car. I just wondered what Max thought he'd do with the real car once he had it?"

The CHP officer replied, "My guess is that it would have disappeared into a storage facility. We found paperwork for one just a few miles away from here in Morgan Hill. Then the substitute would go to Oakland

and be on its way to England. Eventually, the owner would learn of the theft, the insurance company would get involved, and the thief might give the car back after a payoff and a promise of no prosecution."

"Sounds logical to me," Kitty said. "Let's get the paperwork done so I can go home and get some sleep." With that, she started up the Infiniti and started to follow the Santa Clara deputy to the substation. As she headed toward Cochrane Road, she remembered her promise to Detective Bumgarner. As he answered the phone she said, "It's all over for now. I'm on my way to the sheriff's substation to make my written statement and then home. Thanks for the backup, and I'll call you next week."

"Okay, Kitty, drive safe on the way back and again, well done. Oh, I'll get ahold of this Dalglish fellow if he's still in Monterey and let him know about all of this. He'll need to rebook a lot of travel back to England. Talk to you later."

Epilogue

Monday, the 27th of August, and Kitty was up and on the move early. By nine a.m. she was at the Enterprise shop to return the Infiniti SUV. At home again by 10:30 she called Detective Bumgarner to learn what the next legal steps would be.

He told her that the District Attorney for Santa Clara County was prepared to offer Max Shepherd a "deal." Under penal code section 487 he could be sentenced to prison for three years for "grand theft auto." There is an "enhancement" to the sentence based upon two factors. First, was there evidence that the car being stolen was going to be kept by the thief for a period of time? The rental agreement for a storage facility, within three miles of the crime scene, was probable proof of that intent. Then there is the "Ferrari enhancement." In California, if the stolen vehicle is worth over $250,000, two more years are added to the prison sentence. So, Max could be facing five years in prison, or less if he took the plea deal and saved himself and the county the legal fees and time spent on a jury trial.

Also, Santa Clara was prepared to add jail time for the concealed weapon he was carrying. All this would be the subject of bargaining by the D.A. and Max's lawyer, which would take place on Tuesday. Kitty hoped that there would be no trial and her involvement would end soon.

Then Bumgarner told her about the charges that Max would face in Monterey County. The weapon he carried was now in the Sheriff's office, and there had been a lucky break. The bullet which had put Brown in the hospital had passed through him and, after a diligent search, had been found in the ground near the crime scene in Seaside. If the ballistics test was conclusive, then Max would be charged with assault with a deadly weapon (ADW). That alone would get him up to four years in prison. In California, however, ADW with a firearm and causing bodily injury, adds anywhere from three to ten more years to the basic four-year sentence.

Again, all this would be decided by bargaining between Max's lawyer and the D.A. of Monterey County. The goal would be to put Max in prison for a long time without the cost of a trial and the burden of selecting a jury. Kitty would be a key witness in a trial because it was she who had first observed that Max had a concealed weapon.

Bumgarner assured her that he would be keeping her informed as to the deals which might be reached in the two cases, as would the D.A.'s of both counties.

It was noon, and Kitty knew that she had to talk to Gus. She called the Pacific Grove police station and found that his duty for the day was on the front desk. When she proposed dinner, Gus said she should come to the station in the early afternoon because the chief wanted to talk to her. She agreed to come by the station around 1:30, as she had to go by the post office and pick up the mail which was being held for her.

The trip to the post office proved worthwhile. She received an envelope with paper work from California State University at San Jose which, when completed and returned, would have her enrolled in the on-line Master of Library Technology program starting in mid-September.

She was at the police station at 1:30, and Gus took her straight to the chief's office. She was greeted not only by the chief but what looked like half of the P.G.P.D. The chief said, " Ms. D'Literie, I was never fooled by that 'confidential informant' story, but you are the best amateur detective I've ever met." He went on to tell her that she should call Nigel Dalglish as soon as possible, before he left for England.

Before she left the station she called Dalglish, who was effusive in his thanks for preventing the loss of his C-Type Jaguar. He offered to pay for the restoration of her Jaguar in England, but Kitty declined, preferring to give American craftsmen the work. Dalglish said that she should send the estimate for the work to him, and he would cover the cost. He told her that he and his wife would be in Monterey until the Jaguar was released to him. If she decided to have her car restored by the factory in England, it could be flown there with the C-Type. Kitty promised to call for an estimate from the American restorer, XK Restoration in San Luis Obispo.

Dalglish also added that Lloyds of London, his insurer, would be calling her sometime the following day. Insurance companies often pay a reward to the investigator who recovers, or prevents, the theft of insured property.

On Tuesday afternoon she met with her "Bow Street Runners" in the library conference room. She brought the young men and women up to date on the Max Shepherd case, and, with her thanks, paid them for the time they had given to the cause of finding Max.

She had another call to make to Detective Bumgarner at the sheriff's office. He told her what had been offered as a plea deal to Max, and that the district attorney's office had contacted his family about his arrest. The D.A.'s of both counties had decided to merge the two cases into one, with the trial, if the plea deal was rejected, to be held in Santa Clara County where Max was being held. There would, of course, be no trial if he agreed to the reduced sentences they were offering him.

Bumgarner had another question which had been posed by the sheriff of Santa Clara County. It was, "What do we do with the evidence, the Jaguar replica, after he goes to prison?"

Kitty replied, "It could go to one of two places. Either it goes to the collection of a man named Dred Maxim in North Las Vegas, or to the Peterson Museum in Los Angeles. It's the best replica of a C-Type Jaguar anyone could want to see."

Bumgarner also asked her for the name and address of her attorney in Los Angeles. He planned to send a letter to him and the judge who would hear her appeal to have her felony expunged. He would be indicating in the letter that she had acted in a way that prevented the loss of an extremely valuable auto, and her conduct was deserving of the removal of the felony conviction for her one crime so many years ago. Kitty thanked him, somewhat tearfully.

Kitty, as she had promised Nigel Dalglish, called the well-known Jaguar restorer in San Luis Obispo. The owner of XK Restoration, Jason, would not estimate the restoration costs without seeing the car. He assured her it could be done for the same cost or less than the factory, which had charged as much as $400,000 for a full restoration.

Finally, in the late afternoon, she called Gus and set up a dinner date for that evening. They would go to the Fishwife, where they had first dined together what seemed like years ago. She told him to do one thing, which was to find a CD of the movie "The Thomas Crown Affair." He responded "Oh, that's the one from the 1970's with Steve McQueen."

"No, I want the one from 1999 with Pierce Brosnan."

"Why?" he asked.

She replied, "We'll watch it and eat some popcorn, and then you'll see what it has to do with Max Shepherd."

Dinner at the Fishwife was as enjoyable as that first date some four months before. As she picked up the bill and prepared to leave she had one more request of Gus, one which surprised him. Kitty said, "I've got the bill on this date, but next month, around the 15th, I want you to take me to dinner at the Inn at Spanish Bay."

"That's pretty specific as to time and place," Gus replied. "What's the occasion?"

"You've never asked, because you're a gentleman," Kitty replied. "It will be a big deal for me, because then I hit the big 'Five O.' Yes, it's my fiftieth birthday, and I want a little celebration."

"I'm happy to say that I'll make that reservation," Gus said. "Now, let's go to your place and watch this old movie you wanted me to see."

And so, with an old movie about art theft, and a large bowl of popcorn, on a summer evening, the Tale of Two Jaguars came to an end.